MY TIME TO SHINE

MY TIME TO SHINE

Edd McNair

URBAN BOOKS LLC
www.urbanbooks.net

Urban Books LLC
10 Brennan Place
Deer Park, NY 11729

ISBN 1-893196-72-0

First Printing October 2006
Printed in the United States of America

10 9 8 7 6 5 4 3 2 1

Submit Wholesale Orders to:
Kensington Publishing Corp.
C/O Penguin Group (USA) Inc.
Attention: Order Processing
405 Murray Hill Parkway
East Rutherford, NJ 07073-2316
Phone: 1-800-526-0275
Fax: 1-800-227-9604

PREFACE

He worked with the skills and patience of a chemist. The look in his eyes let me know that it wasn't the right time for conversation, no time for error. One mistake could mean thousands of dollars lost. Peering past the Pyrex dish, baking soda, and other items that sat beside the white gas stove, I watched as he sprinkled water on the contents and mixed until it blended together to take the form of thick oatmeal. As he brought it over the short-lit fire, it melted down and changed in consistency to a thick syrup-like substance. He took a dinner fork and began to whip it until it began to harden again.

I moved closer, close enough to see veins appear and begin to travel to the middle of the gooey mix at a rapid pace, just before he tossed it on to a napkin to drain. I stood there staring in amazement. He never broke his concentration or even acknowledged the fact that I was there, until he picked it up, put it in a bag, and tossed it on the scale. In front of me sat one of the ghetto's most powerful drugs and biggest money-makers. He smiled as if he'd just found the cure to all the world's problems—or maybe just his.

CHAPTER 1

"Big Apple"

It was the beginning of the summer. Not even August yet and the temperature was running 93 degrees, with humidity reaching 100. I was laying on one of the dingy-ass mattresses, in deep thought. If it wasn't for the slight movement of the draperies, I wouldn't even know a breeze was trying to blow. I stared at the open window with the missing screen being held up by a stick. I sat up and reached for the towel to wipe my face.

The year was 1986, and I was supposed to be graduating. But so many obstacles stood in my way. Twelve years of school and not a damn thing to show for it— not a piece of paper, not a ceremony. Nothing, except for the knowledge I retained in my head.

I got up and walked downstairs. I could smell the hair chemicals as I approached the stairway. I strolled down the stairs into the living room, where my brothers and cousins were sitting, sweating it out, damn near gasping for air.

My mother was doing a Jheri-curl in the kitchen so

she could get that twenty-five dollars, even though her feet were swollen and her hands ached from arthritis. She was dead tired and still hadn't fully recuperated from the heart attack that almost claimed her life four months ago.

Now, she was racing against time, trying to finish up so she could run to the hair supply store, because she still had a full head of weave to sew in at six. Never did she stop striving to take care of her boys.

On the other hand we tried to do what's right, me and my brothers, but it gets hard at times. She always said if our dad was here that we wouldn't be putting her through half the shit we did. We'd sit, listen and keep our mouths shut, out of respect, but in reality we didn't give a fuck what he said or thought at that point in our lives.

All the beatings we went through. The extension cords that he used to swing with all his might until it wrapped around our arms and legs, leaving strings of welts creeping up our legs, arms, and backs. Not forgetting the many times we'd heard her scream out from pain as he slapped, kicked and beat her, as if she was his motherfuckin' child too.

When she finally decided to leave him and moved to Lake Edward, a section of townhouses separating Norfolk and Virginia Beach, she knew—and we swore in our hearts—that if he ever came anywhere near her again we would bury him. Actually we might not have sent him to an early grave, but he would have definitely spent some time in Norfolk General Hospital recounting his actions.

My oldest brother was now nineteen and stood six feet. He was weighing in at about one hundred and eighty, thirty pounds lighter than me and ten pounds lighter than my little brother, who stood only five seven, an inch shorter than me. I was seventeen; my little brother was three years younger—his thick, muscular body made him look more mature than I.

Over the years we sat and watched our mom go through pure hell with this selfish, no-good niggah. All he had to do was show his ugly-ass face around our house and he'd be gone from here. Plus, we had seen Mom make "ways out of no ways." He didn't do shit, and to really think about it, we didn't even know him.

But we couldn't dwell on yesterday. We had to figure out how to survive and eat today.

Right now I had to figure out how to restore the lights and water.

Going through the turmoil of getting our lights and water turned off month after month, we learned a few tricks of the trade. If my mother had some hair to do, we would go out to the meter and take the plastic off the receptacles, and put it back in; then we would have lights. Going outside with a wrench and turning the water back on so everyone could take cold showers was also a regular occurrence.

This worked from time to time and kept us going for a while. Then one day we went out, and Virginia Power had taken the meter and put on a special lock, which could not be removed. Mom was really upset. She sat in the dark, crying and praying, believing that the Lord will make a way.

Yes, God will make a way, and I believed this, but while my mom waited on her prayers to be answered, my brothers and I had another plan.

Junie, my oldest brother, was sitting on the broken-down Cutlass in front of the house, when I came out.

"Where you headed to?" he said.

"Nowhere. How the hell am I going to get from *A* to *B*, with no goddamn car?"

"Walk your big ass."

"Yeah, right."

"Dee, when we first moved out here from Campostella, the neighborhood was about forty percent white. Now there ain't a white in the neighborhood. More drugs and bullshit have started to come in, and being in the midst of all this shit is for the next motherfucker, not me."

"Go buy you a house in Georgetown and a big Cadillac and call it a day," I said. "Just send us some money for these bills over here every now and then. Don't forget—these bills don't stop."

Georgetown was a neighborhood in Chesapeake, known for its well-to-do black families.

"I'm serious, man. I'm tired of this shit. Tired of Virginia," he said.

"And?"

He looked over at the spot where his Honda used to sit.

"I didn't only bust my ass to pay for my shit, but I also had to pay personal property tax—whatever the hell that is."

The mechanic across the street had just looked at my shit and told me what it was going to take to get on the road again. All I needed was eight hundred to fix it. But I guess I wasn't moving fast enough, so the city had my shit towed away then had the audacity to charge me seventy-five dollars to get it back—not to mention the ten dollars a day for storage. *I'll never get my shit now.*

"Who in the fuck gave them the right to take it?" he said, looking frustrated.

Life had dealt us a raw deal, but it wasn't only dealt to us. It seemed like it touched most cats in the neighborhood.

"If you had come out in the middle of the night and shot that bitch, you'll be the one locked up," I added.

We laughed to keep from getting upset, but it was a shame that shit like that went on and nothing was done.

"But life goes on, baby. We can't stop. What?"

It was July then, and by the end of August, my big brother was gone. That left me, standing beside Moms, trying to make things come together. Now, when the light bill was behind, she looked at me. When the water bill came, she looked at me. When rent time came, she looked at me. I guess the burden had fallen on Junie for so long, all he wanted to do was get away and try and make it on his own.

I thought about going in the military, to allow Uncle Sam to take care of me and my family, but they only wanted young men with diplomas, so that killed that idea. So I hit the streets and found a job.

Over the next two years I worked six jobs: security; washing cars as a lot attendant; cleaning rooms as houseman in a hotel; loading trucks for a food distribution company; and telemarketing—for two weeks.

Nobody was paying shit, but it kept my momma's shit on, and food on her table. And it kept my little brother focused on other things, instead of sitting around at 15 and 16 years old, wondering how bills were going to get paid, how he was going to wash before going to school, how he was going to iron his clothes before going to school, or how he was going to eat.

I wasn't making a lot, but I wanted my peoples to be all right. I wanted my little brother to have peace of mind so he could accomplish what me and Junie never did—graduate and get a high-school diploma. He had to. And I was going to make sure these bitches, money, and drugs didn't fuck up his judgment.

* * *

By the summer of '88, things weren't much better, but we were surviving. I was twenty and working in Chesapeake, making a little paper. I'd moved to Arbor Glenn apartments out in Chesapeake. Trying to get from Lake Edwards to Chesapeake was hell. I was working every day and didn't have shit.

Black, my little brother, was grabbing the few clothes and shit I was buying, because of our money situation. I didn't mind, because he was still in school and I knew what it was like. When I was at Bayside High School I caught a few jokes because of the shit I wore, but I knew Moms was doing the best she could, with three boys and no help from our sorry-ass pops.

My little brother was my heart. I would roll with a lot of things, but fucking with him brought out so much rage within me. I swore that I would do all I could to make sure he had.

Black, on the other hand, couldn't take the jokes. I don't know if it came from the suffering and hardship of growing up. Maybe it was just his personality. He always said that if anyone ever came out of their mouth wrong or disrespected him in any way he would kill them. He had always made statements like that since he was young. His family was all that ever mattered to him. He would go to all ends to look out for his family, but fuck everybody else in the world, as long as his peoples was alright. There was never a doubt in my mind.

Summer was ending, and I was still scraping and trying to maintain, going out occasionally for peace of mind. What better way to relax your mind than going to the club, meeting girls and finding someone?

At the time, everybody called their hanging partner *stickman*. My stickman at the time was Dog. He was real. You didn't have to be a thug-ass niggah for me to hang with you, because that wasn't me. But I had to know, if some shit kicked off, I wasn't going to be left holding the bag. Dog was from Norview, projects in Norfolk called Oakmont North. His family (his mom and her five sons) moved to Lake Edward in '85, and we'd been tight ever since.

My other stickman was Big G. He was more like me than anyone I had ever met. He'd moved to Lake Edward in '82, and we didn't start hanging until '85. Once we got to know each other, we were inseparable. Big G was from Brooklyn. He was a down-ass niggah, and it didn't take much to get him going. Especially when he started drinking, Dog and I knew some shit was about to kick off.

Summer was over and hanging out late, drinking, riding down to the beach, trying to fuck every tourist we could, had come to an end. Now it was time for Norfolk State to resume.

I was just chilling after a long day of work, when I heard a knock at the door. I got up wondering who the hell was knocking at my shit because my peoples usually called first.

"What's up, Dog?" I asked, opening up the door to let him and his company in.

"Nothing, niggah. Just stop through. Are you by yourself?" he asked in a low tone.

After I nodded yes, he proceeded to come inside.

"This is my girl MiMi I'm always talking about," he said, knowing he had never mentioned her before, "and this is her girl Tina. This is my niggah, Dee. Tina's here for orientation. She'll be going to State. She's from DC and wanted to meet one of my boys."

We all sat down for about twenty minutes. Dog was

always known to get girls to relax with jokes and conversation, and he'd always say, "Get a little juice in them and we'll be all right."

A few minutes had passed, and Dog got up and went in my spare room. I eventually made it there. We had no money, so our game had to be tight, knowing the event would be talked about later, when we got back on the block. You didn't have to fuck every time, but you had to represent. And if you weren't fucking, you had better keep the extra wheel occupied so your stickman could. Don't get the wrong idea. We didn't have sex every time somebody brought an extra girl along, but you knew, no matter what she looked like, you had to keep her ass company until your partner got his.

I finally got me a car—an Escort. I felt like everything was picking up. One Thursday evening, I stopped by Mom's house. She was cooking, as usual. Between my mom and my aunt, somebody was always cooking dinner. My aunt stayed in the apartments, while my mom lived in the townhouses, and we were always very close.

My aunt had four boys: Tee, Boot, Lo, and Dre. Tee was my age, dark skin, pretty smile—if you didn't get along with him, you had a problem. Boot, on the other hand, was a tall dark-skin brother with a body to make the women scream. The boys in the family always tried to encourage him to be a dancer, but it wasn't his style. If your girl had a friend that you were trying to keep occupied, Boot was your man. The 'ho's never complained, when it came to Boot. Dre was laid back, didn't give a fuck, usually sipping on that syrup and down for whatever.

Now my little cousin Lo was like Black. Walked around like he was mad at the world. By the time he was fifteen, he had been in two group homes, Tidewater Detention and Beaumont in Richmond. He had two counts of assault, which got him tossed out of school. Hardly a week had passed, when he was hit with a strong-armed robbery charge and two counts of malicious wounding.

When the family asked him why he kept getting into trouble, his reply was, "I got to get mine or die trying."

Tee and Dre left home right after school to join Uncle Sam's Army. Boot and Lo stuck around. They felt their mom couldn't make it without them, but Auntie was so strong, nothing could ever keep her down. They just wanted to get money another way, outside of working hard every day and not having shit to show.

Through the years, we watched these two sisters put pennies together and create miracles.

While Moms finished cooking, I figured I would stand outside and catch some air. Boot strolled up. "The neighborhood is going to shit, huh?"

"No bullshit! Mad shit going on."

"Where's Black?" he asked.

"Seen him coming up the street. He'll be here in a few."

"When Lo be home?" I asked.

"February. You know he gone dread."

"Auntie gonna make him cut them when he come home."

"She don't care. All she said was she just want him to know how to act so the man don't keep putting his ass away."

By this time Black came rolling up with his stick-man, Little.

"What's up, niggah?" I asked, giving him a pound.

"Nothing, man. Give me your car keys. I need to make a run."

"Don't be long. I got business," I said, handing him the keys.

"I don't want to hear all that shit," he said, getting in the car and pulling off.

Minutes later Big G and Dog pulled up, pumping straw hats. They jumped out the car with Michelob in their hands, talking about, "What's up? We going to the club?"

"No, fool," I said sarcastically.

They knew there was no way in hell I was going to miss the Big Apple on a Thursday night. Time was flying, and parking was hell if you weren't there by eleven. So I dipped home and threw on my gear.

Thursday night at the Big Apple, you came to impress, no half-stepping. I pulled out my olive green baggies that I'd bought from J.C. Penney's, my black pullover shirt from GAP, and my black patent leather shoes from Harding Shoes at Coliseum Mall in Hampton.

I arrived at the club about twelve. Just as I thought, there were no parking spaces up front. Actually there was no parking anywhere, so I parked down the street.

As I was going through the parking lot, I noticed MiMi, Tina and two girls trying to find a parking space.

"Hey, Dee," MiMi said.

"How you ladies doing?"

"Fine. I know I get a dance, Dee," Tina said.

"Of course. I'll be inside."

About this time something happened that really

caught my attention and changed something in me forever. Directly in front of the club sat two orange cones. Security came out and moved both cones so two of the prettiest 325i BMWs could park, a white with chrome rims and a blue with gold rims. They didn't park in parking spaces, but in front of the club.

Two young men stepped out of the BMWs, wearing baggy pants, silk shirts and enough jewelry to open their own jewelry store.

Four girls came prancing up, looking good as hell, and my mouth dropped. MiMi and Tina were nice, but these girls were dimes, head to toe, the kind niggahs dream of fucking.

One of the girls asked them to get in the club.

The guy responded by saying, "Y'all, bitches, crazy as hell! Better carry your ass and get the fuck out my face!"

The girls kept walking and laughed it off, but they had to feel embarrassed.

I asked myself, "How does a guy make such a degrading remark to a black woman as fine as she is and get away with it?" This was something I couldn't understand any more than these guys being able to park their shit in the front of the club and not in a parking space.

Once inside the club, Big G and Dog were leaning on the bar and handed me a Long Island Iced Tea. Girls were around them, so I came up and joined in the conversation. The conversation ran smooth, and I talked enough to make an impression. The drinks kept coming, and I was feeling real nice. I also knew that, because they had gotten there before me, Dog and Big G had to feel it more than I did.

I danced a little, but I kept checking out the guys who were driving the BMWs. These guys were fascinating. They were sitting at a table, where some other guys had joined them. The gear they sported was no joke. They had pieces of jewelry, not like the other two, but they were shining.

Through the night I saw many girls going to their table, just to speak and stand around, waiting to be talked to, but these guys paid them no attention. They were just sipping on champagne and joking amongst themselves.

I came off the dance floor and went over to where Big G was standing. I knew he was feeling nice because he was getting tired of people bumping into him, which was impossible to avoid, with the crowd.

Dog comes out of nowhere, "Damn! It's some bitches in here," he said.

When we talked, we sometimes referred to girls as *bitches* or *'ho's*, but never in a disrespectful manner, and never to their face, like the niggahs in the BMW did.

"You ain't lying, niggah," G replied.

"Yo, Dog," I said, "who them niggahs at the table where all those bad-ass 'ho's are standing around?"

"I don't know them, but they got those two nice-ass beamers. I think those niggahs from out Grandy Park. I don't know, but I was picking this girl up from out there and I saw the cars."

"The cars are definitely the shit, and the bitches are riding them niggahs' dick."

"It's that money, niggah," Dog said. "Them niggahs got money."

"Fuck them niggahs," said Big G. "The next motherfucker that bump into me, I'm gonna bust they motherfuckin' ass."

"Chill out, G! You getting ready to fuck up the pussy, dog," Dog said quickly.

"Let's get one more drink . . . then we out," I said.

Dog grabbed us all three more Iced Teas. As long

as we were with Dog, we could drink free all night. Dog was kicking with the bartender, and she looked out.

It was getting late and they were calling for drinks. Drinks were served until two, and the club closed soon after. Besides, G was fucked up and just a minute off somebody's ass. We weren't trying to get in no shit, but if Big G started off we would back him up. The only thing was, it wasn't like the earlier years. It was late '88, and niggahs were starting to die. All you were hearing about was how niggahs were dropping from gunshots. Fair play had gone out the window.

We stayed until the club closed then stood outside to catch whatever we could to carry back to the crib. I noticed one of the guys with the BMW coming out the club, a bad bitch tagging on his shirt. He opened the door for her, and she got inside. His partner came out and was standing beside him talking.

Another guy came walking up. As he walked past them, the guy with the white BMW walked up to the guy and asked him if he needed to see him.

The guy replied by telling him no, and before the guy could get another word in, he caught him in the jaw, yelling, "You trying to play me for soft." Then he hit him again.

I stood there asking myself, "How can a grown man allow somebody to punch him in his shit and do nothing?"

The third time, the guy with the white BMW punched him so hard, the guy fell up against the car and a .45 automatic hit the concrete. The driver of the white beamer picked it up and put one in the chamber.

Before he could shoot the guy, his partner grabbed his arm and told him, "Not out here. It's too many people."

The guy stood there looking like a bitch, with fear in his eyes.

I left there with what Dog had said in the club ringing in my head. "Them niggahs got money. It's that money."

Over the next several months I saw many changes. Now that Norfolk State was back in session, mad niggahs was coming in from New York and New Jersey to Norfolk to go to school or to take niggahs to school. Norfolk was beginning to blow, and young boys were coming in from everywhere, trying to get a piece of the pie.

First it was only the New York and Jersey kids making moves, then came the Washington, DC and Maryland crews. They never could get along, and it was always some kind of shit kicking off in the streets of Norfolk or on Norfolk State campus. New York kids were running Reservoir Avenue, and Jersey kids were running Spartan Village. DC kids were running Marshall and Corprew Avenue, along with the football team.

Then the Jamaicans out of New York came and started running their business across the Campostella Bridge, swamping the South Norfolk area.

Most of these guys came down to go to school, and all of these areas were all in a one-mile radius of the campus. Park Avenue ran right past the campus and had generated a lot of business over the years, catering to the college clientele.

Everybody got their hair cut at Kappatal Kuts on Park Avenue and their cars washed at the hand car wash on the corner of Brambleton and Park Avenue, just because, it was convenient while they got their haircut.

Also, if you drove some fly-ass shit and wanted

everybody to see, that was the place to be. People would always hit the mall before going to the club, football games or any other event.

Military Circle Mall was the hangout spot. People would go to Lynnhaven Mall and shop, go home, and get dressed to go to Military Circle. The kids from up North always liked to go downtown to Granby Mall. It gave them that inner city feeling of the outside shopping, but some shit was always kicking off downtown.

There was a lot of shit going on, because everyone was trying to make their money. Every morning you picked up The Virginia Pilot/Ledger Star there were reports of deaths and shootings. An abundance of young men came from up North with the mentality that they were coming to Norfolk to make money, and they did. But many came thinking that Norfolk niggahs were slow and that they were going to over-charge them or rob them. Many New York and DC niggahs went back home "boxed up."

As months passed I saw many things. I observed and paid attention to how big-money kids acted, and how they carried themselves. I saw that they only fucked the finest girls. They spent money like it was water, always handling their business first; bitches came later. Whatever it took to make that money, they did.

It was not all good, but I wanted it—nice cars; fine-ass girls; fly-ass gear; nice jewelry; and money to blow. I wanted to shine. I set out to get in with the big boys, and all I needed was time. Time to ease my way into the league of the big money-makers.

CHAPTER 2

"Black"

Black was in his last year of school, and Lake Edward was becoming a hot drug area. He was out there every day, so it kind of pulled him in. I started seeing little knots of money, new sneakers and gear, so I asked him, "What you doing out here?"

"Just selling a little bit, to keep things going," he said.

"A little bit can get you a lot of time. You need to make a choice—either stop fucking around, or go all out so you'll have something to show for your paper. Niggahs ain't playing out here in these streets, especially those New York niggahs coming down South to get it."

"I'll be finishing school soon; then it will be summertime, and shit blows in the summer. The only thing is, this niggah trying to pimp me by giving me these little-ass fifty blocks, and I'm not making shit off them," he said, showing me six little beige rocks.

"You got trust in me, right?" I asked.

"No doubt," he answered quickly.

"Work with me then. Every now and then when I go out, let me hold a knot. I'll spend about twenty or thirty dollars and I'm going to get in with some real niggahs, but I'm going to need your help. From now on when we shop, instead of buying two or three shirts from the GAP, let's buy Thalhimers and Polo, and instead of buying two pairs of sneakers, let's get a pair of Bally's. Let's start looking like money."

It wasn't easy, but he agreed.

Money was real tight. But I knew I wanted glitter and gold and I wanted my brother to have glitter and gold. Our time to shine was coming.

I got a weekend job so I could fix my little Escort up so that it looked like I had some money. I went to DJ's on Tidewater Drive to buy a tape, and behind the counter they had Africa-shaped medallions swinging from a gold rope, both gold-plated. I had seen many of the boys from up North wearing these ropes, so I bought one. Somewhere in my travels, I heard that if you put clear fingernail polish on it, it wouldn't change color.

It was May '89, and Black was graduating from Bayside High in a month. It was a done deal. He really had to fuck up not to get this piece of paper now. I stood back looking at my little brother, knowing that nobody's momma or daddy was as proud as I was. He had accomplished what neither of his brothers could . . . or maybe what *I* couldn't.

Junie was smart, but the need for money and other things that we went through as a family may have interfered with his focus in life. I, on the other hand, went to school but hated it. I possibly could have given it the extra push to get it done, but I hated being there. I could read, write, add and subtract. Most important, I could comprehend whatever the fuck I read.

Presently I focused my attention on the blazing hot streets, wanting to make a name for myself. I still didn't have much but was starting to stand out with the little I had.

I was working two jobs and, on my weekend job, met two guys that would contribute to my achievements. One was a kid from New York. His mom lived in DC, and he ran in the circle with kids from DC and New York. This kid would ask me for rides sometimes, and I would drop him off in Spartan Village, at a crib with these guys from DC.

Soon after, I was invited in and introduced. Now I was chilling with Trent and Phil in the townhouse. Trent and Phil had all of Spartan Village locked and were moving their way to Park Place, with half of the university's football team holding them down. There was always several niggahs at the house and girls lying around, not to mention those two pretty-ass Rottweilers that stood guard at the gate outside.

When we stopped over, people would be hanging, drinking, and smoking weed like there was no tomorrow.

I saw and met a lot of heads. Now when I saw these same guys out, they would recognize and show love. The girls I was meeting would automatically characterize me as a hustler, by association.

The other guy was a barber, Slim. He worked at Kappatal Kuts on Park Avenue. Slim was the one cutting all these big money-makers' heads, so they would see me getting a cut every Thursday, preparing for the club. Many times I'd be chilling in the barbershop, and these guys would come up there to show Slim their new cars and sounds. That was always important. I would compliment niggahs on their new shit, and they would act all nonchalant. But I knew different. Niggahs liked for other people to recognize their shit. These guys were proud of the material shit they had accumulated from hustling.

Once I had met this guy showing Slim his sounds, when I pulled up. Slim called me over to check out the sounds also. It was a red 325i BMW. I had seen the guy around and heard he had real money. Young-ass niggah from Huntersville housing projects off Tidewater Drive. The kid's name was Tracy. Little, short, dark-skinned kid, with gold fronts.

After showing Slim and me his sounds, he wanted to be next in the chair. But my appointment was up after the guy in the chair. Tracy said he would give me twenty dollars and pay for my cut if I let him go next. Of course, I had no problem with that. He offered me a ride with him so I could check out his sounds. We rode around the corner to Far East, a Chinese restaurant on Princess Anne Rd.

In general conversation I questioned the fact that he was from Huntersville. I was asking him questions about how a niggah from Norfolk made so much money. What could I lose?

All he could say was he didn't want to fuck with me like that, but he would school me in conversation. He said, while pulling on a joint, "I have peoples in New York and I go there and score. So I know my prices. But for a niggah trying to get over, like the New York niggahs who come here, if they're straight on prices, I'll buy from them rather than take the trip. If they try to overcharge and fuck me out my money, I'll tell them I'm buying. Then I'll stick up their motherfuckin' ass. They can accept it or challenge me. If they challenge me, I'll send them back

to New York in a fuckin' box! Live or die! I don't give
a fuck! That's their mentality towards us. Now I'm
the same fuckin' way."

I was sitting here with a killer, and instead of being
shook in any way, I was trying to pick this niggah's
brain, learning all I can about getting this money. My
only agenda was for my mom, brother and myself to
never see those broke-ass days ever again.

It was Thursday night again, and I pulled in front
of the club. I noticed that the blue beamer that usually sat in front wasn't there, only the white one.
From hanging around the barbershop and car wash,
word was that Art, the driver of the missing beamer,
had gotten caught up at the Norfolk International
Airport with kilos of cocaine taped to his body, while
coming in from Cali. As I stood there looking around,
I realized that those BMWs weren't shit any more.
compared to the shit I saw in the parking lot now—
red Jaguar; pretty white 740i BMW with deep dish
hammers; 190 Mercedes Benz sitting on chrome, with
a full kit. Not to mention the Volvos, Corvettes, and
other nice shit that stood out.

When I entered the club now, with Bally's on, buttoned down polos, and my thick gold chain, niggahs
would give me dap, and bad-ass bitches would give
me hugs instead of waves. Instead of just speaking,
now they were having conversation. Those who I
thought were out of my league or untouchable now
moved my way, trying to find out on the sly my name
and where I came from.

I went to the bar and got drinks for me and Slim.
There were a few other money-makers around, so I
asked if I could get them something, playing the role
of a big spender—I had to play the role, if I wanted

the part. I ended up spending about thirty dollars, but I had my brother's knot of one hundred and fifty, with about thirty singles on the inside. I made sure that when I paid for shit, niggahs and bitches got a good look at the knot. I peeled off two twenties to pay for the drinks then went to chill with my peoples, G and Dog.

The club was hype. Ricky T, popular local DJ, had the club rocking.

All of a sudden, niggahs started arguing. I saw this little, light-skin guy slap the shit out of this tall, kinda stout guy. Before the stout guy could do anything, this thick, dark-skin kid came across the club with a chair and split the guy's head open. He fell, and blood streamed down his face as the two guys made a quick exit. The lights were turned on, and the club was closed for the night.

Two weeks later, while in the club, I heard gunshots in the front by the door. Everybody started to panic and run. As we eased out the club, the small light-skin kid and one of his other partners lay dead in a pool of blood in the doorway. His man who split the guy's head open with the chair lay injured.

They shut down the club after that, and when it reopened, it was strictly twenty-five and older. It even had a new name: BROADWAY.

It was summer time. The girls were hot, and my phones were ringing off the hook. I got a call from this girl. She said that we had met at the Big Apple, and she wanted to spend some time. She wanted me to come out Oakley Park, projects in the Campostella area, and pick her up at 12:30 at night.

Most of the Norfolk projects were really drug-infested, and it was one way in and one way out. You heard about niggahs dropping everyday. Every morning *The Virginian Pilot* would print something like: "Man shot in the neck out Grandy Park"; "Murder in Kappatal Kuts on Colley Avenue."

One of the most shocking was, "Four bodies found dead in a Volvo in the Norview section of Norfolk." Kids were getting stabbed in the head on basketball courts in Diggs Park. Bodies were being found all around Lake Edward. If they weren't by the dumpsters in the alleys, they were being pulled out the lake. All this shit was going on, and she expected me to come out there and scoop her up.

I told her, "I'll check your ass tomorrow during the day, unless you got a ride."

I remembered my mom going out Oakley Park to visit her peoples. So I stopped at my cousin's house when I went out there. It usually worked out that if you knew somebody nobody would fuck with you. While out there, something caught my eye. There was a kid with dreads sitting under a tree selling fifty blocks like he was the candy lady. I called Black to tell him because he had said the niggah he was dealing with was trying to pimp him. He told me to get one and bring it to Lake Edward. When I got to the crib he took one look and flipped. He found out that the niggahs out there put some shit on it called "come back," which made the coke larger after it was cooked. Because the shit was still good and the twenty-block was slightly larger, the fiends went for it.

Summer was heating up. It was about 98 degrees. A lot of drugs were being moved in Lake Edward, and Black was wide open. He was buying at least six fifty-blocks a day and making money. Soon the Jamaican under the tree wanted to give us good prices on ounces. His seeing our faces on a regular basis began paying off. He gave Black his number so they could connect. Now Black worked even harder, moving ounces by the day. He was now selling to everyone that was on the corner with him, pumping fifty blocks.

Everything was going well. Black was making money and shining a little more, but not the way I wanted. I still had a long way to go. I was doing more shopping at Granby Mall, because they had all the New York fashions. I used to frequent this store called Zig Zag, the only store in Norfolk that I knew sold Bally's. I had just started buying hundred-dollar shoes while Black was definitely buying hundred-dollar sneakers.

Black bought himself a Ford Tempo and was making moves fast. Now that he had a car, he was able to move all around the Beach and not limit himself to the Lake Edward area. He never played in Norfolk too much. That was my domain.

Black had started dating this girl in Lake Edward and was over there more than he was at home. Her mom was real chill with it, especially when he started paying some bills. She was real down-to-earth and knew the streets and how to get over. She and Black became real tight, and he was holding his shit in her house. That was real convenient.

My regular job had shut down after I had quit the weekend job. So here I was with free time on my hands and money in my pocket. I wasn't moving any drugs because Black wasn't having it. Even though I was older, he always said, "Moms got to have one of us around at all times. So if I get caught up, you got to hold shit down. So don't fuck with nothing; I'll look out."

Black couldn't get enough drugs. He was running a lot and didn't have a lot of time. One day he told me, "Dee, I need weight. I'm making money, but I'm running too much. If I had weight, I could sell weight and stop fucking around hand to hand with fiends. I can run less and make more."

Between looking out for me, hitting his girl's mom off with paper, and taking care of shit at Mom's house, he was getting a little frustrated. He had also told me he didn't like fucking with those Jamaicans out in Oakley Park because it was getting hot out there, and he couldn't understand shit them niggahs was saying sometimes.

One time, one of them copped an attitude. In a matter of days I had bought us two guns. I took one and gave the other to Black. I wasn't working and was spending most of my time running the streets. There was no telling where I was going to end up, so I felt I needed it.

CHAPTER 3

"Making Connects"

I had accumulated a train of bitches. A few times I found myself in a pressured situation, because they weren't all living single lives. But with my gun on my side and one in the chamber, it eased the tension.

Big G, Dog, and I were hanging in Club Royal Blue, a nightclub off Little Creek Road, and Barry's, off Military Highway—both in Norfolk. Going to the Royal Blue changed the course of things. Hustlers were few at this club. You could count them on your hand—unlike the Big Apple. The girls were definitely easier because they were used to kids in the military and their pockets just weren't as deep.

I remember going to Royal Blue every week and seeing this one particular guy. He was light-skinned, well-built, with gold fronts in his mouth. Every time he smiled, all you saw was gold. He wore a lot of jewelry, including a Rolex that glittered with diamonds, and always dressed to impress. He drove a 190 Mercedes Benz, chromed out and "kitted" up. It used to belong to Duke, but he was moving on to bigger and better things on the low. Even though his man Art had got knocked off, he was still making money. All you had to do was listen to the bitches. They knew who had the money.

Mr. Royal Blue and I would often say hello to each other, but conversation never clicked. Then one Thursday I came in the club and saw Slim standing over there talking to him. I went over and bought a round of drinks. Of course, girls were all around. Mr. Royal Blue was known for running women, and Slim—ever since I had known him—always kept himself a bale of 'ho's. We all kicked it for a while.

I was hoping he would get relaxed so I could kick it on the business level, but it never escalated to that. About 1:00 a.m. I decided to find my peoples, Big G and Dog. Black was looking out for me. And whenever we dipped out, I would make sure Big G was straight.

The next day I went to Kappatal Kuts and talked with Slim. Our conversation was usually about bitches, but today it was about putting me in with Mr. Royal Blue. He told me he was going to give him a call and hit me later. About 10:00 a.m. He had set it up for me to meet him at Kappatal Kuts Saturday at noon.

I called Black and told him to meet me at mom's house. I knew things were going well because, when he came through the door, he was rocking new Guess shorts, Fila T-shirt, pretty white Fila sneakers, and his new gold chain he'd bought at Fine Jewelry in Best Square Shopping Center off Military Highway.

"What's up, fool?" I asked.

"Nothing, niggah. What's up with you?" asked as if he was in a hurry.

"What are you ready to buy right now? Tell me how much weight and a good-ass price."

"Big eight, for twenty-five hundred," he said.

"I'm talking to this kid from Jersey tomorrow for you. I met him through Slim. You know and I know that he's going to try and play middleman. So whatever that Jersey niggah prices are, Slim gonna add something to it. So what you want to do?"

"Run with it and let me know what he can do. I'm ready. Right now I got to run. Tia's in the car," he said walking downstairs.

Tia was his long-time girl that he lived with in Lake Edward along with her mom. Black was always known to get his share of ass, but through making money in these streets and living at Tia's mom's house, he wasn't making a lot of noise. Tia kind of had him locked down. He wasn't missing anything, because Tia was nice. She had a light-brown complexion, wavy dark-brown hair, thick breasts and a tiny waist, with an ass that kept banging for days. I knew he cared about her because he told me that he had to snatch her ass up about two times. Any other girl he would have just cut them loose before he let them get to him like that.

I met Mr. Royal Blue at Kappatal Kuts as planned. This time he was driving a champagne-colored BMW with a kit on it. He pulled up and told me to get in.

"You wanted to talk to me," he said with his northern accent.

I climbed in and stated my purpose. "Me and my peoples are buying ounces at a time and paying like seven hundred, but looking to find a big eight for twenty-five hundred."

Actually we were paying nine hundred an ounce, and he probably knew that, but I had to play my hand as I saw fit. I had learned a lot, fucking with those kids from up North.

"I might be able to do three thousand, but twenty-five hundred, I don't think so," he said smiling, fronts gleaming.

I wanted to say, "Yo, niggah, I'm real! Teach me what you know," but I kept my poise, knowing once I put Black in he was going to handle his business.

"Too high, man. Work with me," I said.

"Tell you what—if you can do twenty-eight, I'll front you the same."

"Sounds good. Let me holler at my peoples," I said.

"Just call Slim. He can get in touch with me. It's like that all day."

I called Black from the Spur on Brambleton Avenue. I knew he was at Tia's house sleeping; noon was too early for him to be up.

I didn't like the phone, but I just talked real short.

"Hello," her mother said.

"Where Black?"

"Hold on. We throwing some shit on the grill later. Are you coming through?" she asked.

"No doubt," I said.

Seconds later Black came to the phone. "What's up?" I could hear the sleep in his voice. he says.

"Niggah say twenty-eight and he'll double what you want."

"What?" he said, as if he couldn't believe what he just heard. He was awake now. "Niggah gonna front a big eight!"

"It's on you," I said. "Tell me something."

"Now, I'm getting up."

I went in the barbershop and told Slim to hit his man and call me at Tia's house to let me know something. I went straight there, and it wasn't forty-five minutes before the phone rang.

"Hello," I said.

"Yo, Dee! It's Slim."

"What's up?"

"Come on through and check me out. I'll be looking out."

Black and I jumped in the Tempo and ran up Brambleton. Slim came out and sat in his car. Black went over and joined him.

In minutes we were back on the interstate, headed to the crib, a quarter of a kilo under the seat.

When we got to Tia's house Black pulled out his scale.

"Dee, this shit is seven grams short," he said. "Know what too—I don't like my money going through so many hands. I counted it up myself and I know it's straight. If your man say that it came up short, I'm going to go up to the barbershop and put a bullet in your man's head. I'm not bullshitting at all. I believe that niggah will do twenty-five, but your boy getting middleman pay. I'm going to hit that niggah off Monday with his paper."

"That fast," I said.

"I'm going to give Little two, but then I got to stay out there because he let niggahs fuck him out of sales."

"What about your boy Mark?" I asked.

"Mark scoring from June, and June's prices are nice. If I meet his prices, Mark will be paying what I'm paying. Sometimes you have to do that. You get Mark money for a big eight then you go in buying nine and maybe he'll front you nine."

"Can a niggah handle a half a brick?" I asked.

"I'm a worker, niggah," he yelled. "What's up?"

"Who else out here is handling shit like you and Mark?"

"Dink making just as much, if not more, but he's

doing most of his business out Plaza Apartments and Friendship. It's wild as a bitch out both of them motherfuckers. That reminds me—I forgot to tell you that I need a gun," he said.

"Where the other one?"

"I keep that in the car because it's straight and if the man stop me he can't fuck with it. I'm talking about one that's not registered, preferably with no bodies.

"You won't believe what your crazy motherfuckin' cousin did." he said. "They robbed a niggah out Bayside Arms projects, off Witchduck Road, and then went out Bridal Creek to buy from this niggah Wil and robbed him. Lo shot that bitch in the shoulder. That happen Wednesday, and last night those Bayside Arms boys came out Lake Edward blasting."

We started laughing.

As I walked out the house headed home, Black walked out behind me. I got in my car, threw up the peace sign and yelled, "Be safe, fool."

"Coming back later?" he asked. "They throwing some shit on the grill about eight.

"Oh yeah!"

"I'm going to change my pager number Monday. Then I'm going to give you mine and get me a new one because sometimes I need to get in touch with you *pronto*. I also want you to move back out this way. Fuck Chesapeake! Find a spot out here by the first and let me know."

I left and went home. I had about seven messages on my machine. I only cared to hear two. My girl called to say she was getting off at five and was coming through.

The other was from Tara, with her sweet, tender voice. "Call me if you find time. You've been on my mind, and I really miss you."

Now my main girl, Venus, was just too sweet. We

had been dating since high school. She was petite, and fine as hell. Looked like a baby doll and always dressed casual but cute—never anything too provocative. She was from the College Park area of Virginia Beach. Her parents had a big home, which impressed me, and as we became closer, I found out that I was her first. I was in love, but this last year I was getting kind of bored with her.

Tara, on the other hand, had just graduated from Booker T. Washington High School in Norfolk, off Park Avenue. She was shorter and darker than Venus, but just as fine. Her body was perfectly sculpted for me. Her breasts were the perfect size. Small waist and a phat ass that stuck out like God had truly blessed her. She had a strut, not just a walk. Her nails were perfectly done, and her hair looked like she just stepped out the beauty salon—long in the back, with a layered cut. She reminded me of those fly-ass bitches who were on Duke's dick and hanging around Mr. Royal Blue, but this was mine. Sex the first time was unforgettable. We stayed in for two days straight, only coming out for food.

We had been seeing each other for about two months, whenever we found time, which was quite often. We had met at Harlem Nights, in Hampton. This was a players' club, no half-stepping allowed. Every big money-maker from Norfolk to Richmond frequented this club.

One Thursday, Big G and I left Royal Blue early and went across the water, just to check out the parking lot party. All the girls at this club were new to us. Quite a few of the bitches went to Hampton University. They were top of the line, but with attitudes, unlike Norfolk State girls. When Big G pulled up in his new Maxima, all eyes were on us. Before pulling it off the lot, he had a kit, rims, and factory tint all financed in the price. He went straight to Discount Auto Sound and had the sounds knocking. With the sounds screaming and the Maxima clean, we looked like moneymaking hustlers on the prowl.

I saw Tara talking to this slim, dark-skin kid leaning on a white Saab. He had on black slacks, red silk shirt, red Bally's, and a display of jewelry on his neck, wrist and hands. I figured he was a money-maker because every time I went downtown to Granby Mall to Zig Zag I would see him. He had a bright yellow Milano, chromed out, looking like some shit a niggah would kill for, no doubt.

All of a sudden, this girl came out and pulled Tara's arm, letting her know it was time to go. Big G was on them. He pulled around before they could get in the car, and a toot of the horn stopped them in their tracks.

I got out, hoping my appearance would do most of the talking and the Maxima would finish it up. I saw her eyes go from my bright gold Bally's, to my dark Fila jeans, past my blue-and-gold, striped polo shirt, straight to Black's new gold chain I was wearing.

Conversation flowed, and we all ended up going to breakfast at Denny's, off Newtown Road. We lucked up because these 'ho's were from Norfolk and they had to go back to our side anyway.

We hooked up the next day and the weekend that followed. I did everything that I said I would do if I ever got a girl like her, but she had a surprise for me. She showed me remarkable skills and fucked my head up.

After about a month, I let her know that if she ever even attempted to fuck with another niggah, I would split her goddamn skull. Beyond a shadow of a doubt, I meant it.

Venus stopped through about 5:30 p.m., and I was

lying around like I was so tired. We talked for a few. Then she climbed in bed, and I sexed her up royally, as usual. Things had become routine. I still cared for her, but my head and life were moving fast. I made an excuse about things I had to do and she was gone—with an attitude. I didn't care.

As soon as she got in the car, I was on the phone, telling Tara to be dressed. I let her know that I was coming through in about thirty minutes and we were going to a cookout.

We arrived at Tia's house, and her mom put Tara to work. Her and Tia moms hit it off quick and fast. When Black came in and saw her, he gave me a pound, as if to tell me that I had done good. Real good.

The 10:00 a.m. phone call woke me up. It was Black on the other end talking about, "We're waiting on you, fool. Moms got pancakes, sausages, and getting ready to drop eggs in the skillet right now. I don't know if shit going to be left. Boot and Lo on their way around here now. Come on, fool."

I got to Mom's house and went straight to our room. Black followed me. When he came in, I asked him if he was going to see Mr. Royal Blue today. He answered by pulling twenty-eight hundred out the drawer.

I pulled out a .38 and a .45 automatic.

"This kid I know from Foundation Park projects in Campostella took me to Lincoln Park projects in Portsmouth and introduced me to this guy they call 'Fence Man.' The guy said they didn't have bodies on them, but all I can say is don't get caught with them."

"I don't give a fuck because this .45 getting ready to get bodies on it. Little got some peoples coming from Richmond, trying to buy half a brick. I'm going to take Lo and Jay and see what these niggahs know. If I get these niggahs, I won't need Mark. I'll be able to buy my own half by Friday."

Thursday came and Big G and I were in the club as usual. I was in the back shooting pool with this bitch I definitely didn't mind getting with.

Then someone hits me in my side.

"What you drinking?" he asked.

"Ice Tea," I said.

"All right, I'll be at the bar," he said.

I finished my game, telling the little shorty that I would be back, so I could go get my drink and scream at Mr. Royal Blue.

"How you feel, baby?" he asked.

"Fine. You know that," I answered, giving him a pound.

"How was everything?"

"Fine, except we were a quarter short," I told him.

"For real," he said with a surprised look. "Damn, I'll take care of that shit next time."

"Good looking out. Check this—I might be trying to get a half. What can you do for me?"

"Ninety-five hundred, if you coming like that. I don't want to hold a brother down. If you can blow, I want to see you blow," he said.

"With that much cash, partner, I want that shit to go from my hand to yours. Too many things happen when money travels."

He laughed and grabbed a napkin to write his pager number and code. "Hit me when you ready. Hey! You know shorty you were shooting pool with? That bitch is nice. She's married, and she'll fuck quick. Don't sleep on it," he said.

I went back and finished talking to the girl and wrote down my pager number for her. I even gave her a code, like the big money-makers did. I wasn't really in a club mood.

My mind was on Black and Lo. I knew he told me that he was meeting those niggahs from Richmond in Newport News tonight, and I didn't know how shit was going to turn out. Richmond niggahs were known for acting up just as bad as Norfolk kids.

I got with Big G, and after a few more drinks, we were out. He knew something was on my mind, but at this time, I couldn't speak on it. He knew everything that was going on, but if something went wrong, it would be better left between blood. If some things got repeated, Black could lose his life or his freedom. And if anyone hurt my brother in any way, there would definitely be some slow walking and sad singing behind them.

I got to the crib about 1:00 a.m., paged Black, and received no call back. I sat there with my stomach churning, not being able to sleep. Then about 2:30 a.m. the phone rang.

"What's up, niggah?" Black said.

"What's up, fool?" I responded in a nonchalant manner, not letting him know I was glad to hear his voice or that I was sitting around, worried half to death.

"Call your man in the morning. It's on!" he yelled, all hyped up.

"For real," I said. "I talked to him earlier tonight, and he said ninety-five."

"Hell, yeah! Call that niggah early in the morning. We on now, fool." Then he hung up the phone.

I was feeling so good I jumped up, threw on shorts, T-shirt, and Reeboks, no sock, and headed out. Where I was going, no fly shit was needed.

I got to the Casablanca on Princess Anne Road about 3:00 a.m. Alcohol was still being served in white foam cups. The law was to stop serving at 2:00 a.m., but at the Casablanca, anything goes.

This club was wild as shit. You could get anything you wanted in the back. You had kids selling weed, cocaine, and heroin. Whatever your pleasure, they had it. It was no surprise that almost everybody was packing their shit, when they went inside. Many, many niggahs had lost their lives in this club, but every hustler in the Tidewater area made it his last stop, before calling it a night.

It was made up of a small bar, DJ stand, a small dance floor that stayed packed until the club closed, and two pool tables in the back room. In the back there was the scent of "woos"—crack in weed—and "yes-yes"—cocaine in weed—burning.

Niggahs would always be gambling in pool, cards, craps, or the new game that the niggahs up North brought down, Cee-lo. I wasn't familiar with the game, but this particular night I was standing watching while about five big money-makers were playing.

The guy with the yellow Milano who was talking to Tara was heading up the game. They called him "the bank."

He looked up and saw me. "Put your money up, niggah," he said. "The same way I'm going to break these niggahs, I'll break you. I don't give a fuck who money I take. It's all good."

"Can't get my paper on some shit I don't understand."

"I'll take it as I teach you," he replied.

Some of the guys started laughing—the ones who weren't losing.

This dark-skinned girl standing beside me told me not to play that shit.

I asked her why.

"The game is too fast to learn while you're playing," she said.

"Can you play?" I asked.

"I know how, but I don't. Niggahs out the park play all the time," she said.

"What's your name?"

"They call me Ce-Ce."

"Know what, Ce-Ce—I've seen you many times, mostly at the Big Apple."

"Yeah, I've seen you too."

She had more gold hanging from her neck than any niggah I'd seen—gold bracelets bundled up on one arm, gold bangles running up the other, and rings on every finger. I hadn't seen too many money-making bitches. She either had a niggah making plenty of money or was doing her own thing. She was fly as hell and knew it, and I was attracted to her. But once our conversation got going, it was like talking to one of my boys.

We talked until it was time to go. She gathered up her crew, and we all walked out joking and talking. I had never met so many cool-ass bitches. They kicked it and talked like they were down-ass niggahs, and I really liked that shit. She asked if I was going to check out a new club in Portsmouth called David's on Saturday.

I told her that I might come out, but I really didn't fuck with Portsmouth too much. Then I asked her if she was going to put me on with one of her girls I was eyeing. She had no problem there.

Then I realized something—cool as she was and as many girls as she swung with, why try to get with her? Just kick it as friends and then fuck all her friends.

I got to my mom's house about 10:00 a.m. Friday. Black was already there reading the paper. I looked at the front page: "Two Virginia State University Students Murdered in Newport News."

"Damn, niggah. What's this?" I asked.

"That's Lo and Jay—shit happen real fast and kind of got out of hand," he said.

"I heard that. But damn!"

"Damn nothing! Fuck them bitch niggahs! I don't

give a fuck about them! They knew the game when they got in it. Now let's make this motherfuckin' money!"

What could I say? He was paying the bills, and he was right. Nobody gave a fuck about our family, but us.

I got the phone and paged Mr. Royal Blue to see what was up and when. "Yo, this is Dee."

"Can I talk on this line?" he asked.

"Yeah, it's straight."

"Do you know where Newpointe Condos are? Behind Food Lion on Newtown Road?"

"Yeah!" I said.

"How long will it take you to get there?"

"I guess about thirty minutes," I said.

I could have gotten there in five, as close as I was. But where I was wasn't his business.

He gave me an address and, in a half hour, me and Black were going into a condo out in Newpointe.

Two guys were already there. Mr. Royal Blue introduced them, and I introduced Black.

"Can you handle a whole brick?" he asked.

"For sure," Black said.

"How much time you need?"

"The weekend," Black answered.

"From here on out, you'll call me, but you'll be dealing with them," he said.

"I'm going to give my brother your number, and he'll use my code, but from here on out, you'll be dealing with him," I told him.

Couple months passed and business was good. Black was now buying a whole kilo of cocaine a week. Mr. Royal Blue was still fronting him whatever he bought. I had given up the apartment in Arbor Glenn and moved out Campus East. I got a two-bedroom townhouse and laid it out with Black's help. He wanted a spot where he could just chill, smoke weed, and answer his pager without interference from Tia and her peoples. He really cared for her, but he needed his privacy to hook up with other bitches.

Black had traded in the Ford Tempo for a burgundy Acura Legend. When I told him I could get this pretty black Pathfinder that I had seen, with the Escort and fifteen hundred, he talked shit to me.

After hearing me talk for about a month, he gave in and went to take a look.

"I like this bitch here," he said, driving the Pathfinder off the lot. "Where we going?" he asked in an excited voice.

"Home, niggah," I answered.

He asked again, sparking a blunt he had pulled out of the pouch of his hoody.

"Wherever, fool. I'm riding," I said, laying my seat back.

I was just lying around and heard the door open. I jumped up. Nobody had any business just walking in my house.

"Fuck you jumping for, fool? Be done jumped up and got beat down," Lo said, acting all serious.

"Fool, you better carry your ass."

"Where Black?

"I don't know," I answered.

"He told me to meet him here in fifteen minutes and that was thirty minutes ago. Both of y'all motherfuckers on some bullshit. I'm about to stop fucking with you."

"Give me some dish detergent so I can wipe this shit down," Dog yelled from outside.

"What's up, man?"

"Put these in the freezer," Dog said, handing me a twelve-pack of Michelob. "Big G on his way around here. I just talked to him."

"What time we jetting out Northside Park?" I asked.

"Shit . . . I guess about 5:00 p.m. We'll see when Big G gets here," he said.

Every Sunday there was a routine. We would go out to Northside about 5:00 p.m. or 6:00 p.m., chill until the sun went down, go by Norfolk State, come home and chill until 11:00 then head to the Cotton Club.

We stood out front awhile, cleaning up our cars, then grabbed another twelve-pack and headed out to the park. Just like every week, the McDonald's and Burger King across from the park were jammed pack, and the line to get on the park was backed up.

I was with Big G, and our other boy, Terri, was with Dog. These days we weren't packing up in the car, because we all were on the prowl. You couldn't pick up no bitches, being four and five deep in a car.

After parking and pouring our beers in cups, it was time to find something. There were so many bitches out, it was pathetic. We kicked it, drank until we were feeling real nice, and collected as many numbers as possible. The girls impressed me out at the park, but very seldom did I find something to make me flip out. My peoples saw it the same way, but we were all out for a good time.

"Let's get ready and roll by Norfolk State," Dog yelled.

Without hesitation, we were out. Now out by Norfolk State, the environment was totally different. We saw more women—the kind with kids at home, but still looking good and more conservative. Most of the cars belonged to niggahs from the military: Cutlasses; Hondas; Maximas; and Camaros. And guys were clean cut, pumping fade haircuts.

The niggahs by Norfolk State were thuggish, pants sagging, shirts off, with beards and goatees. Many were straight rugged, looking as if they hadn't shaved in days. We would hear sounds banging out of the Mercedes Benzs, Acuras, BMWs, Volvos, 300ZXs and Corvettes.

The bitches were wearing damn near nothing. They would come to us and see what we were getting into. Niggahs used to fight for a spot in front of Twin Towers, one of the girl dorms on campus. Usually the girls didn't have shit and really wanted to get off campus. We all had different pick-up skills, which had expanded from watching each other over the years. Everybody's approach was different, but reliable.

Dog preferred light-skinned females. He would talk to them and ask them about going to Waterside for a walk. They would walk around looking at the shops, and he definitely had to get them something to eat because they were always hungry. Then he would get something to drink and head to his crib.

Big G was always into music. He would usually offer something to eat, which usually worked, and something to sip on. Then they would ride around and pump his sounds, while talking about getting up, and head to his crib. He preferred brown-skinned girls with big asses. The girl definitely had to have a big ass.

I liked girls from up North, Jersey or New York, preferably from the inner city. I didn't give a fuck about their color. I liked ass, but it didn't have to be all that. A woman's breasts were what caught my attention and made my dick hard as a fucking rock. The girls from up North just had a laid-back attitude, like the girls I'd met in the Casablanca. It was like hanging with your partners, except you could fuck them. Every time I would touch them, and they would speak with that northern accent and sweet voice, I knew they weren't my partners.

Most of them liked to smoke weed. So, we would cruise to the beach, while getting lifted, then stroll the boardwalk down by 50th St., where there wasn't much traffic.

When I stood there, hugging them, watching the moon sit on the water, it usually got them. I was bringing them something they had just seen on television, something unreal. They weren't used to that shit. I knew it worked because, as many times as I had done it, it was still a beautiful sight to behold.

Afterwards we would grab something fast to eat and carry it back to the crib and see what's up.

We didn't fuck like we wanted to all the time, but we kept going back to campus, picking up different bitches over and over.

We ended up at the Cotton Club as usual. Dog was on the dance floor, and Big G was chilling with me over by the pool tables where all the money-makers were. I was rocking some green Bally's, beige slacks, green silk shirt, and Black's new herringbone that he'd bought from Super Star Jewelry. I was seeing quite a few new money-makers popping up on the scene, hanging around the pool table.

I put my quarters on the table, and the guys playing quickly turned to me to let me know that their particular table was a hundred dollars a game.

"No problem. I'll bet," I responded.

I wasn't a shark or anything, but I knew these niggahs couldn't beat me.

Bitches were all around the table.

We started playing, and the crowd got larger as the game progressed.

I waited until the perfect moment to enhance my

image as a money-maker. I told one of the wait-
resses—actually the finest waitress, who I also wanted
to get with—to bring me three shots of Hennessy, a
bottle of Moët, and some champagne glasses. I paid
for it with a phat-ass knot. I turned where everybody
could see and peeled off four twenties and said,
"That's you."

That meant she could keep the change. She was
impressed and thought I had paper like those other
niggahs. (Later on we fucked.)

With bitches looking on, I knew I had them. It was
just a matter of saying the right thing to get whatever
I wanted. Bitches were now approaching me, but that
attention quickly faded when the game started.

The guy who I'd seen driving that pretty red
Jaguar was getting ready to play the slim, dark-
skinned kid with the white Saab for thirty pairs of
Bally's. I don't know if he had thirty pairs, but whenever I saw him—and I was clubbing almost every
night—he had on a different color.

Ce-Ce came in with her crew, and they joined Big
G and me. Dog broke out because two girls that he
was sexing and one that he had been trying to get
with were in the club. In most cases he would have
said, "Fuck them bitches." But once you establish a
stable of ass that you don't have to go through any
trouble to hit, it's better to just leave sometimes and
call it a night.

Ce-Ce had put in a word for me with her girl, and
our conversation was flowing. After another round of
drinks and a few more laughs, Ce-Ce's girl, Stacy, and
myself was out. We went back to my house, with the
help of Keith Sweat.

After about thirty minutes I was in my bedroom,
putting it down, representing LE.

I knew we would hook up again. I had been

through my share of women, and usually after fucking once or twice, I was done. But she had this trick she did with the muscles in her pussy, making them contract at the perfect time. That shit had me open. I dropped her off in Ingleside, a housing project off Virginia Beach Boulevard, gave her my pager number, a code, and I was out.

I realized it was about 3:30 a.m. With no job to wake up to, it was still too early to go to bed. I decided to stop by the Casablanca, just around the corner.

I was in the back shooting pool, when this girl with a beautiful complexion and long hair twisted up into a bob started talking. Her body was well-proportioned and impressive. She was wearing a short skirt and rayon blouse, with a bra that was too small and flimsy. It couldn't even begin to support her large firm breasts, which jiggled every time she moved.

After several drinks, I sat there thinking that Stacy had satisfied me, but as I kept staring at those breasts, my dick let me know that Stacy hadn't done shit.

We ended up going to my spot and smoking two blunts. It was almost 5 a.m. I reached for her hand and headed for my room.

"What you doing?" she asked.

"Don't even front. You know what's up."

"I didn't come over here for that."

"Why the fuck you come over here at four in the fuckin' morning then?"

"I just wanted some company. If it's all that, you can carry me home!" she yelled.

Before I knew it, I had snatched the bitch up by her neck and slammed her to the floor. Then I picked back up and slammed her head on the wall so hard her body went limp as she struggled to keep her balance.

"Who the fuck you talking to, bitch? Huh?"

"I'll do it. I'll do it," she muttered.

"I know goddamn well you are."

I grabbed her by her neck with my left hand, pinning her against the wall, while releasing my dick with my right hand. I slammed her on the couch, pushed her panties to the side, and jammed myself inside her so hard she tried to scream. But the force of my hand on her throat would not allow the scream to come through.

I wasn't inside her five minutes, when my body began to shake as I let loose.

I stood up, threw her twenty dollars, and told her to get the fuck out before I beat her ass to death. I told her a cab was on the way and to go stand on the corner. But she was moving too slow.

I then snatched her up by her hair and pushed her out the door, kicking her in the ass to get her from in front of my crib.

"Carry your ass, simple bitch," I yelled, before going back inside to call Beach Taxi.

CHAPTER 4

"Better Life"

I woke up the next afternoon with my head banging, still feeling fucked up. I thought about what had happened the night before and figured I must be losing my mind, letting myself get out of control like that.

The ring of the phone was pissing me off; I had ignored it most of the morning. *Who the fuck could this be calling and letting the phone ring off the hook?*

"What!" I yelled, answering the phone.

"Who you screaming at? Better check yourself," the familiar voice said sternly.

"What's up, man? Long time," I said, forgetting about my headache and all. "Damn, Junie. Where the hell you been?"

"Taking it easy. I was in Atlanta for a minute, then Florida, came back to Carolina, and now I'm in New York with Little Sister and Big Bro. You and Black need to come up here. I met these guys who got something real going on, but you got to come with some paper."

"Better scream at Black," I said.

"No, *you* need to check this because the people you know can use this. This money is too slow for little brother. You would have to convince him to buy into it; you can build a clientele off the people he knows too.

"It's for sure. If you can get him to come off about fifteen G's, this shit will come off. Anything less than that you'll be running back up here too fast. I'm going to give him a call and see what he says. You follow up. I'm going to be in Washington DC with this girl Friday and Saturday. You and Black come up. I need to see my brothers."

"We'll see. Call back later."

I didn't see Black until the following evening. He was in Elizabeth City with my cousin Pat. Pat and his boy, Rod, were chilling with these bitches from Elizabeth City. Pat said the girl he was chilling with had peoples that could move whatever they got their hands on. All he needed was a steady flow of product to lock shit down around there. Pat was hoping Black would show him some love and put him on.

Black went down to meet niggahs and check it out. Everything seemed to be all right, but Black was cautious. He knew that Pat sometimes came with a lot of shit and looked at his boy, Rod, as a counterfeit-ass niggah. Any new moves with new people could always come back to haunt you, but it could also turn out to be very profitable.

Black called Boot. He was going to have him go with Little to serve Pat and Rod.

They met at Greenbrier Mall. Pat and Rod bought nine ounces, and Black fronted nine. Pat wondered why Black didn't serve him, but he knew Black had his reasons.

The following Tuesday, Lo came over and was talking to Black about a bitch he was fucking with from Lake Edward named Dieta. She was young and "bad as shit." Lo had been fucking her awhile—since high school—but they had become friends and still got down like that.

She was living with a money-maker from New York. He had come down with the mentality that Norfolk bitches were slow, and some were—but not all.

Dieta had been hanging on the corner with niggahs for a long time, smoking weed, getting fucked up. Her mom was a fiend that Black used to trick up sometimes. Dieta was all about money, and this niggah was not coming off. She was telling Lo that he wanted her for running around, making trips, and for the pleasure of fucking whenever he wanted. He was scoring his shit from New York and using Dieta and her girl Roxy as mules.

Roxy was young, not all that fine, but had a banging-ass body. She was from Long Island, but had lived in Aragona Village, Virginia Beach for years. Everybody thought she lived in Lake Edward, as much as she was always out there.

Dieta told Lo that her man would score for other New York niggahs and that the night before leaving he'd have about one hundred thousand in the house.

Black started yelling, "One hundred G's! One hundred G's! Now that's some real dough there! I'll kill any motherfuckin' niggah for that!"

"But we won't have to. This shit is easy, fam. We're going to just go in and straight rob this niggah. She said him and his man leaving Thursday night after the club so they can be in New York Friday morning and back in Norfolk by Friday evening. We go in about 12:00, scoop up the hundred G's, and we out."

"Where those bitches going to be?" Black asked.

"Deita's the only one who lives there, and he's sending Roxy and her to New York tomorrow so they can mule that shit back while him and his man follow."

"Where is the house?" Black asked.

"Off Indian River Road, in Rosemont Forest, I think," Lo said, confused.

"We got to scope that shit out tonight and see how we going to do this. Shit sounds too easy," Black said, staring at Lo.

"That paper looks good, don't it, fam?" Lo asked.

"Yeah, but that's all you thinking about. I'm considering everything else. How can I come back and tell Auntie something happen to her baby?" Black asked, laughing.

"You're right. All on my mind is that money. If I knew for sure a hundred G's was in there right now, I'd kick in the fuckin' front door blasting!" Lo said, acting out the scene.

We laughed, but he was dead serious.

"You don't think that bitch is going to fuck you, do you?"

"No," Lo answered quickly.

"Why—because she sucked your dick and said she loved you?" Black said, going out the door laughing.

"All of them suck this dick," he said, grabbing his crotch.

I ran outside to catch Black before he pulled off. Lo was headed down the street in his MVP, with Shabba Ranks blasting.

"You talk to Junie?"

"Yeah, he paged me from New York. That niggah just want some money," he said.

"I don't know. He's been known to come up with some shit to get over," I replied.

"Yeah, right—and plus I don't have fifteen G's for him to fuck up. Even if we do go, it won't be until Friday night. We'll have to wait and see how things fall. I need you to call ADT and put that alarm shit on the house. Not tomorrow, today—while you ain't doing shit—you need a motherfuckin' job. You also need to find us another place for us to chill. Find some bullshit to serve niggahs, where everybody can hang out because you always got your bitch up in here."

"Ain't no bitches here. Don't make a niggah stand up to get knocked the fuck out," I said.

"Shit, don't make a niggah reach up under this seat," he said, acting as if he was serious.

"How much we spending?" I asked.

"Two bedroom for about six hundred. Tell Tara don't say shit to Tia about going to DC because if I go I'm carrying Shereena. You haven't met her. You wasn't home last time, when I brought her here and was knocking that ass out the box," he yelled, speeding off and shaking his head.

I watched the Acura roll away with smoked tinted windows, two-thousand-dollar chrome rims, and sounds to run you off the block. My brother definitely looked like a money-maker, rolling away in his phat-ass load, talking on his cellular, and shining like the sun.

It was Wednesday evening. Me and G was sitting in the crib, getting lifted, talking about bitches as usual. Boot came in looking for Black. Black wasn't in, so he paged him.

"What's up?"

"Boot paged you. Hold on a minute," I said, handing Boot the phone.

"Your peoples haven't seen me yet, and they said they were going to get with me yesterday," Boot said. "I paged him early this morning, and he was kicking some bullshit about he fronted some niggahs and the police ran up on them. Talking about he waiting for them to get out of jail and he'll call me. I've paged him, and he ain't call back."

"What they owe? Fifty-six hundred, right?" Black asked.

"No, sixty-two," Boot said.

"Hell, yeah! That's right. Stay there. I'll be there in a minute. Tell Dee not to go nowhere," he said, hanging up the phone.

"Black said he'll be here in a minute, don't go anywhere."

"Who the fuck is he? Black can kiss these nuts."

We all burst out laughing. I was talking shit, but I didn't leave.

Black got there about an hour later with Little. They were high as shit, with a blunt and forty-ounce in hand.

"Come on, let's bounce. Get your keys, Dee. We're taking the truck," Black said.

Big G broke out and agreed to meet me at Mitty's about 11:00. Mitty's was a club on Bonney Road, connected to the Omni Hotel in the Beach. Mostly whites hung out there, but you'd also find a few sisters with careers.

We jumped in the truck and headed to Elizabeth City, about forty minutes away. Black just wanted to ride and show Boot where the niggahs lived, and we would come straight back. He came in, paged Pat twice, back to back, with no response. He grabbed the cordless as he talked on his way up the stairs.

Five minutes later he came back down. "Lo and Jay waiting at McDonald's on Newtown Road. Get with them and take care of that shit."

They all met up. Lo and Jay followed Boot and Little back to Elizabeth City. They were sitting across

the street, when Pat and Rod came out joking and
playing. The girl's house they came out of was Rod's
sister and Pat's girlfriend. The girlfriend had two
kids by Pat and was pregnant again. Rod's grandmother lived there also, but she was laid up, kind of
sickly. Black had given them the run-down.

Little and Boot got out the car, and walked over.
Lo and Jay were sitting in the car looking on, ready to
blast if Rod or Pat did something stupid.

"What's up, man?"

"Heh!" Pat said, startled.

"Don't you niggahs need to see us?" Little said.

"I talked to Boot earlier," he said.

"But I paged you like three times and you ain't call
back. Black paged you twice about an hour ago, and
you said, 'Fuck him too.' "

"Naw, man, I told you I was going to get with y'all
as soon as the niggah got out. That will probably be
early tomorrow."

About this time Lo walked up and stepped real
close to Pat and Rod, much closer than Boot and
Little. "Fuck all that bullshit, niggah. Picture this
scene real clear—we going to go up to Kentucky
Fried and get something to eat. We'll be back at this
house right here in one hour. If you motherfuckers
not standing in front with my goddamn money," he
said, lifting his shirt, "me and these two nines, and
my man in the van"—Jay held up his twelve-gauge
and cocked it—"and his motherfuckin' pump are
going to kick in your shit and blast your entire family—the kids, your girlie, and your motherfuckin'
grandma. I don't give a fuck! This nine will put her
ass to rest. One hour, and I believe my shit is fast."

Pat ran in the house, blowing up Black's pager.
Black called him back immediately.

"Goddamn, cousin. What's up?" Pat yelled.

"What the fuck you mean?" Black yelled back.

"How you going to send niggahs like that at me? I'm your fucking cousin," he said.

"That wasn't my shit, Pat. I didn't have it at the time you were begging me for it, so I told my other peoples to look out. And here you are throwing shit in the game. Now that shit is between you and them. Don't mix me up in it."

Black then hung up the phone laughing. "Bitch niggah scared now. Lo went down that bitch acting like he in Vietnam and pulled his card. Crazy niggah."

I damn near choked on the smoke, I was laughing so hard. After pulling myself together, I asked him if Lo was going to do anything to him.

"I told him not to, just get my money. But I saw him and Jay earlier drinking that 'knotty head' gin straight out the bottle. You know how that shit can get a niggah acting."

Two hours later Boot and Little called Black from Bennigan's. They had been paid the money and said they planned on calling again, without the drama.

I jumped up Thursday hype for some reason or another. Tara had come through late the night before, but after those blunts and sipping on Hennessy with Black, any bitch that didn't have a car to bring me no ass, I wouldn't get. I had told Venus about Tara the night before because I just got tired and didn't give a fuck anymore.

She cursed, fussed, gave me sad stories about how she wasted years fucking with my trifling ass. She said she should have left me when she saw I wasn't going to graduate from high school, which should have shown her that I wasn't going to amount to shit.

"I know why you didn't leave me," I yelled back just to fuck with her. "Because I got a long tongue and I long-dicked ya."

"You're a stupid-ass niggah! I'm being serious and you joking. I hate your black ass, you stupid bitch," she said screaming, out of breath, and crying.

"If you act right, I'll give you some of this dick some time, but being rude, I'm going to—"

She didn't even allow me to finish. "Know what? Nothing good can come of you. I mean it and I promise you this will come back on your ass."

I felt bad, but she didn't understand that people and feelings change. I still cared, but not like she wanted me to.

"Tara, get up. Tara," I said, "get the hell up."

"Why?" she asked.

"Because I got business. Now put your shit on so I can get out of here."

"All right," she said and continued to lie there.

I went downstairs in the kitchen to get the ice water jug and came back upstairs.

"You're a hard-headed-ass girl." Then I poured it on her head.

She jumped up yelling, "Goddamn, Dee. You stupid-ass bitch."

Before I knew it I had slapped her in her mouth, and she fell back on the bed. I grabbed her by her neck and began putting pressure across her windpipe. "Don't you ever come out your motherfuckin' mouth at me like that ever again! I'll kill your motherfuckin' ass in here! Do you understand me? Do you understand?" I said it with such rage, I scared myself.

"Yeah!" she said, with her eyes wide and watery.

The phone rang, and I went to go answer it in the living room.

"What's up?"

"What you think, niggah?" G yelled.

I knew he was in a good mood too. That meant the day was going to be all good.

"Come scoop me and let's go to the mall and get some lunch. My treat, fool," I said.

"Buy me something, fool. Shit, I'll eat a sandwich," he said. "Can I get a shirt?"

'We'll see, fool. Just bring your ass. I'm waiting on you."

Tara was pissed and wasn't saying a word to me. Since her girl had dropped her off at my house, I gave her the keys to the truck, reached in my pocket, and peeled off three fifties for her. "Here, go get your shit done and find something to wear to DC in case we end up going. I'll give you a call later."

She got up and headed for the door.

"I don't get a kiss or nothing?"

"No—kiss my ass."

"See you later or something," I said sarcastically.

"Kiss my ass," she said and slammed the door.

Big G showed up a few minutes later.

"Where Black?" he asked.

"How the fuck should I know?"

"Because his car is in the driveway, dumb ass."

"Oh! I didn't know it was out there."

"Bring your ass, fool," he said, as I set the alarm.

Lo had a fiend's car and picked up Black from the house. They rode out Rosemont Forest to check shit out. Dieta's Sentra and a black Cadillac Alante convertible was parked in the driveway.

"That's that niggah shit?" Black asked.

"No, he drives that Sentra," Lo said laughing.

"I know that's Dieta's raggedy-ass shit," Black said.

"Dieta was saying that one of his boys came down here with him. It's like five of them."

"Yeah, that's what you call a clique. Those type niggahs make all the money," Black said.

"What you mean? A whole lot of niggahs?"

"Yeah, but a lot of real niggahs. Ones where every niggah is moving weight and making money. They all buy together and get a good-ass price. Check this out. Right now I'm paying twenty thousand for a whole brick. My man I fuck with from New York say shit up because there's a drought. Them niggahs there put all their paper together, like one hundred thousand, go to New York and get like seven kees [kilos]. When you buy weight like that you buy powder, bring that shit back, and cook it up. See, you got some niggahs, that's all they do. Cook dope and make big money. That shit ain't easy. But if you know how, you got a skill. Usually whoever cooks it knows how to make it come back with extra weight, and you making money already. So you need to learn how to do that shit.

"Man, when they bring that shit back, they divide it and work. No bullshit, because next trip is coming fast and you don't want to be the one they waiting on. That's why I'm trying my hardest to blow Little and Boot up. If I could blow them up, get you to handle your shit, and get Mark to come my way, that shit will be off the hook."

They had rode by twice and was heading home.

"That niggah shit nice," Black said.

"That shit butter, niggah."

"I want me a motherfuckin' house big as hell, just like that joint there."

"For you and your girl Tia," Lo said.

"Fuck, no! For me and my goddamn brother. He don't do shit, but I got to take care of his ass. Man, me and my brother will have a ball, put a pool back that bitch, cookouts for the crew all the time, and mad bitches and blunts."

"Dieta said that niggah bought that shit. She said he dropped fifteen thousand."

"Naw, I don't believe that. A niggah get locked up dropping that much cash," Black said.

"When he came down, some other niggahs turned him on to this realtor who handled all their shit like that. She said he took care of all his peoples, some shit called non-qualifying loans and land contracts.

"For real. Tell her to find out his name. Then again, I don't trust them crackers."

"This is a brother handling this shit," Lo said.

"I heard that shit!"

A few minutes had passed, and Lo was sitting there asking Black, "You pay twenty G's for a whole brick?"

"Yeah," Black said.

"You charge me fifty-one hundred for a quarter kee, you only making a hundred dollars off me?" Lo asked surprised.

"You, my peoples, your family and mine are in the struggle together. Family is everything! Everybody else is just there," Black said. "I heard that shit somewhere."

"That shit is true as hell. Truer than a bitch."

"This your thing, niggah. You bringing Jay?" Black asked.

"Fam, this is a family move, and I want to cook out every day."

They gave each other a pound—thugs' way of showing love—then relaxed and thought about the night.

Big G and I had just dropped his car off at the car wash on Brambleton and were walking over to Kappatal

Kuts across the street. Girls were in the parking lot selling T-shirts. Niggahs were hanging out in front. The kid with the white SAAB and some more ballers were next door at this little bar called Goldies, playing Cee-lo.

"Niggahs getting shit clean at the car wash. The Royal Blue gonna be packed."

"Fuck the Blue. Let's check out that shit in Hampton."

"It's on you, niggah, but I ain't driving."

"Man, you got to! If I drive, I got to call Tara. She going to have to bring the truck over and then she going to want to stay the night. I know she'll catch an attitude if I tell her she has to go home, and I don't feel for the drama."

"Yeah! And I don't feel like hearing your drama. You got more shit," he said laughing.

What I was saying was true, but my boy knew that I didn't want to drive and would try to talk my way out of it.

We got cuts, and I picked up two T-shirts from the girls at the table. I started to try to talk to one, and before I could get going G yelled, "Them bitches ain't trying to talk. They hot, been out here all day, and a thousand niggahs already asked them for some ass. They smile like they down, but ain't nobody getting shit."

"Thank you," one of the young girls said.

As we were picking up the Maxima, I saw the guy with the red BMW, Tracy, from Huntersville. He had pulled up to get his shit cleaned. He was now driving a long, pearl-white 560SEL Mercedes Benz with deep-dish hammers. This kid was blowing up, and I wanted to experience that fame. Pushing wheels like that, all niggahs saw was money.

Me and Big G stopped at the weed spot on Reservoir

before heading back to the house. We were sitting looking at videos, when Black came in. He didn't say shit, but just ran upstairs and shut the door.

It wasn't unusual, but that night I knew what was on his mind.

It was about 10:30 p.m. when G went home to change.

I jumped in the shower quick and ran over my beige Polo khakis. I had just had them tapered and hemmed. I threw some Murray's in my hair and tied up the do-rag, after throwing on my Ralph Lauren boxers, Ralph Lauren khakis, Ralph Lauren socks, and a Polo belt by Ralph Lauren, all compliments of the discount Polo shop in the Industrial Park area, not like high-ass Thalheimer's.

I topped the outfit off with cream Bally's and a cream shirt, pulled out my gold Citizen, gold bracelet, and threw on Black's gold chain. With two squirts of Eternity cologne I was set, ready to scream at the finest bitch.

I went in Black's room. He was lying across his bed, with the lights out.

"Let me get some change," I said.

He sat up fixing his eyes from the light. "Look in my pocket, those jeans on the dresser." He had changed clothes. He sat there with black Timberlands, black jeans, and a black hoody was lying across the bed.

I reached in the pocket, took the knot out and counted it. "Six hundred. I'll bring your change back," I said.

"Turn off the light," he said, lying back down.

"Hit me later," I said, shutting the door.

I was standing in the door with LL Kool J shit rocking, when Lo pulled up with the same car he had earlier. He was wearing black jeans, black Reebok Classics and black T-shirt, his dreads pulled back. They were getting pretty long for the length of time he'd been growing them.

"Black upstairs?"

"Yeah," I said, going out the door. "Yo, make sure you niggahs be safe."

"In and out. In and out. Some simple shit," Lo said.

Big G and I got to the club, fucked up from sipping on Hennessy all the way to Hampton. Going into the club, which was packed as usual, I noticed that, just like many other clubs, there were cones in the front. I was thinking that you really got to have props to park there. I noticed that many clubs reserved the spots up front for the phat-ass foreign shits.

Black and I had come a long way. I didn't agree with robbing a niggah for his shit, but I did feel like we could use it a little more than them.

We ordered drinks, and I sat there staring at all the fly-ass bitches and the big-time hustlers.

I wasn't crazy about Moet because it got you fucked up. But the hustlers drank it, and I wanted to shine too.

Ce-Ce came strolling by, looking fly as shit, with four other girls. They had been there awhile, because they had drinks in hand that were just about empty.

I pulled her elbow. She turned like she was getting ready to get an attitude. Then she looked and smiled, opening her arms to give me a hug.

"What's up, baby?" she asked.

"Just chilling, girl."

"I see you are. Dee, this is Tonya, Shanice, Boo-Boo, and Lady," she said, introducing me to her crew.

Tonya stuck her hand out, and I quickly told her, "I don't shake girls' hands. I hug them," I said, pulling her to me and hugging her, along with the other three. I hugged Boo-Boo last. "Goddamn! I ain't letting Boo-Boo go. She staying with me," I said. "Where your man?"

"He ain't here," she said.

"I don't want him to come in here and go to your ass."

"Shit. Ain't none of that shit going on here."

"I heard that."

"Here," I said, passing her a champagne glass.

G quickly gave her friends one also and started to pour.

We sat there talking for a second before I suggested that Ce-Ce, Boo-Boo, and I hook up for lunch.

Ce-Ce gave me her pager number and leaned over towards me. "Boo-Boo and Stacy are kind of tight."

"Me and Stacy just friends," I said.

"Niggah, please! My girl told me she gave you some pussy."

"What else she say?" I asked smiling.

"I ain't fucking with you tonight, Dee," she said and walked off smiling.

"Oh! Boo-Boo, you just going to walk off. No kiss or nothing," I said with a serious look.

"I'll give you a kiss tomorrow when we go eat," she said smiling.

"You see that silk skirt, niggah? Them little tiny draws, titties all in a niggah face. You know I gots to hit that shit," I said to G.

"Body was banging, but I like Shanice," G said.

"Why you didn't say shit? Bet I hook that shit up tomorrow. My niggah scared to ask for some ass," I said jokingly.

He just stood there with his eyes barely open, fucked up.

"Hey, Dee," a familiar voice came from behind.

"Hi, baby. How are you?" I asked.

"Fine. Can't you tell?" she said with confidence.

"Most definitely," I said, with a smirk.

"Have you seen Tara?" she asked.

"Yeah, I hollered at her earlier," I said, not volunteering too much information. I was trying to see where she was going. "When the last time you seen her?"

"It's been a while. We don't swing like that too much no more," she said.

"Why is it that your man won't let you out?"

"I don't have no man. It's just me and my son. I live in University Apartments near by Janaf Shopping Center now."

"Yeah, yeah. I know where that's at." Now it was time to test her. "My man stays out that way. We have to drop him off when we leave here. He lives in the houses over there. I would stop by and say hi, but it might be too late," I said.

"After I leave here and we get something to eat, I'll probably be up 'til about 4:00 a.m.," she said.

I was thinking that she wants to get with the program. *I probably shouldn't, but maybe I'll just stop by and say hello.* "I'm riding with my boy. If I stop you'll have to carry me home."

"What time will I see you?" she asked.

"I'll check you about three."

She gave me her address, phone number, and strutted off.

I was standing around checking out all the hustlers in the club, wondering which one Black was getting while they were out having a good-ass time. I figured they might get something, but I couldn't even imagine the niggah getting one hundred thousand. It was unheard of.

Then the niggah with the SAAB came up on me. "It's some bitches in here," he said.

"True, bad-ass 'ho's," I added.

"They ain't shit though. Nasty, stinking-ass, broke bitches. "Know what, man?—I could stand here for thirty minutes and probably point out thirty bitches I've fucked in the last year," he said, opening up an opportunity for me to find out about Tara.

Question was, Did I really want to know?

"Couple weeks back, I saw you talking to this girl out front. Brown skin, fat ass, layered cut, with it long in the back. Bitch got dimples. What's her name? Tam . . . Tia . . . I don't know."

"Tara," he said.

"Yeah! Tara," I said. "I saw her in here a couple times. She seem all right. I know her ass is fine."

"Yeah, I been knowing her for about five years. She used to talk to my man Pooch. You know Pooch?" he asked.

"I don't think so. I know a lot of niggahs by face and not by name."

"Yeah, I know what you mean. He's from New York, drive a blue 300E. He fucked her for a while, traveling back and forth, but he had a wife Up Top, so it was just a thing. He said she was starting to get all serious and shit. I know a couple niggahs she went out with, but they ain't say shit about her. She must not be coming off that ass like talking about it."

That definitely made my night.

"See those bitches there." He pointed at five girls walking in a line through the club. Each of them had their hair done to perfection, not a strand out of place, nails done, sexy-ass "fuck-me" clothes, and bodies that filled out each outfit like it was painted on, phat enough to make any niggah weak.

"Don't even fuck with them bitches. They from Norview, where Dog was from. Them bitches so money-hungry, you better do more than hustle. You better be CEO of a corporation to afford them 'ho's."

We started laughing, gave each other a pound, and he stepped off.

It was about 1:00 a.m., and Black hadn't paged me. I checked the pager to make sure it still worked. My stomach started churning, but I was telling myself shit couldn't go wrong—except no money be there.

The sweet perfume of a young lady in front of me broke my concentration.

"What's your name, love?" I asked, touching her back.

"You don't have to touch me," she said.

"It's not all that, baby. Please believe me," I said.

"Naw, you ain't all that," she said loudly, with her hand on her hip.

"Know what—you better carry your ass, bitch, because I'll punch you in the back of your fuckin' head and drag you through this club. You don't know me, you ignorant bitch."

G grabbed my arm. "Naw, this bitch crazy. She best carry her ass."

"Look, asshole. Here comes Tara," G said.

The other girl and her friend started walking off.

"What's up, baby?" Tara asked.

"What's up? What the hell you doing up here?" I asked directly.

"I came over here with Dina and Nita," she said.

"Who drove?"

"She did," Dina said.

"What's up, Dee?"

"Nothing, Dina. Where Nita?"

"She over there with Psycho," Dina said.

"I hope he don't beat her ass up in here. You know that niggah crazy."

"If she scared of him, she ought to leave him alone," Tara said.

"There you go with that bullshit—running your mouth all in other people business," I added quickly.

"Sorry," she said, smiling and hugging me. "Nita going with Psycho, and Dina riding with them because they going to Norfolk and it's closer to dropping her off. Are you going with me to your house?" she asked, looking too good.

I was thinking about her girl I was talking to earlier. I wanted to hit that shit. It was going to be too easy. I was close to being in love with this girl and couldn't see her driving back across the water by herself. I also didn't need the headache of other bitches coming up, playing stupid games.

"Yeah, but I was just getting ready to leave. Big G and I been fucked up all day, and my head hurting."

"I hope you're not too tired, because you have business to take care of later," she said sarcastically.

"Bring your ass, girl," I said, putting my hand on her neck and guiding her out the club. G was right behind me.

CHAPTER 5

"Ready to Blow"

On the other side of town Black and Lo were on their way to Rosemont Forest, both deep in thought. Lo was thinking about the money, and Black was thinking about what could go wrong.

"Black, you know how you say the cliques do?" Lo said.

"Yeah," Black answered.

"If we get a hundred G's, we got to give Dieta hers. After that, just give me like ten G's and take the rest and work it. Just hit me off with weight, and I'll make enough to buy when you buy. That way I'll maintain forever, instead of taking cash and blowing it all."

"That's the move, and we all can stay rich. But I don't know niggahs like that to go up top and score," Black said.

"I know this niggah, Red, from New York. He be out Lake Edward, always over at Mark house. Say he Mark cousin. I think Mark was talking about going in with him. He be scoring a whole brick. They know how to get it back here and everything," Lo said.

"If we get this paper. I'll make that run, no problem," Black said.

They pulled on to the side of Exxon, on the corner of Indian River Road and Lynnhaven Parkway, and parked. Lo had two 9mm, and Black had the .45 and the twelve-gauge shotgun.

"Let's do this," Lo said.

They entered the house through the back sliding door. They got upstairs to the rooms where Dieta said he kept his safes.

"I'll take this room, and you go in there," Black whispered.

Lo pushed the door open, expecting the room to be empty.

A tall, slim niggah was in the bed with a fine-ass Latino girl. He jumps up, but Lo quickly slows his roll by putting the nine in his face.

"Lay down, niggah. You better not make a sound. Where the money, niggah?"

"Oh, please!" Don't shoot! Please! You can have it. Just please don't shoot!" he begged.

"Where the motherfuckin' safe?" Lo asked.

"Money in the top drawer! Please, man, come on!" the slime niggah in the bed pleaded.

Lo pulled the drawer and saw nothing but stacks of money. He turned to the guy, who was still in the bed beside the girl, and put the gun to his head. "Where the rest? I know it's more. It's two safes, niggah! Don't play me!" Lo said, raising his voice.

"In the other room," he cried.

Those were the last words he would ever speak. Three shots rang out, and the Latino girl let out a scream.

Black, in the other room, felt his heart drop to his stomach. His knees buckled, he couldn't swallow, and his eyes got fiery red. He moved slowly towards the room, thinking it was Lo who got shot and was waiting for the owner of the house to come running out. He entered the room real slow and saw Lo. "Damn, niggah! Shit!"

"Bingo, niggah! Bag this shit!" Lo said.

"What happened?"

"Fuck you think?" Lo said. "The niggah was home fucking."

Black threw Lo the book bag with the money in it already from the safe in the other room. "Check the other safe," Lo said.

Black walked over to the closet and popped the safe. It was empty.

"Let's go, niggah," Lo said.

They both were standing there looking at this beautiful young woman sitting beside a man, half his brain on her lap.

She was shaking and crying. "Please, please, please!" was all her soft voice could put out.

"Sorry, mommy. I can't get locked up over no bitch talking," Black said.

One shot to the chest sent her against the headboard. Another one to the head made her funeral a closed casket and assured him she wasn't going to talk.

They never stopped running until they were in Campus East with bundles of cash lying on the bed. They sat staring at each other for about ten minutes, not a word said.

I was coming through the Hampton Tunnel, when I received a page, "804 555 3333333." "Eight O Four" meant Campus East, and "3333333" meant bring your ass right now, it's a family emergency. Since I was already on my way home, I felt there was no need to stop.

When I arrived at the house, by the time I hit the

third step, Black and Lo were standing at the top of the stairs, their guns in hand.

"Who you with?" Black asked.

"Tara," I said.

"Take her in your room and make sure she stays," he said directly.

I told Tara to get her shit and that if she wanted something to drink to get it now. She went in my room, turned on the television, and began to undress. The sight of her dark-green lace panties and matching bra made me ready to climb in the bed with her instantly, but I wanted to see what my peoples had done.

"I'll be back up in a few. Don't come downstairs for nothing. Niggahs trying to take care of some business." I gave her a kiss and shut the door.

"Yo, niggah, we straight. Come on," I yelled to Black and Lo.

They came downstairs and dumped a bag on the table.

"Goddamn, make sure that door is locked and set the alarm," I said, getting up and taking the phone off the hook. I cared for Tara but, with this much paper at stake, didn't want her calling nobody in on my team. My head was fucked up. Never in my life had I seen so much cash.

"Jackpot, niggah! What's up?" Black said smiling.

"We got this from the New York lottery. Our number hit," Lo said, as we all started laughing.

"Ready to count, niggah?" Black asked.

"Get to it, baby," I said quickly.

"Shit. I don't even know if I can count this high," Lo said laughing.

By the time we had finished counting, we had set up ten-thousand-dollar stacks. Black counted, "1, 2,

3, 4, 5, 6, 7, 8, 9, 10, 11, 12, 13, 14, 15, 16 . . . one hundred and sixty thousand dollars."

"Goddamn," I yelled.

"Hundred and sixty G's, cousin. Are we getting ready to blow or what?" Lo said.

"Or what, niggah. Or what?" Black yelled. "So what's up, Lo?"

Lo got two bags from out the kitchen, opened them up, and picked up two stacks. "Twenty thousand. That's for Dieta."

"That's all she get?" Black asked, confused.

"Yeah! We only got eighty G's," Lo said seriously. "She was looking for twenty and that's what she getting. Twenty!

"I'll take twenty, and you take twenty." He put his twenty in the other bag and pushed Black's to him. "That's leftovers, Dee. You can have that."

They both bust out laughing until they were bent over.

"You know what that's for, Black. Handle your business, niggah," Lo said. "Put that shit up. I'm getting ready to call Boot so I can take this fiend shit back."

"Lo, I'm going to DC tomorrow, and we'll be back late Sunday. So scream at your boy, and we'll sit down and talk Monday," Black said.

"Bet," Lo said.

"We going to get us another crib next week too. We need a spot where niggahs can come to handle business and feel good. We going to keep about five or six heads in the crib at all times and packed with artillery. Niggahs are getting ready to blow. Call Junie in the morning and tell him to set up rooms at the Marriott. That's where I'm trying to rest. No more half-stepping, big brother. No more."

"How you know it's a Marriott in that area?" I asked. "You ain't never been out of Norfolk."

"Shit. Just tell him Marriott. I don't give a fuck. As long as that shit got a buffet in the morning and a bar at night. That's how we living now," Black said.

"That's how you living. I'm going to go put this money up, make this 'ho' get out of bed, and go spend about three days in Motel 6," Lo said.

He then left, and Black and I sat there smoking a blunt.

"Next week I'm gonna get with this niggah Lo know, he Mark cousin from New York. We gonna try to go up there and score. Whatever I buy I hope I can come close to doubling it after I cook it up."

"Do you know how to cook?" I asked.

"No, but I will find out or pay somebody."

"Going Up Top to score is a big move, niggah. What's up?" I asked.

"Yeah, but I've been waiting for this. I'm going to handle this shit. "How you feel, niggah?"

"I'm all right."

"Here," he said, throwing me ten thousand, "how you feel now, niggah?"

"Rich, niggah! Rich!" I said with a big-ass smile.

I was on the phone with Tara, when Black beeped in. "I'll be there in about half an hour. It's 9:45 now. Look, be ready to bounce because I got this shorty with me and I don't want Tia riding by. This hooker is nice."

"Yeah, right! Just bring your ass," I said.

"Fuck you, fool! Check you in a minute."

I clicked back to let Tara know that we would be out in thirty minutes and she better bring her ass or get left. She was there in fifteen.

I stood there watching her get out the truck.

"Thought I was going to be late, didn't you?" she

asked without letting me answer. "I just had to get this top to throw on tomorrow morning." She was holding a long beige top and some spandex-type pants. When she came in full view, the black silk top, her jeans fitting like they were greased on, and her black high-heel, open-toe sandals had me totally fucked up. I stood there thinking that this girl had inched her way into my life enough to make me spend money on her and—to top it off—drive my shit. What the hell was I thinking?

"By the time we get there, you'll be able to put on that same shit tomorrow," I said.

"Naw, you put that same shit you got on tomorrow. When I get up and wash the kitty, I have to put on clean clothes so I feel clean and fresh all over."

We laughed, walking through the house.

It was something about her that made me think, *Damn, I enjoy her, and she is so very special that I want her to be part of my life forever.* I didn't want to marry her right now, but I wanted to do something to attach her to me forever.

"Who Black carrying?" she asked.

"I don't know—why?" I asked quickly.

"Just wanted to know which one of his 'ho's he bringing. He bought Tia that raggedy-ass Chevette that she be driving around in, and he gives her money. Like that's supposed to keep her occupied while he running with other bitches."

"That ain't your motherfuckin' business; I'm your goddamn business, and that's what you worry about. Don't fuck around and end up sipping broth because of your fuckin' mouth," I said sternly.

"It's still wrong, Dee. I see your brother ain't shit, but you probably ain't shit either. You just know how to hide it good. You better believe, though, if I think another bitch is in here and your truck out front, I'm coming in. I will bang on the door, set off the alarm. I don't care, but you will open the door."

"Girl, I will come out and go straight to your ass."

"Whatever," she said. Then she turned soft. "Dee, where is this relationship going?"

"It's progressing, baby. It's progressing."

"Dee, I'm over here all the time. Why can't I be here with you permanently? I love you and I don't have any desire to be with anyone else but you."

"My brother stays here too. What's up?"

"He don't care. I said, 'he ain't shit.' I didn't say I don't like him. He treats me sweet as hell. At first he wouldn't say anything to me, but now he talks the hell out of me about his girls."

"You be telling him shit and hooking him up with your friends. Then you say he ain't shit."

"That ain't my business, Dee. I know who looks out for me. Shit. I'm here all the time anyway."

"We'll see, baby," I said softly. "I'm glad you love me too because I don't want you to ever fuck up. If you ever play me, girl . . ." I said, shaking my head, ". . . just don't ever play me." I gave her a long passionate kiss. Those came few and far between.

I hardly ever kissed any of the girls I fucked and didn't want to kiss her. For some reason it felt good.

Just as I thought I might have time to get a quick one in, I heard the keys in the door lock.

"What's up, fool?" Black said.

"Not a thing."

"You ready, girl?" Black asked, yelling at Tara.

"Shut up, Black. Hello, I'm Tara," she said, directing herself to Black's company.

"My bad, my bad. Shereena this is Tara and my brother, Dee. Let's go, fool. Time to bounce."

"You got weed?" I asked.

"I just got a half from out the way, but it ain't rolled," he said.

"I got some rolled, niggah."

"We straight then. Let's bounce."

We all climbed in the Acura. Before we could even cross the Hampton Roads Bridge-Tunnel, the car was filled with smoke.

Shereena and Tara were talking like they had known each other for years. Shereena was about nineteen, but her face and body easily said twenty-five. Her breasts were large but firm. Her ass wasn't real phat like other bitches I had seen Black bring to the crib, but it was nice. Her skin was flawless, not a blemish in sight, her makeup perfectly done like a professional model, her eyebrows arched and her lips lined in black. They made you want to lean over and beg for a kiss. She had colored her hair to bring out her light skin. She looked very attractive and had a very pleasant attitude, a sign of real maturity.

We were all just rolling, with the music jamming. Every time something came on we liked, we would raise the volume until the car shook.

"Where the hell y'all think you at?" I asked.

"I thought I was in *Harlem Nights,* as loud as you were pumping that music," Shereena said, smiling.

"For real, girl," Tara added.

"This is the goddamn club. Pump that shit up, fool," Black said.

Since I was driving, I handed the phone to Black to page Junie because we didn't know where the hell we were going.

"You have to put the phone on roam," I said.

"You never been up here before?" Shereena asked.

"No," Tara answered for us all. "Why? You have?"

"Nope, but these girls from the shop come up here all the time. They said it's a lot going on."

"Damn right. All the shit happens where the President rest his head. How the hell do he sleep?" I asked. "Junie been up here before, he'll know what's up."

Just then, the phone rang.

"We talked his ass up," Black said. "Hello."

"What's up, my brothers?" Junie asked. "Where you all?"

"We just pass Potomac Mills," Black answered.

"Dale City," I yelled. "Where the fuck he at?"

"Tell that niggah I said shut up," he said.

"Where we coming to?" Black asked.

"Stay on 95 and come straight into DC. Follow 14th Street signs, and the Marriott is on Pennsylvania Avenue, on the right side coming in. We're in room 630. You all are on the same floor," Junie explained.

"Is that shit all that?" Black asked.

"You can't get much better," Junie said with a very serious tone. "Check you in a few."

"Hey! Get the number and room number. In case we get lost we can call him back direct.

How far are we anyway?" I asked.

"He said we're about forty minutes away," Black answered, after he hung up the phone.

We arrived at the Marriott with no problem. Bellmen were standing in front, ready to grab our bags. We all held on to our shit. We weren't used to no shit like that.

As soon as we walked in the girls were like, "Damn!" and slapped each other's hand.

Me and Black looked at each other with the same expression and just smiled.

"Excuse me. Can we ring a guest?" I asked the lady at the front desk.

"Sure. There's a phone right there, sir. Just dial the room number."

I made the call, and he said he would be right down.

"Thank you," I said.

Black and Shereena were looking in a restaurant on the same floor.

The elevator doors opened, and out stepped the long-lost brother and one of the finest women I'd ever seen. Tall, light-skinned, long hair with no weave and pushed back in layers. She was wearing an olive, short-fitting skirt, beige sheer hose, beige heels, beige blouse, and an olive blazer that fitted like it was tailor-made. She looked about thirty—like a real woman.

My brother stood there looking just as fine with his olive slacks, black shoes, beige shirt with cuff links and a silk tie with olive, beige, and black designs.

"What's up, my brothers?" he said hugging us.

"You, niggah. You the one looking like you just stepped out of *GQ* magazine," Black said.

"For real. And she looking like she getting ready to go to a photo shoot for *Essence* and what not," I added. "This is Tara and Shereena. And you are?"

"Jacqueline. Nice to meet you all," she said with her northern accent.

"Let's take care of these rooms," Black said, nudging me and motioning for Junie to come along, leaving the ladies to talk.

"So why you didn't bring Tia?" Junie asked.

"Man, that's my girl, but she fusses too goddamn much. I wasn't in the mood for that shit. I came to have a good time," Black said.

"Who is that?" Junie asked.

"That's my new shorty. I think she might be around awhile, if she acts right," Black added.

"Fuck all those bitches. Let's get these rooms," I said.

"Where Venus at, niggah? I know you ain't let her go," Junie said.

"She gone. She didn't know how to take care of this dick. Bitch got to know how to handle this dick. If not, she's out of here," I said.

We all started laughing.

"How much are the rooms?" Black asked.

"Parking and taxes, about two hundred and thirty," Junie said.

Black reached in his pocket and pulled out a knot. "Here's a thousand. Take care of our shit for tonight and tomorrow," he said. "How did you pay for yours?"

"She put it on her American Express," Junie said.

"Well, remind me, and I'll give it back to you later. Take care of this right now."

Junie went to take care of the rooms and brought us our keys.

"The sixth floor, right?" Tara asked when we all got on the elevator.

"There's a lot of blacks working here," Shereena said.

"Shit. Them motherfuckers ain't black. They open their mouth and you can barely understand what the fuck they saying," Black said.

"They're black," Jacqueline said. "They're just not black Americans; you can find every nationality here in DC."

"We going to put this shit in the room and then grab something to eat downstairs," Black said.

"Another restaurant is on the seventh floor. It's got more of a bar atmosphere, with a pool table."

"That's what I'm talking about. Meet you all there in twenty minutes," I said.

Tara and I entered our room and couldn't believe it. The rooms were like apartments with a king-size bed, refrigerator, wet bar, and big-screen television with every channel possible.

"Dee, they have an iron in the closet and paper to fill out to get your shit sent to the laundry."

"Did you see the coffee maker, coffee and a damn sewing kit? Check out the view," I said, moving over by the window.

"This is nice," she said, easing over to me.

"Who wouldn't like this?" I asked jokingly.

We relaxed on the bed, enjoying the fact that we could lay back sprawled out like eagles and not touch each other.

The hard knock on the door brought us back. It was Black and Shereena.

"Let's go, niggah. I'm about to fuckin' starve," Black said.

"Where's Junie?" I asked. Before I could get it out good, they came out of their room.

"Are my little brothers ready?"

"Both of you are bigger than him, but he calls you two little brothers," Jacqueline said.

"They know what's up," Junie said.

We all laughed and walked down to the restaurant.

Being with my brothers gave me a feeling that only someone with brothers could understand. I stood back and I watched them laughing, joking and having a good time.

The girls were drinking, eating and trying to play pool, enjoying me, my brothers and our money. I and my brothers knew that, with money, we could do this as often as we wanted, with whomever we wanted; but without money, these bitches wouldn't pay us no goddamn mind. We felt that, given time, you could make a girl fall in love, but sometimes it took money and nice things to attract their attention and indulge in conversation.

I remember hearing once that a woman didn't want a broke-ass man. All a man had to do was make money and women would be there. Damn if that shit wasn't true.

Before we knew it, it was 2:00 in the morning, and the bartender was cleaning. He asked us to make this our last game.

"Do we have time to get one more drink?" Black asked.

"No, sir. It's that time already," the bartender answered quickly.

"All right, how much is the bill?" Black asked.

"Ninety-seven dollars and seventy-three cents."

"I got it," I said, reaching in my pocket and handing him two fifties. "You sure you can't take six more drinks out of this?" I asked, holding out another fifty. Even if he charged us, he would still have a twenty-dollar tip, which he could've easily pocketed, as he had already counted his register.

"Three Iced Teas and three Hennessys," he said smiling.

"Money moves everybody—not just niggahs in the hood," I said to Black, going back over to the table.

We talked awhile, finished our drinks, and called it a night.

The ring of the phone woke me up. I was trying to ignore it, but they kept letting it ring.

Tara picked it up.

"Junie said he was getting ready to go downstairs," she said.

"What time is it?" I asked.

"Eight thirty," she responded.

"Shit. Tell him I'll check him about 10:00."

She hung up the phone and fell back to sleep.

About 9:30 we heard banging at the door. I got up, peeked out the peephole, and didn't see anyone. The knock came from this other locked door.

"Goddamn! These rooms joined together!" Black yelled.

"Yeah! Let's have a party," I said, wiping sleep out of my eyes.

"Let's go eat, fool," Black said. "Get the hell up, Tara, right now."

"Get out, Black! Get out! I was up when Junie called earlier," she said.

"Stop lying, girl. Your ass was knocked out just like the rest of the lazy-ass motherfuckers in the other room," I said.

"Niggahs don't know we don't get up before noon," Black said. "We'll be ready in about thirty minutes."

We went down to join Junie and Jacqueline. They were sipping coffee and waiting patiently, carrying on a deep conversation.

"Good morning, everyone," Jacqueline said.

"How you all feel?" Junie added.

"We're doing great," Shereena answered for us all.

"Everything on the buffet, and they make omelets however you want them," Junie said.

"Six buffets then," Black said, directing his comment to the waiter.

After eating we decided to go to Georgetown and shop. We pulled the Acura in front of the hotel.

While waiting on Junie and Jacqueline, Shereena and Tara had gone upstairs. Shereena came out wearing a long, colorful dress and a pair of sandals; Tara had her little set on that she'd shown me the night before, with new white Reeboks, no socks. Both looking cute as they wanted to be.

"Don't my bitch look good," Black said, as they approached the car.

"I like the way she wears her makeup. Maybe Tara will pick up on that shit," I said.

"Yeah, that shit is nice. I like it too," he added.

No sooner had they climbed in when Junie pulled up with Jacqueline's 325 BMW convertible.

"Ooh, that's cute," Shereena said.

"I'll look good driving that shit, wouldn't I, Dee?" Tara said.

I ignored her.

"What that bitch do?" Black asked.

"Junie said that she had her shit together. She's an accountant at a law firm," I said. "You know he always said he wouldn't fuck with no bitch that couldn't look out."

"I heard that shit," Black said.

We went into Georgetown. It was hell trying to park. We decided to park on *M* Street and then walk back down to check out the rest of the shops on Wisconsin Avenue. We stopped at this Polo shop on the strip. Two stories of nothing but Ralph Lauren shit, ladies on the second floor and men on the first floor.

I came out with polo khakis, about four Polo shirts, ten pairs of different-colored Polo socks, and shoes. I also picked up sweaters.

Black bought sweatshirts and fifty-dollar Polo belts. We were trying to live.

We didn't stop again until we hit Up Against the Wall. This store was all urban street gear: hoodies; Guess jeans; and T-shirts with names we never heard of. Black ended up spending about five hundred.

Our next stop was the Benneton shop on the corner of Wisconsin Avenue. That was where Shereena and Tara wanted to look. Together they spent about five hundred and came out all smiles. On Wisconsin there were several leather shops, shoe stores and jewelry shops. The girls ran over to the shoe shop with the intention of meeting us in about twenty minutes.

We rolled into the leather shop with just the intention of looking. They had nice soft leathers, two-tone leathers, ranging in all colors.

Black got a beige leather and a black one. Junie grabbed a long three-quarter black one. I had a short black one, a long black one and a three-quarter beige one.

"Twenty-five hundred for them," the Arab-looking store owner said.

"Too much," said Black.

All the tags added up to be about twenty-seven hundred.

"Twenty-four is the best I can do," the man said.

"Let's do it like this," Black said. He pulled two knots of paper out his pocket and took off the rubber bands. He put all the twenties together and slowly laid them on the counter. "Two thousand—that's what I got for you. What's up?"

"No. Can't do it. Too low," he said.

"OK, then. I saw some other shops. Let's see what their prices look like, and we'll be back," I said to Black. Junie and I laid our coats on the counter and walked out. Black did the same.

"Twenty-one, my friend. That's the best I can do without taking a loss," the man said in a sad voice.

We knew he was bullshitting, but everybody got to make theirs. I threw another hundred on the counter, and we left out.

We met the girls standing over by some Africans selling costume jewelry, fake-ass Rolexes, Gucci, Polo watches, Guess watches and even fake rings with 14K written inside. The girls had about four pairs of shoes apiece.

Across the street was a big jewelry shop, which

caught everyone's attention. We put all our things in the car and pulled over by the Jewelry Center. This place was like Kay Jewelers, Zales, Reeds, and J.B. Robinson all rolled into one. Looked as if everyone was trying to compete. The herringbone that Black paid eight hundred for at Super Star Jewelry, he saw for four hundred. Bracelets, rings, chains, everything was half the price it was in Norfolk.

I bought a fat herringbone with a nice charm and matching bracelet. Tara was looking at bracelets, bangles, and rings. I had never spent a lot of money on a bitch but always liked the way Ce-Ce shined when she came in the club with all the gold. That shit looked good. So, I bought her a smaller herringbone like mine—only slightly longer—for three hundred, three matching bracelets, five bangles and six rings.

Black bought Shereena a nice herringbone for three hundred but nothing else.

When we came out, Tara looked at me and was all smiles. "Thank you," she said.

"Don't thank me. Just let me know you appreciate it by being good to me and playing fair. You understand what I say?"

"That's easy," she said, blowing me a kiss.

Right then I knew that I loved her and her fucking up could cause her to lose her life.

We were walking towards the car when, all of a sudden, Black told me to give Tara the keys so she could pull the car around.

We ran back to the Jewelry Center and bought Tia a small link chain with a little medallion, three bracelets and a nice gold watch.

"Think she'll be all right?" he asked.

"No doubt, niggah," I said. "You trying to keep them all happy."

"Man, I've fucked a lot of girls, but there's those

select few that just know how to keep this dick happy. Keep the dick happy, and I'm happy."

"You're a simple niggah," I said.

"Naw, I'm a serious niggah," he said quickly as we went to the car.

"We going to the mall," Junie yelled from Jacqueline's car.

"Hell with the mall. Let's get some of these street deals," Black said.

"This ain't no regular mall," Junie said. "This mall makes Lynnhaven Mall look like Pembroke Mall." (Pembroke was a very small mall in the beach area with not many stores.)

"Yeah, right," I said. "We'll follow you."

We followed them for what seemed like a fifteen-minute drive, but actually I thought we were headed back home.

This mall was right outside DC, in Arlington, Virginia. We pulled into a garage and went up several stories to enter the mall.

This was like something I had never seen. There was a Macy's on one end, Nordstrom on the other, and about five stories of stores and boutiques I had never heard of. We strolled through, slowly checking out everything.

Junie was the only one spending at first. There was this store with nothing but expensive ties. My brother got five silk ties and at the next store bought matching slacks.

We all decided to go separate ways and meet downstairs at Ruby Tuesday in an hour. I saw maybe a shirt or two. But everything was dressy, and I wasn't trying to buy dress shit at that time.

Me and Tara went into Macy's. We were looking at all the expensive name-brand clothes that we had never heard of before.

I wasn't about to pay the price on that shit, until we found a Donna Karan dress. Tara tried it on, and I couldn't say no.

When we went into the shoe department, she found a pair of shoes that went perfect with the dress, but I had already put out two hundred on a dress. I wasn't about to pay three hundred for no fuckin' DKNY shoes.

At first I was like, "Shit," but when she put on the dress and the shoes, I had no choice. My girl was fine, and the outfit was made for her.

Afterwards, we went straight to Ruby Tuesday. Everything else was strictly window-shopping. We sat there for twenty minutes waiting on them.

When they arrived, the girls automatically started showing each other their bags. Shereena got three outfits and two pairs of shoes—designer shit with designer prices. Jacqueline had two plastic bags over her outfits that were on hangers draped across Junie's shoulder. She had found her a pants suit, Jones New York and a skirt and blazer, all compliments of Liz Claiborne. It was the first time all day that she smiled like the other two girls.

Black slipped Junie the money for the rooms, plus a little something for his pocket. He was definitely straight.

The day was winding down, and everybody was tired. After grabbing something to eat we went back to the hotel.

"I'm going to get in the Jacuzzi for a few," I said, "then I'm going to sleep to about 9:00 a.m. What's up?"

Everybody agreed.

We all sat in the hot tub until our skin was wrinkled, but a dip in the pool quickly cooled us off. Then we all jumped back into the hot tub, hugged our girls, and just relaxed.

"This is the life. I could do this every day," Black said.

"Yeah, but back to work Monday morning," I said. We all started laughing.

"You work hard, baby? I know you do," said Shereena.

"What type of work you do?" Jacqueline asked seriously.

"Pharmacist at the Naval Base," Black answered.

"Where did you go to school?" she asked.

"Old Dominion University. You heard of ODU?" Black asked.

"Yes, I had a girlfriend that went to Norfolk State."

We all sat there and never even smiled. If Junie didn't talk to her, evidently he didn't want her to know.

"What you do, Dee?" Jacqueline asked.

"Real estate investor. I buy damaged properties, fix them up, then put them right back on the market."

"Oh! So Edward's the only one in school, working on his masters."

Me and Black turned our head towards Junie. Guess our big brother had accomplished quite a bit since leaving home.

"Yes," Black said, "he's the only one at this time."

"I'm hot. I'll meet you in the room," Tara said as she turned and kissed me.

The other two followed.

"I'll be up in a minute," Junie said.

"All right, smart-ass black man with the masters degree," Black said laughing, "what you know good?"

"There's three things. First thing is cellular phones. Niggahs in New York are fixing phones where you can make all the calls you want and never pay shit."

"Bullshit," Black said.

"Well, not *never* pay. But you pay a flat fee up front—like two hundred dollars—and make all the calls you want, anywhere you want, and talk as long as you want. The number will last about one month. You can call out, but no one can call you. You can buy the chips from Radio Shack, but the machine to do it cost a lot. The guy will show you how. They're not on that shit down south. All you have to do is buy the machine, and the same person will sell you numbers by the month or each time you run out of them."

"Sounds good. You already got this set up?" I asked.

"Yeah, all you got to do is come to New York and meet him," he said.

"What's up?" I said, staring at Black.

"Sounds good. It will move, no doubt."

"The second thing is, I met this guy that deals with birth certificates and social security cards."

"What?" Black said, sitting up and smiling.

"Yeah, he has so many, he said he'll sell them for three hundred each; that's the set. If anybody need a new identity, got bad credit or on the run, this can change who the hell they are. All they have to do is go to DMV and get an ID or a license. No problem."

"What they sell for on the street?" I asked.

"You can get a thousand easily—fifteen hundred if a niggah desperate. Everybody want these but can't get them."

"Third thing is the biggest. Her brother live in Manhattan, Uptown, but the niggah got spots in Brooklyn, Queens, Jersey and even some spots down South locked down. I met the niggah about two months ago, and he said he just put workers in Hampton. I figured if you meet him directly, you could get New York prices in Virginia."

"You sure this niggah large like talking about it, or is he fronting for the next niggah?" Black asked.

"Check it. Her peoples been in the shit a long time, from the dad to the uncles. Her brother grew up with her then went to live with their father. That's when she said he blew up in the drug trade. She doesn't fuck with them too much, but every now and then he stops by and lately we've been getting together on some things. I was talking to him, and he wants to fuck with somebody down there. You need to meet him."

"What you got set up out of this?" Black asked. "Don't leave anything out. New York niggahs are dirty, and everybody out for self in this game. So don't pull us in and we end up getting shit. Tell me everything! We fuckin' family! Fuck him!" Black said seriously.

"This is for real. I'm looking at you two to set me straight. I'm telling you all now I want to go to Florida. All I need is a spot and a car. Right now the girl is looking out, so I'm stuck in New York, depending on you two to get me out."

"What about Jacqueline?" I asked.

"Niggah, please! What the fuck I look like? Bitches walk out of niggah lives every day. I got to get mine so I can stand," he said.

"Dee, you going to New York Monday. Talk to his boy about the phones and other shit. Meet with that girl brother and see what kind of prices we can get down our way and then check prices if we travel. Junie, you make plans to get up out of there because if we start fucking with him and some shit go wrong, niggahs might end up meeting Lo and Jay—and that ain't good," Black said, getting out of the Jacuzzi.

When I got to the room, Tara had showered and was lying across the bed with just a towel. "Are you going to lotion me down?" she asked.

"No question, baby," I said. "Turn over and move the towel."

She removed the towel.

I squeezed some lotion onto my hand, gently massaging her back and rubbing it into her skin in circular motions. I put lotion on each arm and shoulder, massaging her gently, but firmly.

When I moved down to her lower back, she let out a moan to let me know I was doing all right. Squeezing more lotion onto my hand and rubbing it around to make sure it was warm, I calmly placed my hands on her buttocks and slowly caressed each side, as if I was kneading bread.

I moved down her thigh, and as I rubbed in the lotion, lightly ran my finger across her moist vagina.

She jumped but quickly relaxed as I finished her legs and got to her feet. She started to squirm and let out a sigh when I stopped.

"Turn over," I said softly.

I started putting lotion on the front of her legs, lightly rubbed her stomach and leaned over and kissed her breasts. My mouth found her large nipple. I gently sucked it and ran my tongue around it in a circular motion, then gave the other breast the same attention. I then slid my tongue down to her stomach, following her hairline straight to her love. As I eased my tongue up and down, I felt her body tremble. So, I slowly lifted her legs and reached up and took her hands.

As I sucked and flicked my tongue in a rapid motion across her clitoris, she squeezed my hands and let out sounds that I'd never heard. Her body began to shake and jolt, then she collapsed as if she didn't have a drop of energy left in her body.

I told her to be still, while I moved on top of her and slid my hard erection inside of her.

She slid her arms under mine and held me so tight, I felt as if I was part of her.

As my thrust speeded up, she began to spread her legs wider and squeezed me tighter. I got a feeling that went from my feet and made its way up my entire body until my body trembled in ecstasy.

Tears ran down her face as I leaned back.

"What's wrong with you?" I asked.

"I don't know. I really don't," she said. "Just hold me, please. Just hold me."

We lay there in each other's arms and fell fast asleep. It was the most peaceful sleep I had in a while.

About 9:00 p.m. the phone rang. It was Junie wondering whether we were going to eat dinner downstairs or at this real nice restaurant that Jacqueline knew across town in Union Station.

"I'm getting in the shower. You coming?" Tara asked.

"Give me a few," I said. I got up and knocked on the door that separated me and Black's room. "What you going to do?"

"Whatever, man," he answered, hitting a blunt. "Junie said we can go downstairs and catch the train to the restaurant," he said.

"Where's the train?"

"The train picks us up downstairs in the hotel and drops us off in Union Station, where the restaurant and movies are located."

"Fuck a goddamn movie! I can see a movie at the crib."

I sat and rolled a blunt then jumped in the shower before Tara could get out. I started trying to play, but we didn't have time. I promised to finish later.

After we got dressed, I sat on the couch smoking. Suddenly there was a hard knock at the door.

"Get that, Tara," I said.

"Their finger is over the hole," she said.

"Let them stay the fuck out there then and get my shit out my bag."

"You brought your gun?"

"Hell, yeah! I don't know these motherfuckers up here and I'm going to carry it on the train with one in the chamber."

She looked outside again and opened the door.

"Come on. B. Smith's closes at 11:00 p.m.," Junie said.

"Who the hell is B. Smith?"

"She supposed to be a model or still is. Well anyway, she opened a restaurant in Union Station, and it's all that," Jacqueline said. "And to top it off, she's black."

"I heard that shit," I said. "Knock on that door and tell Black to come on."

Black came out and started hitting the blunt. "We out, fools. Let's go."

We got downstairs and purchased tokens. As the doors opened and we got on the train, Black told us that he should have brought his shit.

Junie and Jacqueline laughed, but I knew what he meant and was already prepared.

We arrived at B. Smith's, and the atmosphere was unbelievable. We came in through a cocktail room, as they called it. We were seated and treated with real class and courtesy. The building was very spacious, and the ceilings were real high—like in very old government buildings. The service was remarkable, and the prices were not exactly reasonable for the food.

The food was prepared perfectly, and it arrived hot and on time. But it wasn't like Moms'.

We didn't think it was that great a spot, but I kept it in mind because it was definitely a place to impress someone.

We caught the train back and went straight to the bar.

After a few drinks and a couple games of pool, we were all in our rooms by 1:00 a.m.

The next morning we packed and went down for breakfast. We sat and talked about how we enjoyed the weekend and each other's company.

Jacqueline invited us to New York for a weekend. She seemed like the perfect woman, but me and Black knew we would probably never see her again. All the goodbyes were said, and we left.

Black and I looked at each other, as Junie went the other way. We hated that. We were family and felt we shouldn't have to part. I really missed my brother and prayed that God would take care of him and one day send him back home to us.

The drive home felt much longer than going to DC, but we pumped sounds, sparked blunts, and had some in-depth conversations to pass time. We got back about 4:00 p.m. Black pulled in front, Tara and I got our things, and he was gone.

I took Tara home about 8:00 p.m. I told her I was tired and had to go to New York in the morning to take care of some business.

She didn't want to go, but she understood.

By 9:30 p.m., Big G was at the house sipping Hennessy and getting lifted so the head would be right.

"Enjoyed yourself in DC?" G asked.

"That shit was nice. Not a bad little city to hang out in," I said. "Black said we all going again. Next time it's just the crew, and you know we gonna have a ball."

"Fuck DC, niggah. Ain't nothing like Norfolk," he said.

"You right, fool. Ain't nothing like home."

CHAPTER 6

"No Stress"

I caught a flight out the next morning and arrived in Newark, New Jersey about 10:30 a.m. Taxis were lined up, so getting to the hotel was not a problem.

I jumped into a yellow checkered cab. "Take me to the Marriot Marquis," I told the cab driver.

He just nodded his head, which was wrapped in a lavender turban and said, "Sure."

We ran into traffic going through the Lincoln Tunnel. I tried to make conversation, but he wasn't trying to talk.

I saw bums and homeless people in Norfolk all the time, but as we came out the tunnel by the New York City Port Authority, I saw bums in the trashcans, trying to eat the food others were tossing away.

Once at the hotel, I decided to page Junie right away to let him know that I was waiting.

He arrived at the hotel about 2:00 p.m. with the guy issuing social security cards and birth certificates. This guy looked like he was straight business. He was wearing a nice gray suit, with shirt and tie, but when he reached his hand out to greet me, I saw the gold cuff links.

That really caught my attention.

The man had no facial hair at all. The first thing I thought was, *he could be the police*. But Junie said he was straight, so I rolled with it.

We all walked into the hotel restaurant, sat at a table, and ordered drinks.

"So what you have for me?" I asked.

"If you need new identity, I have it," he said with an African accent.

"Yes, that's what I'm looking for. Can you help me?"

"Birth certificates with matching social security cards for five hundred each. Let me know how many you want," he said.

I could barely understand what he was saying, but I looked at Junie. "I thought you said three hundred," I said.

"No, no. Three hundred for him, five hundred for anyone else," he said.

"Look, that's my brother. We're one; what you do for him, you do for me. I'm prepared to get ten from you right now. My money is his money. If you can't do three hundred then time is being wasted. If so, you can count on this like the 15th and the 30th just like the military checks," I said as he smiled.

"All right, let me go to the car."

He came back in carrying a brief case. It was nothing unusual. Many other businessmen were in there with suits on and papers sprawled out across their tables.

I was feeling good about how business was being handled.

He sat down and handed me a folder with ten birth certificates and ten social security cards. Junie was sitting beside him, so I gave him the three thousand.

As Junie slid it to him, he put it in his briefcase and stood up. "Take care," he said.

"Look, I need a number so when I'm coming in town you can meet me. This is my place, always."

He passed me a card with his business phone on it. "I'm there every day, Monday through Friday, until 6:00 p.m.," he said.

I took the folders up to my room. "Where's your other partner?" I asked Junie.

"I just paged him. He should be on the way."

The phone rang.

"What's up?" I asked, knowing it was Black, because nobody else knew I was there.

"How's it going?" he asked.

"One down and two to see," I answered.

"Look, Dieta and her girl are still up there. They just talked to Lo and they got a rental. I told them to pick you up about 7:00 p.m. from the hotel and you ride back with them. I don't want you trying to bring the machine back on the plane."

"No problem," I said, hanging up the phone.

I knew the other guy was going to have to come upstairs because he had to show me how the machine worked. Junie went downstairs to wait on the guy.

I was waiting about half an hour, when there was a knock at the door.

"What's up, God?" the young black guy asked with his northern accent. He didn't look to be more than twenty-one.

"Chilling, son," I answered.

"I got the machine and five phones with numbers. I'm going to show you what's up, and afterwards you buy what you want and the rest I'm out with," he said, talking real fast.

"I'm going to do one for you, so watch carefully."

It didn't take long, and he let me make a call, letting me know to dial the area code first.

I paid him for the machine and the phones then got his number so I wouldn't have any problems reaching him.

"How often you coming, son?" he asked.

"At least twice a month. I got to see how they move."

I put everything in my bag and sat it by the door. Looking at Junie he knew it was time to call Jacqueline's brother, J.B.

It wasn't until 6:00 p.m. when J.B. arrived. We all sat down, and he ordered some Remy.

"Talk to me, kid," he said. "What's up?"

This guy reminded me of Mr. Royal Blue, light skin, gold fronts, and dark black curly hair, with a low cut.

"Trying to do some business," I said.

"What you looking to do?" he asked.

Before I could answer he stood up and told me to take a walk.

"All right, talk to me," he said once we got outside.

"I'm in Norfolk and I want to score. But I want New York prices," I said directly. "If you got peoples in the area?"

"Check it, son—if you come here I can look out, probably around sixteen five, but if you score from my peoples in Hampton, then you looking at eighteen or nineteen thousand."

"I'll buy five straight up, if I can get them for seventeen in Norfolk, and that's guaranteed. You give me about a month, and I'll be coming like that every week."

"I can do that, but if you don't come like that, my man is going to tax you. Believe that."

"Here's my number and his. I'm going to call him and let him know to expect your call and what's up, so use code 362. When are you trying to do this?" he asked.

"Probably in the morning. Depends on the time I get back home."

"You coming to do five, right?" he asked.

"Yeah! It's time to blow, baby," I said. "I hope he's ready."

"He will be. Don't even worry."

I went back into the hotel and sat with Junie. We both downed our drinks and went to the room.

The girls were there at seven like clockwork, and we were back in Norfolk by 1:30 a.m.

They dropped me at my mom's in Lake Edward. I paged Black, and he was there in minutes. He dropped me off at the townhouse and took the phone I had done already.

"I'm going to hold this on the corner tonight, and each time somebody's pager goes off I'm going to let them use this and set this shit off. Hopefully by the morning we'll have five or six sales," he said. "How much these things going for anyway?"

"Two hundred and fifty for my phone and two hundred if they have their own. But it has to be a flip."

"All right, I'll be here in the morning. What the other niggah say?"

"Seventeen if you buy at least five, eighteen or nineteen for anything less. And if you go to New York then he'll do sixteen five."

"When can he do it?" he asked.

"Tomorrow morning. I got the kid's number in my pocket. So I'll check you in the morning."

* * *

The next morning Black was downstairs counting money when I came down.

"Help me count this. I want to be sure because I don't need that short shit."

We sat and counted eighty-five thousand-twice—then paged the guy in Hampton.

He called back immediately. "Yeah, who is this?" he said.

"Dee."

"The kid from Norfolk?" he asked.

"Yeah, I met with your man up top, and I'm ready. Just waiting on you, god," I said, remembering the terminology that the other kid up north used.

"Meet me at Bennigan's by the Coliseum Mall at noon. I'm driving an old Maxima."

I told him to look for us in a Honda hatchback.

We put the paper in a bag and left. We went to a hair shop on Chesapeake Boulevard, by Oakmont North, where Shereena worked. He left the Acura, took her Honda, and we were on our way to Hampton.

"Got your shit with you?" I asked.

"Yeah, but I hope it don't come to all that," he answered. "I just want to make this money."

"Yeah, but we don't know these niggahs. And they might just want to take this money."

"Why? You got your shit?" he asked.

"Damn right, and one in the chamber. I'm not taking no chances with you little brother. You all I got."

We gave each other a pound and prepared to handle our business.

We met at Bennigan's, and he had us follow him to a spot out McGruder Commons. When we parked he introduced himself as Plush.

"I'm Dee, and this is my brother, Black," I said, handing Black the bag. "I'll be right here. Watch yourself."

They went into the house and about ten minutes had passed. I was sitting there looking at everything that moved and everything the wind blew. It was early October, and the weather was going back and forth. A car pulled behind me, and two guys got out. I jumped out the car quickly.

"Don't park behind me; I'm getting ready to pull off."

One guy walked in the house, and the other moved the car before going in himself.

A minute later Black came out, and we were on our way back across the water, five kilos of powder sitting in the back.

"Niggahs got a money machine," Black said. "He saw the paper, called them other niggahs then started counting. We gave them eighty dollars too much."

"Eighty out of eighty-five thousand. Shit. We did good," I said.

"Yeah, but I ain't trying to give nobody shit. Them niggahs seem pretty chill. He suppose to try to get me a money machine next week."

"I heard that shit," I said.

"Those niggahs who came inside brought the shit with them. They said for me to tell my peoples to relax. They said they thought you were going to start blasting," he said laughing. "If I heard any shots, I would of plugged them niggahs with several holes getting up out of there."

We got to the house, and Black was on the move. He wanted to get the coke cooked up and on the street quickly.

He told me that he needed a spot to meet niggahs. So he took one of the birth certificates and social security cards and got a new ID. He then went and got him a townhouse out Stoney Point on Newtown Road.

He kept all his coke in the townhouse, and that was where Boot and Little lived. They weren't wild as hell and didn't fuck with a lot of 'ho's. They were just two laid-back young niggahs trying to make money, and Black was seeing that they did.

Black let Lo and Jay move into the apartment because that's where he would meet niggahs for transactions, and with them there, he wasn't worried about anything kicking off. He knew shit was safe.

By December, Black was still buying five kilos a week, cooking it and bringing back seven kilos.

My mother's lease was up in Lake Edward, and so was auntie's. Lo decided he wanted to move auntie and get the apartment to pump out of in Lake Edward. Black figured that was the move, and he did the same to mom's townhouse.

We all met with a realtor, Freddie Mac. He worked for a big company in the area and knew Dieta quite well. (It seemed like after the sudden death of her boyfriend, she wanted her a man with a real job. But it never stopped her from breaking Lo off some ass on the regular.) Boot and I met with Freddie Mac and he showed us six houses in Virginia Beach.

Two of them caught our attention because they were in the same neighborhood. The places had just enough space for moms and auntie to feel comfortable and not be scared. Both of the houses were non-qualifying, and we had to put down four thousand to close in two weeks.

They were in and settled by Christmas, with two new cars: a Ford Escort; a little Toyota Corolla that Black had got Moms.

By the time New Year's came, we had two crack

houses out Lake Edward and a stash house in Stony Point.

Black kept everything going at the other two spots, but him and Lo was taking the extra two kilos and breaking them down, only selling half ounces. They were more than doubling their money. They were selling a half an ounce for six hundred and bringing in over forty thousand off each brick, out of each house a week.

They had some young boys from Lake Edward, Bayside Arms, and Plaza working out the houses, and shit was moving quickly. They were there day in and day out. The houses were always open for business. These young boys were making money, a lot of money. Black and Lo were definitely getting rich, seeing more money than ever.

The young boys they had working for them looked up to them and wanted to be just like Black and Lo. They were becoming ghetto celebrities, and I was enjoying the ride.

I was running to New York twice a month like clockwork. I was doing about twenty phones a month, and selling birth certificates and social security cards as if they were drugs. For every hustler, thug, and regular person who had fucked-up credit and needed a new identity, I was the man.

I only went to Black for big paper. I was shining with my own paper now, but he still paid the bills. I decided that this year I was going to accomplish some things instead of just partying.

My New Year's resolution was to buy me a house, get a new car, and start a business. When I had told Jacqueline that I was a real estate investor, I liked the way that sounded, so I wanted to find out more about it. Plus, I was seeing quite a few people get locked up and even more losing their lives to the drug game, and I didn't want to see Black, Lo, Boot, and even Black's main man, Little, go out like that.

I was talking to Black and told him of my ideas. He was all for it. He said that making money and having a good time was all he had on his mind.

I had heard him talking about selling the Acura and getting a Lexus. I told him that he couldn't have a Lexus and continue to live in Lake Edward. His Acura was loud enough, and I told him not to draw any more attention to himself than he already did.

I was explaining to him to get a business first; then, buy houses with garages like the guy out Rosemont Forest.

He told me to take care of these things fast because he was stacking a lot of money and too many people knew where we were resting our heads. People were starting to get jealous, and he was becoming the talk of the hood.

I knew I had to get going because he was too busy handling other business, and I didn't need any stickup kids running up in the crib on us. I knew that when niggahs and their families got hungry and their kids don't have, all morals go out the window, and there's no limit to what they'll do—including blasting me if I stood between them and their paper.

I went to see an attorney to know the ins and outs of opening a business. My objective was to put away some of this money Black was making. I went downtown on Freemason to the law firm of Madison, Robinson, Williams, and Fulton, who are all black attorneys. I had heard of them because Madison and Robinson were two big names in the city. Most of the time when you heard of a big-time hustler getting knocked off, you would hear that he obtained Robinson and his team as his defense attorneys. I decided to get one of the attorneys and put them on retainer for myself and my little brother.

My attorney advised me to incorporate my business and use the name of my corporation for anything I did.

It cost five hundred to start my corporation. I figured anything that I was real serious about would go under the corporation name and everything else would be under my new identity.

It didn't take long for my corporation papers to come from Richmond. B&D Corporation was our new entity. I wanted to open a club, but the paper wasn't there. I decided instead to go with a spot where people could hang out, eat, drink, and entertain themselves with games and pool tables, a sports bar.

I found a building close by, right in the shopping center off Newtown Road. After talking to the owner, I realized that it was the perfect spot.

I went to the courthouse to find out the procedure. What I thought was going to take weeks was going to take months. I didn't only have to get permits, but I had to get a trade name, get an application for pool tables, apply for an alcohol license, and get a health inspector in before serving food.

Meeting with City Council to see if they approved of my business was farther down the road, but I even had to run the shit in the paper, in case the civic league had a protest.

First, I thought this was more trouble than it was worth. But I knew this had to be done not so much for myself, but mainly so Black could hide all the paper he was bringing into our world.

By February, our corporation was set. B&D Corporation was legal and in the system. The first thing I did was make myself President and my moms Vice President. Black said don't put his name on shit, which was understood.

I called Freddie Mac to let him know I needed to see some homes. He showed me five houses that were older and needed work. I quickly let him know that when I wanted some investment property I would let him know.

Right then, I wanted to see some fly shit, and money wasn't standing in our way.

Next time we got together he showed five more. It was hard making a choice, but I narrowed it down and picked two. They were in a section of Virginia Beach called Salem Lakes and Rock Creek. Both were beautiful homes—three bedrooms, two full baths and a half bath downstairs, separate living room, family rooms with fireplaces, and formal dining areas. And they both had attached garages.

The one out Salem Lakes was ten thousand down, and the other was fourteen thousand down and take over the loan.

I told Freddie Mac, "I never knew you could buy a house with no job and no verification of income."

He quickly let me know that as long as you had the cash, you could purchase whatever the hell you want.

As long as I had the cash, he had the houses.

I told Black about the houses, and he agreed. But he still didn't believe it could be done. So he told me that if I could get one, he wanted it with a pool—for pool parties and cookouts.

I called Freddie Mac to let him know that I needed to see some homes with swimming pools. He showed me three: two of them had pools; and one was on a golf course, with a pool and tennis courts in the complex.

I ended up buying the house on the golf course in Glennwood—three bedrooms and a loft. When you entered the front door, you had an open foyer, with stairs to your right. To the left in the corner was a fireplace. The ceilings were high, and in the center sat two skylights that allowed the sun to brighten the room. The living room and the dining room ran together, which created a perfect great room. The kitchen was off the dining area, with a door that led to the two-car garage.

The home I picked out for Black was also in Virginia Beach, in a section called Larkspur, about ten minutes away from me, off Independence Boulevard. He had three bedrooms, with a room over the garage. The living room and dining room were formal, and there was an enormous family room with a fireplace.

There were built-in book shelves and a wet bar in the sunken family room, which had doors that led to a deck that stretched across the entire back of the house. Directly behind the deck was an in-ground pool. The home had hardwood floors downstairs, but wall-to-wall carpet upstairs.

It was well worth the thirty thousand that we had to put down, but was still pretty steep, compared to my fifteen thousand.

I bought both homes under B&D Corporation. Freddie Mac set it up where I made an offer with seventy-five hundred and then came with seventy-five hundred to the closing table for my house.

Black's house was bought under a different system, because it involved so much cash. He made his offer with five thousand and agreed to bring five thousand to the closing table. He then agreed to pay the sellers five thousand a month until the thirty thousand was paid.

Freddie Mac was a genius, definitely somebody we had to keep on our payroll.

By the end of February we were closing on the houses. Black had safes in the house out Campus East, each filled with stacks of money. He had given me the combination to them all, but I was only allowed to go in one.

I got the money to carry to closing and my keys the same day. After closing, I called Black, and we rode out to both houses.

He flipped when he saw them. "This shit is mine?" he asked. "How in the fuck?" he yelled, hugging me. "So how much it cost?"

"One hundred and sixty," I said.

"How much a month?" he asked, looking around, smiling.

"One thousand two hundred and seventy-five."

"Shit, niggah. That's three goddamn apartments. But I need my room over the garage for the pool table, a nice-ass deck. And check out the pool. I got everything I need right here. How much was your shit?" he asked, trying to keep track of his money.

"One hundred and eighteen. I pay eight hundred a month," I said.

"What you going to do with the one out Campus East . . . because I'm not going to pay for both of them motherfuckers?" he said seriously.

"Well, I'll pay for it. I want it to run bitches, I ain't bringing them here or to my shit," I said, letting him know I had my own paper, all the while knowing that he was going to be chilling there also.

But if he didn't fuss when he spent money, it wouldn't be Black. "So, you gonna stay there by yourself?"

"I think I'm going to let Tara move in. She fucked around and let herself get pregnant."

"She ain't carrying her ass to Hillcrest? Or you plan on giving a niggah a nephew?"

"I'm going to keep this one. It's about that time."

"You love that bitch, man," Black said.

"Something like that. She's real sweet."

"I heard that. As long as she makes you happy, do your thing," he said. "Now let's go to Haynes Furniture and lay both these cribs out as if we were motherfuckin' kings. I want some plush carpet upstairs, so when a niggah step down on it, their foot sinks about two feet," he said laughing.

"That shit's expensive as hell," I said.

"I don't give a fuck! Get that shit in your house too. Then, call and get ADT on both cribs. I need Freddie Mac's number so he can meet with Tia and find her a small townhouse or something; and I need to get Shereena a rental."

"Who coming in here with you?" I asked.

"No goddamn body! This is my shit! If I feel like walking around this bitch butt-naked every day and jack my dick, that's what I'm going to do! Plus, if we go out of town and meet bitches, now we got somewhere for them to stay when we invite them here for the weekends. This shit is strictly for the 'ho's."

We left there and went straight to Haynes. We bought five bedroom sets, which included two expensive-ass Henredon bedroom sets, two Thomasville dining sets; Sherill set for my loft; Italian leather for my living room; and Italian leather for his family room and living room. We must have spent at least twenty thousand.

We left there and stopped at Circuit City to get six twenty-seven inch televisions for the bedrooms, and two wide-screens for the family rooms. Black even bought four complete Harmon/Kardon stereo systems.

Our last stop was Q-Masters, to get a nine-foot Brunswick Gold Crown III pool table to go in the room over the garage. We had everything set to be delivered a week later, which would give us time to lay carpet and get alarms put on the houses, amongst other things. Things seemed to be moving in the right direction.

By mid-March we had our homes laid out like models. Black had Tia in a townhouse out Northridge, and Shereena in a condo out Thalia Station. We gave up the rental in Campus East and bought one in Campus East.

Freddie Mac found somebody getting ready to lose their home and only wanted three thousand to assume, so I started my investing before I was ready. It turned out to be just like the one we had in the front.

It became the ideal spot, because it wasn't even a mile from Lake Edward and no drugs were even in the vicinity. That gave Black an opportunity to just relax and chill, but still be close to his money in case anything happened with his business. He was trying to let his crack houses keep bringing in the money, but he knew time was ticking away. It wouldn't be long before it would end.

Boot and Little were also blowing up. Pat and Rod were now buying whole bricks, without putting all the shit in the game. Pat and Rod would come to Virginia and meet Boot and Little at Greenbrier Mall. Boot and Little had told Black that Rod's cousin, who lived in Fayetteville, North Carolina, was trying to score. He said that niggahs were paying almost twenty-six thousand for a kilo.

Black was very hesitant about going farther down South; he wanted them to come here and score. Rod's cousin was trying to score two or three bricks, which Rod couldn't handle. So he was trying to turn him on to Boot and Little. Rod told Little that his cousin had no way to come to Virginia and get it back, so Little was all anxious about being able to sell a kilo of coke for twenty-seven thousand and was getting impatient.

Black told Boot that if niggahs were making money like that, they had a way to come to Norfolk and that it was some shit behind it.

That was all Boot needed to hear.

Little on the other hand felt that the money was too good to pass up, and he was going to show Black. He bought a kilo from Black and asked him to front another, one that he would usually sell to Pat and Rod.

Little went and got Jay and decided to make a move to Fayetteville; they met at a hotel by Cross Creek Mall.

"Check it out, Little—I'm going to stand over there in the cut. If these niggahs attempt to act stupid, I'm taking them away from here."

Jay actually had a plan that when they came up he was going to come out blasting and go back to Norfolk fifty-four thousand dollars richer.

The guys pulled up in a 535 BMW and parked beside Little. Jay stood there waiting for one to get out the car so that he could run up and rob the niggahs, but there were just too many people around to start that shit.

All of a sudden, the driver jumps out the car with nines in each hand and starts blasting. Four shots hit Little—two in the chest and two to the head. He grabbed the bag with two kilos in it and was getting in the car.

With people acting hysterical, Jay ran up with a nine and started blasting into the BMW. The driver had put the car in drive, but four shots to his chest left him slumped over the steering wheel. While the passenger lay with his head back and eyes open, two shots in the neck and one in the head at point blank range definitely sent him to his maker.

Jay opened the door and grabbed the drugs, their bag of money, and took off. He ran to the McDonald's across the street, where he jumped in a burgundy Camaro, and, at gunpoint, made a soldier stationed at Fort Bragg carry him all the way to Emporia.

The guys that had killed Little had twenty-seven thousand in their bag, like they had planned to buy one brick if they weren't able to pull off the robbery. Jay gave the soldier two thousand for the ride . . . and his silence.

The soldier told Jay, before getting out the car, "You didn't have to pull the gun. All you had to do was show me the money."

Jay called Boot and told him where he was, and Boot went and picked him up.

We were all at the house in Campus East, when they came in. Black knew something was wrong. When he told us that Little was dead, a feeling went through my body that made my spine shiver. No one close had ever gotten gunned down before. I sat there with nothing to say. Boot knew it could have easily been him.

Black stared at Jay. Jay gave him both bags; the two kilos and the cash. He didn't give it to him because it was his to get, but out of respect. All the young soldiers in the 'hood respected Black, and that was Jay's way of showing it, which he knew would put him in with Black forever. Black stood there knowing that Jay was a real trooper who could not be slept on.

"I don't believe this shit." Black said, looking at Boot. "Didn't I say don't fuck with it?" Black was talking, but he didn't want answers. He was just thinking out loud. He turned to Jay, holding out both bags. "Which one you want?"

Jay reached out and took the two kilos.

Black walked upstairs. Tough as he was, I could see the hurt.

"Did my motherfuckin' niggah troop like that?" Lo asked.

"Blasted two niggahs, stole the goods, and jacked an Army boy for a ride home. Now, if that ain't a fuckin' trooper, somebody better tell me!" he yelled excitedly.

We all smirked, because a laugh was hard to hold in at that time.

Black came back downstairs with a bottle of Hennessy in one hand and a blunt in the other. "Boot, page Pat and Rod and tell them you'll give them two kilos for thirty thousand. They should jump on it. Tell them you trying to score and you'll give them a deal if they move on it now."

Boot paged Pat, who called straight back and jumped on the deal. They were set to meet at Greenbrier Mall.

Black turned to Boot, "As far as I'm concerned, Rod and Pat turned you and Little on to them niggahs. So they're responsible for their cousin's actions. Go meet them and take Lo and Jay with you. We split the thirty thousand," he said, going back to his room.

* * *

The next morning I woke up to Tara cooking us breakfast. She was strolling around in a T-shirt and a silk scarf. Damn! She looked good to me.

I grabbed *The Virginian Pilot/Ledger Star newspaper.* The front page read, "Two Elizabeth City Youths Found Dead at Greenbrier Mall." I continued to read the article, because it said *slain,* not shot. It said that they were beaten to death with car jacks and their throats were slit from ear to ear. Rod was found in the car dead and castrated. Pat was found dead in the trunk, with Rod's dick in his mouth.

"Niggahs losing their minds these days," I said. "Those niggahs must of went through hell before they died."

"I know. I read it," she said. "I have a doctor's appointment. Are you going with me?"

"No, I have business."

"Is that the way it's going to be for the whole nine months?"

"I don't know, but that's how it is today," I replied.

"You act like you can't do shit when I ask you."

"Don't start. I'm not in the mood for that shit today."

"I don't give a fuck. I'm talking!" she yelled.

Before I knew it, I had slapped her against the wall and slammed her head in the eggs and toast on her plate. "Who the fuck you talking to? Huh?" I yelled, my hand around the back of her neck.

She started crying and yelling, "I'm leaving because you not going to keep putting your motherfuckin' hands on me. You ain't my goddamn daddy!" She jumped up as if she was going to stand up and go toe to toe.

I reached in the drawer and pulled out an extension cord and went across her legs. She yelled every time I swung, "I'm sorry, I'm sorry."

"No, run your mouth now. Talk that shit you were just talking. Like I'm one of those bitches you hang with."

When I stopped, she took off upstairs. I ran up there after her. She fell across the bed crying, with her T-shirt up and her ass out.

Suddenly I was aroused. "Take them panties off," I said directly.

"Hell, no. You fuckin' crazy," she yelled.

"Fuck no. I ain't crazy," I said, ripping them off and jumping on her. I fucked her like a crazed animal.

She struggled, but my weight on top of her gave her no chance.

When I was finished, she got up and started getting her things, yelling she was going to leave. I tried to ignore it, but she kept on cursing and yelling, talking 'bout, if I didn't let her go, that when I came home she was going to be gone.

I went to my closet, got my gun, put one in the chamber, and put it to her head.

She stopped in her tracks, and her eyes widened.

"Do you want to leave? Huh, do you?" I yelled. "I'll help you leave this motherfuckin' world. You want to leave?"

Her eyes got wider, and she said through short breaths, "No, no. I don't."

"Don't fuck with me, Tara. I'm telling you, don't fuck with me. If you try to leave here, I will hunt your ass down, and you'll end up in Norfolk General fighting for your fuckin' life. I mean that shit. That's a fuckin' promise."

I left and went and stayed at Black's house for a couple days. I wasn't worried about her because she had some money. I had also bought her a 200SX, and so knew she could leave if she really wanted to.

I got up early and called Freddie Mac. This was the day I was going to get my peoples some investment property. I wanted something I could fix up and make a nice piece of change to put down on a new car.

I told Black about my idea. He asked me to find three properties because he wanted some new shit also, and the cash we get from that would work.

I ended up buying two houses off 28th Street, in the Park Place section of town, for twenty-five thousand each and found a duplex in Ballentine for thirty-five thousand.

It took me ten thousand and two weeks to fix the houses up in Park Place. It only took four thousand for the duplex, and my handy man had it ready to sell in ten days. I put the houses up for sale for forty thousand each. Sold them both in a month's time. The duplex took three weeks to sell, and it sold for fifty-three thousand.

I had made thirty-two thousand within two months. I bought the homes under my corporation, and I put the thirty-two thousand into the corporation account.

My business idea was coming along, and everything was falling in place. I had signed the lease and set it up so rent wouldn't start until I opened. My tabletop permit was issued. The health inspector said I had to add a bathroom and make them both handicap accessible. That was done in two days. I recorded my trade name and had to wait for the city council to meet. The ABC board told me that I had to open and sell a certain amount of food and show receipts of the amounts being sold before a beer and wine permit could be issued.

Summer was rolling around, and the pool was uncovered. Black was getting it treated. It wouldn't be long before the pool was clear, and the parties and

barbecues would be on. Big G and I were at my
house in Glennwood, sipping on Heinekens and getting lifted. We sat around talking about the new club
in Portsmouth called David's. Everybody was now
going there as Harlem Nights was closed because of
the fighting and shooting incidents that had become
an every-week occurrence.

I remembered the last time I was over there, the
club was still packing out every week with the fliest
bitches. Somebody told me that the kid with the
white Saab had flipped it on the interstate and was
doing pretty bad.

Things happened so fast! I had just read in yesterday's paper that a young man was found dead in his
car at Wendy's on Independence Boulevard, near
the beach. He was shot in the head. Then, I was at
the Casablanca and found out it was the hustler who
drove that pretty candy apple red Jaguar. What were
things coming to?

"What you doing today?" G asked.

"Waiting on Black. We suppose to go look at some
cars." I answered.

"Can't hide that money," G said. "Can't hide it."

About that time Tara came in with her cousin
Dawn. "Dee, I need you to get those bags out the
car." She had just come in from Food Lion. "Better
carry your boy. It's quite a few things out there."

"Hey, Dawn," I said.

"Hi, Dee. How are you doing?" she asked.

"Fine. You not going to speak to my man?" I asked.

"The hell with your trifling-ass friends," she said.

G spoke to her anyway.

She never cared for him, since he had fucked her
girl and never called her again. She hated Black because they went out a few times. Then we all went to
the Poconos. When we got back he never returned

her pages, but every time he ran into her, the first thing out his mouth was, "When we getting up?"

We brought the groceries in and sat them down on the counter.

"How you feel today, baby?" I asked Tara, pulling her to me and kissing her.

"Fine. But my clothes are getting snug on my stomach."

"I have to run out for a few, but soon as I get back we'll go to Lynnhaven Mall and pick you up a few things. You, me, Dawn, and Black," I said, loud enough for Dawn to hear.

"Shit. I ain't going nowhere with Black's black ass."

We laughed and kept going.

It wasn't long before Black and Lo pulled up in a brand-new Acura Legend with thirty-day tags.

"Damn. Who is this?" G asked.

"My shit, niggah," Lo said. "And I got a garage for this bitch to go in too."

"Where you resting now, son?" I asked.

"Out by Green Run High School," Lo said.

"Where you get this shit?" I asked.

"A&G Auto. The man gave me a deal I couldn't re-sist."

Big G and I jumped in, and we were out. "Dawn in the crib," G said to Black, who was lighting a blunt.

"Fuck that bitch. I'll beat that 'ho' ass today if she come with that smart shit. I ain't in the mood. How that bitch looking? I know she looking good."

"You know that shit, fool," I said

"Little niggah out the way want to buy my shit," Black said.

"You going to sell it?"

"Doubt it," he said. "Tia needs a car. That shit she got has had it. I can't have her out there stranded and that bitch carrying my baby."

"What?" me and Lo said at the same time.

"You ain't going to believe this—both of the hookers pregnant," Black said, shaking his head.

"Damn, son. I know you didn't plan it that way, but things occur. Now handle it."

"Man! Shit! I called Freddie Mac. Lo and I met with him early this morning. I'm going to buy this house out Indian Lakes, off Ferrell Parkway, for eight thousand down in Tia's name and let her live there. Then I looked at one in Chesapeake, off of Battlefield Boulevard. Phat-ass shit. But that's ten thousand down. I'm going to get that in Shereena's name."

He finished talking about the shit he had to do, and then out of nowhere he yelled, "I want my Lexus, niggah. Me and Lo saw this blue Lex with Florida tags today. That shit was butter. Two niggahs driving that bitch."

"I saw those niggahs getting out that shit at Military Circle, wearing motherfuckin' Dickies, wearing work shit, and flashing a mouthful of gold," G said.

We stopped and ate lunch at Red Lobster. Red Lobster and the mall was almost an everyday thing. Thalhimer's sales people knew us on a first-name basis.

It was quite a difference going into the stores now. Whenever Black and I walked into Thalhimer's, Beecroft and Bull's, and especially the stores on Granby Street downtown, they catered to us as if we were celebrities, and it felt good.

We spent most of the day checking out cars. Black ended up getting him a black Lexus from the dealership on the Boulevard. As we were leaving the dealership, I rode with Black so he could drop me back at my house.

"I met these guys in Suffolk," Black said, breaking the silence. "They been coming out the way for a while buying. Now they want two bricks. I've served them about three times, and they coming on a regular. I'm moving more shit than you would believe. After I close on these houses for these 'ho's, I want to buy some bomb-ass shit with a two-car garage that nobody—I mean nobody—know about. Then I am going to buy two phat-ass cars to go in both garages. But they'll be strictly for out-of-town use."

"I heard that. We going to fuck around and make Freddie Mac rich," I said. "But he knows his shit. Got to give it to him."

We were riding down the Boulevard, past Phillip Oldsmobile, and saw all the Mercedes and Oldsmobiles.

"Stop over there," I said.

We looked at the different-sized Mercedes and even test-drove one. Black promised that he would have a 560SEL by the time Freaknic in Atlanta came again. I test-drove a black Range Rover and fell in love. I stood there staring at it and debating. Black asked the salesman how much I could get for my Pathfinder if I traded it in, and how much cash I needed down.

We left and went home. All my mind was on was the Range Rover and how I would shine in that bitch! Niggahs would definitely take me as a big money-maker.

Black and Lo dropped me and G off and they kept going. As I approached the door I heard the horn blow and realized it was still Black.

"How much you got in the safe?" he asked.

"About hundred and twenty thou. I ain't fuck with it. I been spending my own shit," I said.

"Trade in your truck and buy the Range under the corporation's name. Write a check and put down fifteen thousand on it," he said. "Don't be looking all sad and shit. Don't think every time I get something new you supposed to. I work every day. You need a motherfuckin' job!"

He started smiling and drove off. I ran in the house like a big-ass kid getting ready to go to the toy store. This was a big-ass toy and an expensive one as well.

CHAPTER 7

"It's All Good Now"

It was kind of chilly out, and I was enjoying my new truck. Time was flying by, and Tara was getting ready to have my baby. She was acting irritable and fussing nonstop, which was wearing my patience thin. I was on my way to Mom's house, and we were arguing. She had gotten in good with Moms and once even told me that if I ever hit her again she was going to tell her.

I told her that I didn't give a fuck because I was grown. But I didn't want to chance it. That would make Moms bring up how stupid my dad used to act and how we felt growing up. I didn't want to get into it with Moms, because she always wins. She wasn't for all that bullshit.

I was traveling down Baker Road, by Lake Edward, when my heart dropped at the sight of the police cars and Black sprawled out on the ground.

"Oh, my god! Is that Black's car?" Tara asked, startled.

There were three Virginia Beach police cars and

two unmarked cars with lights flashing, around Black's Lexus. As I rode by I saw Boot leaned on the car and Black still on the ground.

"I hope he didn't have anything in the car," she said.

"No, he wouldn't have anything in the Lex. He don't even smoke weed in that bitch," I said. "What the fuck they got him for?"

I picked up the cellular and called Tia. I knew he always said that if he ever got caught up she knew what to do.

She was up there in a matter of minutes. I had stopped at 7-Eleven so I could see what was going on. Tia went over by all the commotion.

"Don't worry," Black said. "They like the Lexus and never seen one close up before. Shit they can't afford."

The crowd started laughing. They put him in the back of the car and held them a few more minutes, while they went through the Lex thoroughly before letting them go.

"You're becoming big time now, Black! No more corner action!" one of the police officers yelled, "You're on everybody's list now, big baller."

"Tell you what, officer—you pick up an application from the corner, and next time you stop me, I'll look it over and I might give you some work," Black said sarcastically, before him and Boot got in the Lex and drove away.

We all went to Boot's house in Wesleyan Chase. Freddie Mac had found him a three-bedroom, with two baths, a colonial-style home. Nobody was staying in the townhouse, except for the soldiers pumping out of it. We pulled up, and he had his Toyota 4runner with thirty-day tags and his 300ZX parked in front of his garage, where he had just cleaned them up before Black had scooped him.

"Fuck that," Black said, getting out the car. "Page Lo. I don't want him going out there."

It didn't take Lo long to call back. Black told him what happened and not to go out Lake Edward.

"What we going to do? Sounds like we going to end up closing shop," Lo said.

"No, not yet. I'm going to change up, but keep things out this way. Ten months ain't a bad stretch. It's time for a switch. Dee, I need you to run with me."

I told Tara to go to my mom's, where I'd meet her.

We called Freddie Mac on the cellular to let him know we needed two condos in Newpoint by the morning. As the sports bar was going to be in Newpoint Shopping Center, right in front of the condos, it was going to be very convenient.

Freddie Mac called us early and wanted to meet us at Food Lion on Newtown Road. He showed us four condos, and we took two. He had us signing leases by 5:00 a.m. the following day.

When people came by the houses to score, Lo and Black told their soldiers to tell kids about the new spot. They had gotten greedy out Lake Edward by selling anything people wanted, from sixteenths to quarters. But he wanted the flow of traffic to slow down out Newpointe, so he only sold ounces.

Business never slowed. The police even raided the two townhouses, and all they found was niggahs camping out, with empty weed bags and forty-ounce bottles lying around the house. When this happened they were the joke of the day.

Late that same night, police sent some undercovers in the hood to buy crack from the corner, where about twelve niggahs stood, just hanging out and making sales. Police knew that most of them scored from Black and figured if they couldn't stop his money one way, then they'd make it where he had to come to the corner himself.

After they approached the car to make the sale, the detectives showed their badges and tried jumping out the car. But to their surprise instead of the black youths being scared and running, they took bricks, 2x4s, and iron poles and beat the detectives down. Two were seriously injured, and one was beaten into a coma.

The next day the police had gotten an apartment on Lake Edward Drive the main drive that ran through the neighborhood, and made a mini police station. Twice as many cars were riding through now, and they even had police on bikes.

Black was making plenty of money by just selling weight, but it was nothing like the money that he was getting from the crack houses in the hood or the condos he now had down the street.

The police were really slowing things down.

The next night I ran into Black and Lo at the townhouse in Campus East. They were driving a beige Honda Accord Black got just so he could make moves on the down low.

"Where the Lexus?" I asked.

"Put away. I'm incognito from now on."

Usually him and Lo bust new shit on a daily, but today they were wearing sweat pants, and old Reeboks.

"Me and Lo going out here and set up shop in the back alley. Young boys trying to make sales in front of the police apartment, when all they have to do is move somewhere else. The fiends will find you," Black said, with a smirk.

"Couple days and money will be flowing again," Lo said. "When I go down, niggah, all you going to see is black jackets and DEA hats. And if they don't come correct, straight gun smoke. And I mean that shit. Fuck around if they want to."

Just two days ago we were all at Auntie's house for dinner. We had thought about having dinner at one of our houses, but Moms and Auntie felt better at their house. We ended up having a beautiful time, as always when we all came together, but now the dinners were much more plentiful. You would've thought the mob was having dinner, with all the bomb-ass cars sitting in front of Auntie's house. We all had gotten competitive when it came to our shit. We were buying homes and seeing who would come up with the most extravagant idea. We were buying cars and would battle with custom sounds.

Everybody's most expensive habit was the sports car, and racing. Boot had his 300ZX, which he had just got back from dropping a new engine in, and was anxious to try it out on some real competition. Lo had his 5.0 Mustang that would burn rubber sitting still. Dre had come home from Ft. Bragg with his RX7 ready to run. Tony, meanwhile, had flown in one-way from Ft. Riley, Kansas, and Lo had promised to get him a new car to drive back. I had a Corvette that I hardly drove, but I always had some shit I was getting done so my people couldn't fuck me up.

Dave and Steve, two white boys I went to school with, had a shop. They would take it to the shop and just have fun. They always said they dreamed of having a car and unlimited funds to just create shit, and they had the 'Vette hard to handle.

Black had a black Porsche 911 Carrera, limo-tinted windows, chrome rims, and wide-ass tires. He was fuckin' this white girl who lived down on the oceanfront in a condo out Linkhorn Cove. Her brother, Chad, owned a car shop that only did work on foreign cars. He kept Black's Porsche running tip-top and looking even better.

Chad sold powder cocaine, which he also sniffed. Whenever Black scored, he would take it to Chad to check the quality. That's how Chad got paid. So they looked out for each other. Things must have been going okay because it wasn't too often Black brought his Porsche on this side.

Black rented a home in Oyster Point, on the other side of Newport News. He had built a rapport with his suppliers and, since he was scoring in Hampton, kept most of his shit in Oyster Point and distributed on the other side of the water. He bought the Porsche from JB, and it was clean and ready to run when he got it.

Junie had come home from Florida. He had been there for about six months and was staying in a condo that Black had purchased from JB for him. Junie was driving a beige sleek-ass Jaguar with leather interior. This Jag was built for running.

Before dinner we all went to the stretch, a section of Interstate on 264 going to Suffolk, where there were usually no police. Everybody decided to open the cars up and see who had the most ass under the hood.

We all got back to Auntie's house, where Black was smiling and talking shit. We knew nobody could fuck with him. The only one who had the money to afford to fuck with him was Lo—and he didn't like Porsches.

Lo and Junie were fussing about Boot being in Lo's way. That was the main conversation over dinner.

"Lord, y'all are doing wrong and know you doing wrong racing up them roads. What if the man was out there? Then what?" complained Moms.

"If their asses get caught, they better not call this

goddamn house because I don't accept collect calls," Auntie finished.

We all laughed, but we knew that if either one of them thought any of us was in trouble, they would be there with the quickness. They knew it, and we knew it too. That's something we'd known all our lives because they didn't play when it came to their boys.

It was two days after Thanksgiving, and I was walking Tara up and down the halls of DePaul Hospital.

"Get my momma! Get your momma!" Tara cried. She wanted one of them. I guess I wasn't doing the trick.

All of a sudden my mom, Tia, and Black came through the door. The doctor came in, had her moved to a room, and put her in a bed. She was then hooked up to a machine to monitor the baby. She laid there with the look of pain on her face. We all stood there as my mother held her hand.

"Ma, it hurt so bad," Tara cried.

"I know, baby, but it will be all over soon," my mom said. "Then that little thing will be here kicking and screaming, and you'll never have a moment's peace."

Tara smiled as much as she could, then her mother came in. "Oh Lord, look at my baby," she said. "Are you Okay?"

"No," Tara said sharply.

Moments later the doctor came in and said too many people were in the room. Black and Tia left out. Tara's mom also left. She said she couldn't stand to see her baby in pain.

The doctor took her legs and parted them, asking me to hold one. He then put on plastic gloves and squirted some gel-like substance on his hand. Then he pushed it in her vagina and told her to push.

I stood there amazed and scared at the same time. Tara had told me months ago DePaul was a Catholic hospital. She said they told her the baby's life came before hers.

I didn't really pay it much attention until now. I just closed my eyes briefly and said, "God, please don't let anything happen to my baby."

When I opened my eyes I realized I had only prayed for Tara. So I quickly added, "Or my little girl."

Minutes later, I saw the most remarkable thing I'd ever seen. This wet, slick-headed, little creature came sliding out of my girl's vagina into the doctor's hand. They cleaned her mouth, nose, then made my baby cry.

The doctor never knew I was getting ready to call Lo and Jay. He wrapped her in a blanket and handed her to me. "Congratulations. You have a beautiful baby girl."

I stared down and knew they weren't lying. She was beautiful. I thanked God and Tara. This little girl was here, and she was all mine, something to connect me to Tara forever.

It was Saturday night. I had just had a baby girl and was feeling good. I called Big G and told him to get dressed and meet me at Black's house. It was time to spark up, sip on some Hennessy before going to David's in Portsmouth. He knew how I felt; his girl had just given him a baby girl three months earlier.

We pulled up at David's, behind a white Maxima kitted up, with deep-dish hammers, wearing Florida tags. The chrome sign around the plates read: "Straight From the Bottom, Miami Hurricanes."

I was checking it out when a voice asked, "What's up?"

"Nothing," I said. "Is this your shit?"

"Yeah!" he replied.

"That bitch is nice."

I had seen this guy many times in the clubs, mainly

the Royal Blue. We always talked and even passed pounds while talking to bitches, but never talked on the personal.

"Nice, hell! I like that motherfucker there," he said, referring to the Lex.

I felt good inside because I knew that bitch was all that. That's why I parked directly in front of the club.

It was about 12:15 a.m., and the line was long. So when I parked and Big G and myself got out the Lex, all eyes were on us. My shit was on, and nobody could tell me different. The other hustlers no longer impressed me, acting as if they were the shit. I was now amongst the ranks of money-makers.

All the players felt I was making enormous amounts of money in the game. The only question was who was I scoring from. They were quickly learning where I represented.

Females weren't even a big thing anymore. I felt I could fuck anything I wanted. I knew the shit I was rocking was no joke—two-hundred-dollar Cole Hahn shoes; two-hundred-dollar Perry Ellis slacks; one-hundred-and-fifty-dollar Perry Ellis shirt; my new herringbone and medallion; and matching bracelet and Rolex that Black bought me from Reed's Jewelry in Military Circle.

I had started wearing glasses, so I went out and bought some gold frames by IZOD and tinted the lenses. I was the shit. Just like a motherfuckin don!

My conversation had changed now towards the girls; it was short and direct. I expressed myself with much more confidence because my game was tight and money was flowing like a river.

I remembered before I got paper, my game was all right, but it would have never worked with these money-hungry, fly-ass, pretty bitches with bodies like goddesses. That was what the fuck I liked.

Before, I would ask unnecessary questions: What's your name? Where you from? What you do for a living? Where your boyfriend? Do you want to get a drink? And so many nights ended with a fiend sucking my dick.

With the big money, my conversation was short and to the point. "Get a glass and have some champagne so we can discuss where we going to do breakfast and if we we're going for a late-night swim?"

If it was summer that shit worked, allowing me to have those goddess-like bodies however I wanted. My dick would be served by the finest lips.

Growing up I thought it was all about true love. In reality it was all about the paper.

This guy and me talked for a few, realizing the females were checking our style. He was wearing fly dress shit too, and had a fat cable with a phat medallion on the end. He was definitely a hustler, or his peoples were.

"Got any pull up here?" I asked.

"This security ain't no joke. They don't look out for nobody."

This shit was true, but when we got in, it was on.

"RJ, this is my man, Dee," he said.

"What up, my niggah?" he said.

"Cooling, baby," I said, like a real don, impressed by nobody. "Why? What's up?"

"Not a thing, my niggah. Yo, Kane, tell them bitches to bring two bottles of Moet over here," RJ said loudly.

About this time, Big G came over, and I introduced him as my peoples, so niggahs would know his respect was due.

About six niggahs was drinking, and RJ was spending money like it was water. He had bought two platters of chicken and fries then invited some bitches to join us, knowing real 'ho's always hungry. He said he had rooms at the Omni downtown and wanted the bitches to go back.

As we all left the club, one of his boys went to pull his car to the front. He had the prettiest Lexus I'd ever seen, with Florida tags.

The girl G was talking to and two of her friends jumped in his Lex.

"Come on, my niggah. That bitch belong to you, my niggah," RJ yelled at G.

Kane and his boy, along with two more bitches, jumped in his Max.

"Where you all parked?" I asked.

"Way down there," Melody said.

She was one of the girls we had been drinking and talking with. Them bitches just jumped in those niggahs' cars, not knowing how the fuck they getting back home.

"Can you give me a ride to my car?" she asked.

"Yeah," I said, laughing.

"Naw, those bitches stupid," she said. "Go to his room and then if they don't give up no pussy, he ain't gonna want to carry they ass home. Shit, if I want to give a niggah some pussy, I will. But I'm not gonna give a niggah pussy for a ride home. Know what I'm saying?"

"Yeah," I said, laughing as I slid in a CD, feeling fucked up.

"What's your name anyway?" she asked.

"Dee," I answered.

"Well, I'm Melody."

"I know. I heard your girl call you in the club. Where you all from?" I asked, making small talk.

"Lincoln Park," she said, getting out the car. She got into hers and followed me.

Neither one of those bitches would have won a beauty contest, but they had bodies to kill. Their hairstyles were done to perfection. It was like they'd just walked out of the salon.

When we got to the hotel they already had suites. RJ called me in the back. He said that his man figured I was somebody he needed to talk to. I knew niggahs thought I was a big baller. He went on about how he didn't know what I did to live, but he could beat anybody's prices, especially them New York niggahs.

I knew that Black was paying sixteen a kilo and I knew that it was lovely, so I threw fifteen at him to see how he grabbed it. He did and told me that if I bought at least six he would do it for fourteen, five. He gave me his pager number and a code.

That was my main purpose for going back to the hotel. Then, it was back to them 'ho's. I wasn't really pressed on the bitches and didn't care too much for fucking around with niggahs I didn't know. I told Big G that I was getting ready to roll, but he had his mind on one of those bitches.

"You leaving, Dee?" Melody asked, sounding disappointed.

"Yeah, baby, I'm going to the crib, spark a blunt, fix me a drink and call it a night."

"Don't sound bad," she replied.

I wasn't pressed on no ass. Actually, my mind was on my baby in DePaul. I just said anything to throw her off.

"My man riding with me," I said, pointing to Big G. "You can roll if you let your girl take him home."

"That's my cousin. Hold on." She walked over, and all of them came back. "They're going with us, if that's Okay," she said.

"I heard that," I said, shaking my head and giving G a look as if he were handling his business.

We went to the townhouse in Campus East. I took

the back road from North Hampton Boulevard, through Diamond Springs Road. I didn't want to get stopped, and Black had already told me not to take the Lex out that way.

"Hey!" G yelled from the car, "she's carrying me home. I'll get up tomorrow."

"I heard that, my niggah!" I yelled out.

We all started laughing as we remembered that RJ was saying that all night.

We went inside and rolled two L's. We started smoking and talked for about forty-five minutes. Then, I decided it was time to see what was up because it was getting late. If she wasn't fuckin', it was time to get the hell out.

I moved closer and started rubbing her leg, while talking some bullshit. I leaned over and kissed her neck. As I rubbed her breasts, she sunk deep in the chair and more into my arms. I opened her shirt and released her breasts from the pretty lace bra. I took it into my mouth and then tried to slide my hand up her skirt. She stopped me.

"Is there a problem?"

"I just met you, Dee," she said.

"And," I said. "You know you want to, or you wouldn't have let me get as far as I did."

"I do want you. But what's the hurry?"

I sat there getting pissed. I wanted to yell, "Bitch, I got a girl and it's late! That's the hurry—I just want to hit this ass!"

"Look, I told you I don't have a girl. All I do is sit in the crib, smoke weed, and make all the money I can. I need more and I think I can get that from you. I want a strong-minded woman who knows what the fuck she wants and goes for it."

"I know what I want, but I just rather wait," she said.

"All right, baby. No problem."

We sat there for about another twenty minutes. I told her I better get ready to take her home before I fell asleep.

We hit the interstate and got to Lincoln Park in twenty minutes. She asked me to come in for a few. I was hesitant, but she was persistent about it. So I went inside and sat down.

Some young girl came back downstairs, and Melody walked her to the door. "That's my baby-sitter," she said. "I didn't want her here all night. Come on up-stairs."

I went upstairs and relaxed on her bed. She went into the bathroom. I decided to take off my shirt, so I could take my gun out my waist. I put the shirt around it and laid it on the floor beside the bed.

She walked back in the room, wearing a black lace bra. Her breasts were big, but not real firm. Her lace panties were supporting the phattest ass. Overall, the body was banging, and my dick was throbbing in my pants.

She laid on top of me and started licking my ear lobes, creating a tingling sensation. She moved down to my neck, which made my body weaker. She moved farther down to my chest and started sucking and nibbling; it almost made me whimper. She then pulled off my pants and boxers.

My buddy popped up hard and free.

In one quick motion, she took my man into her mouth, and I eased back on the bed and relaxed. There was no better feeling in the world. She did good, but it was nothing she had perfected.

She then stood up and released those large breasts from her lace bra and eased her big, but firm ass out of her panties.

I thought to myself, *If she don't say a word about a condom, I won't.* I wanted to get inside of her with the rawness.

She walked over to her nightstand, pulled out a condom, put it on and climbed on top of me.

The warm, wet feeling that came down on me almost made me scream. She started moving up and down, side to side, around and around.

As I started to get into it, a knock came at the door. She never stopped, so I ignored it also.

The knock got harder, louder, and more rapid. "They don't seem to be going away," I said.

"They will," she said, continuing to ride like it was all that.

The knocks got harder as if the door was coming in. Then we heard screaming.

She jumped up and went downstairs.

"I know you in there, Melody! Open the motherfuckin' door!" a man's voice yelled out.

She was quiet.

"I'm not leaving! Don't make me kick this shit in!" the voice yelled.

I then pulled off the condom and threw on my shit with the quickness. I put my gun in my hand and waited, scared shitless. My stomach started churning, my leg was jumping, and my heart was beating very fast.

"Go home, Darryll! Go home!" she yelled, "before I call the police."

"Fuck the police! Open the fuckin' door!"

Then, I heard a big boom so loud I thought the wall came down. My heart dropped. I wasn't scared of him. I was scared that I was really going to have to kill this niggah and end up locked up. Then, I would be away from my family, Tara and my new little baby girl, Destiny. All this over a piece of pussy that I wasn't even pressed for. I knew the shit I was in and didn't want to kill this man I didn't even know. But I would if it came down to his life or mine.

I cocked the gun and put one in the chamber. I heard him fighting with her then running up the stairs. All fear was now gone.

I met him in the hallway. He reached out and tried to grab my neck.

Pow! Pow! I fired two shots into the floor.

He jumped back against the wall, with his hands up.

"That shit is between you and your girl, niggah. I ain't got shit to do with it," I said on my way down the stairs and straight out the door. I jumped in the Lex and was out, thinking about how my niggahs would mess with me tomorrow, when I tell them about this shit.

CHAPTER 8

"Black Destiny"

It was a week before Christmas, and I was in the building that was soon going to be my sports bar. The pool tables were in place, and the electrician was hanging light fixtures over each table. I was there waiting on my handy man to come build my counter and make my bathroom handicap-accessible.

A sudden knock at the window startled me. I opened the door for the two guys standing outside. They had walked down from the building at the corner. They came in and asked if this was my spot. We started talking, and to my surprise, I found out that they had leased the largest building in the complex to open up a club. We continued to talk and soon realized that we could help promote each other's business.

They introduced themselves as Lite and Smalls. You could tell by their northern accent that they were from Up Top. I wanted to get to know them on the business tip. Since they were opening up an establishment much larger than mine, I figured they might know something that I could pick up.

We walked down to the club for a drink and discussed more business.

It wasn't long before I had to break out and go meet the handyman.

When I got back Boot was there shooting pool. He and Black were the only others who had keys. I joined Boot for a game, when he started telling me about some beef Lo had gotten into in Lake Edward.

Some niggahs from New Jersey had moved in and started selling. They bought soldiers down from Jersey and quickly set up shop. These guys came out on Lake Edward's corners, selling little weight for less than anybody else. The guys who were buying ounces from Lo and Black then started fucking with these niggahs because they had better prices. So, Lo and Jay caught the niggahs on the corner, and while Lo held them at gun point, Jay and this young hungry niggah named Bo pistol-whipped the niggahs real bad.

Bo was Lo's new soldier. He was sixteen, stood six feet tall, and weighed about two hundred and ten. He was the oldest of four boys, but had two older sisters. Bo never had too much—actually he didn't have shit—but he always hung out, admiring the little hustlers on the corner.

Jay and Lo started going over to his house, kicking with his sisters. One day the girl got out of line, and Lo was whipping her ass in front of 7-Eleven on Newtown Road Bo came up and swung on Lo. Lo whipped the niggah's ass, but he liked the fact that the young boy had heart enough to help his sister even though he knew Lo was straight killer.

Rumors always floated around the neighborhood about Lo's dirt, but the only people who would tell, couldn't.

Lo ended up putting the kid on and taught him how to go out in the hood and make his money. Young boy never had shit and wasn't scared of going to jail.

In no time he was breaking down ounces and making money. He was now wearing new gear on a daily basis and was able to look out for his younger brothers. Before, there were times they sat around hungry, but now it was Kentucky Fried and Pizza Hut on a regular basis.

Jay and Lo really liked his sisters, so they brought the girls to a new plateau. They were hitting them off so they could go to the Magic Comb Beauty Salon on a weekly basis and was buying them shit out of Merry Go Round in the mall.

Bo looked at Lo as someone who came along and not only looked out for him but brought his entire family happiness. He felt he owed Lo, and there was nothing Lo asked of him that he wouldn't do.

After Bo and Jay had damaged the guys on the corner, they rode by where the guys were staying and shot up their cars and house. Lo said they had carried their ass like bitches, leaving their furniture behind.

Black pulled up driving a new white 535 BMW. He came inside wearing some new black Girbaud jeans, Girbaud shirt, black Timberlands, and two gold herringbones.

"Y'all must sell drugs with those pretty-ass trucks out there," he said, trying to sound white. "Get up against the fuckin' wall and spread 'em."

We all started laughing.

"Where you get that new shit from?" Boot asked.

"From Lynnhaven Mall down the beach. The white

girl bought it for me," he said, opening up his coat so we could really check his gear.

"I'm talking about the car, fool," Boot said.

"Oh, I bought that shit so Shereena could have something to drive. Her shit ain't holding up too well."

"Give me her shit, man," Boot said. "I'm fucking with these niggahs out Ocean View, back on 28th Bay, and I don't like driving my shit out there."

"You still fuck with those niggahs in Cambridge Manor?" Black asked. "Because I saw them in Greenbriar Mall when I was with Shereena, and they kept staring like they knew me."

"Yeah, they expanded in Pleasant Park and they trying to come off," Boot said.

"If you front, you think they'll be good for it or not?" Black asked.

"I think they will, but I can't take the loss if they don't. Fuck that," Boot said. "They can keep buying halves like they been doing."

"Front the other half and see what happens. I'll take the loss if they fuck it up," Black told him, having a feeling the kids were good for it.

"What about the Honda, man?" Boot asked. "I need it."

"Let me see what she say. I don't just want to give her shit away."

"Fuck that, niggah! You got that 535 for her. Tell her you giving me that shit and be done with it," Boot said with an attitude.

"Yo, check this—New York kids opening up a club in the corner down there," I said, pointing.

"That's gonna bring bitches from all over and put our shit on the map," Black said. "Make sure you buy a couch that opens into a bed for the office, so I don't have to go far to fuck."

"Lo tell you about that shit he did?" Boot asked.

"Naw, but I heard about it. That girl he fucking brother crazy too," Black said. "I don't care too much for those New York niggahs anyway. Fuck them! Kid I fuck with now talking that drought shit, and now he want eighteen a kilo. What the fuck kind of shit is that?"

"I forgot to tell you—them niggahs pushing the big Lex, I met them in David's the other night, met some 'ho's, and we went up in the Omni and tricked. Niggahs got to talking and said they can beat any price we bring."

"For real, for real. Call him and tell him we want . . . naw, tell him to meet you up here and let me talk to him," Black said, heading for the door. "Let me know what's up and when. I have to go drop Momma off at church and then head out Chesapeake."

Later on that evening I was at home enjoying my little girl. Tara had gone out with Tia to get their nails done.

I was trying to entertain my daughter, but she was paying me no attention. Tara said if she started crying that something was wrong because she wouldn't just cry for no reason at this early stage in her life.

I tried feeding her then burped her. I changed her diaper, and she was still whining. I got real close to her, face to face, and started hollering.

She just stared at me like I was crazy.

I realized it was too quiet; my baby wanted noise. She was going to be a club girl, just like her peoples. I put in some EPMD, pumped it up, and didn't hear another peep. She fell asleep instantly.

I stared at her knowing that in just a few months, she'd have two cousins. *That will be three little ones which Black and I will have to provide for forever.*

"God," I said, "please give us the strength to keep

going, look over us and give us a helping hand. Please don't pull your hand back. Our kids need us, and without you we can't make it."

I was running a lot, trying to get things right for the sports bar, E's Cue—the *E* stood for extravagant. That was how I wanted to portray my sports bar. As an extravagant atmosphere.

I knew all I wanted to do was get the sports bar going, open my investment company, and let the money turn. Too many people were dying, and I was seeing guys I grew up with getting unbelievable time for small amounts of cocaine. I knew if Black ever got caught up, he'd be gone for a long time, something I couldn't even imagine. *That would kill me.*

"What's up, niggah?"

The voice sounded familiar, but it couldn't be my niggah.

"Oh, shit! What you doing home, Dog?"

Dog had been gone for a year. He had graduated from Norfolk State and started in the military as an officer. All he had to do was keep his nose clean and he'd have not just a job or hustle, but a long prosperous career.

"Checking out this new club tonight, Club EnVogue, off the boulevard. It's twenty-five and older," he said. "You going or what?"

"I'm with it, niggah. I don't give a fuck."

"What you going to do, G?"

We both knew he was down.

"Where the liquor at, boy?" Dog asked.

I pulled it out, and we sat and sipped on Hennessy, talking about old times and the good times that were to come. We caught him up on all the bitches we'd hit, the money we made, who was locked down, and the girls that started smoking that shit.

Our heads were just about right when Tara came

home. When she saw Dog and G, I saw the attitude in her face and heard it when she barely spoke.

Dog and G told me that they would catch up with me at Bennigan's. They figured I was going to hear a little something.

I knew it, especially after I'd promised her I was staying in tonight. I walked them outside still talking about nothing in particular, but we were contented.

I was still trying to figure out how to tell her I was going out, without catching hell.

When I came in she was looking at the baby.

"I was rocking that EPMD. She like that shit," I said.

"She do like music. She was whining the other day, and I turned on some music and she got quiet," she said.

"Your nails look good," I said, easing towards the stairs. "I'm going to take a shower."

"For what?" she asked.

"Them niggahs going to the club and asked me to go. I'm not really pressed, but since Dog home I'm going to go up there for a minute. I won't be long."

She fussed and talked shit until I left, but it wasn't as bad as I thought. Maybe because she'd had gotten out for a few earlier.

We were sitting in Bennigan's, talking and checking out ladies coming and going. Then, the doors opened and three of the cutest young ladies walked inside. We asked them to join us, and they did. These girls were as fine as any female I'd ever seen, but they were carrying themselves like they were hanging out with each other, not trying to attract men.

Dog stood up to pull their chairs out. "I'm Billy. This is Dee and Gary."

We always used real names when talking to girls with the mature looks and attitudes, you know, the ones that weren't half-naked or cursing like sailors.

"I'm Kim, and this is Sheila and Monique."

Kim was tall with braids. She was wearing jeans and beige blouse with beige heels. Sheila was wearing a long skirt with boots and a nice silk shirt. She was light-skinned with a short cut and a small frame. Monique had brown skin, stood about 5' 3", had shoulder-length hair that was pushed back. She was wearing a sweat suit with sneakers.

Nobody set out to talk to anyone in particular, but everybody was going to get somebody.

We found out that the young ladies were attending Hampton Institute. Two of them were accounting majors, and the other was a psychology major.

Our conversation just flowed. We were all giving our opinions on world events, good investments, such as CDs and mutual funds, the kinds of jobs in demand, and those with promising futures. It wasn't the usual conversation we used to have with the young girls in the clubs not trying to accomplish shit.

Kim was from Chicago, so the mid-west differences came up. Sheila was from Atlanta, and so we discussed the opportunities the South had to offer and the fact that Atlanta was becoming a mini New York. Monique was from Brooklyn.

Of course, the subject of living in the big city came up. I expressed how I thought New Yorkers were savages.

She quickly took the bait and got offended. She came back at me saying that niggahs from Virginia were too slow to cope.

We kept on until we were in our own little world.

Dog had focused his attention on Sheila, and Big

G on Kim, who acted as if she paid no attention to my necklace and bracelets.

But Sheila did acknowledge the Rolex—I was wearing beige pleated slacks by Liz Claiborne, cream-colored silk shirt, and dark brown leather Cole Hahn shoes. When she talked, she made direct eye contact and was very confident about everything she said. I was really impressed by this young lady.

"Are y'all going to the club?" Dog asked.

"We aren't dressed for the club," Kim answered.

"Go get dressed. You should have on clothes anyway, not sweat suits and shit," I said, laughing.

"Don't start on my girl," Sheila said.

"What time is it?" Kim asked, looking at her watch. "It's only 9:30 p.m. We could go to Hampton and come back."

Before we knew it, they had their things and headed out. We sat and had another drink before heading to the club.

About 11:00 p.m. they came in, all looking like perfect ladies. Monique's tight, short skirt and blazer and the way it hugged her beautifully shaped body kept my attention.

We all sat down, and I asked the waitress to bring me a bottle of Moët and six champagne glasses, three Hennessy's, one Iced Tea, White Russian for Sheila and Grand Marnier for Monique.

I pulled out three fifties and gave the waitress two. I had a knot, but tonight I wanted to portray the businessman, big CEO of B&D Corporation, not a hustler making moves in the hood.

"You have class in the morning, Monique?" I asked.

"Yes, my day starts at 9:00 a.m. and ends about 10:00 tomorrow night. I have to be at Hecht's," she answered.

"Which one? Coliseum Mall?" I asked.

"Yeah."

"Seem like you're pretty busy. I better get all my time in now," I said, standing up. "Do you feel like dancing?"

They were playing some Tony! Toni! Toné!, but by the time we reached the floor, the DJ had started playing "Today."

While Big Bub sang a song about taking your time in life, I held her, and she squeezed me like I was her man. I couldn't resist. "Where's your man?" I whispered in her ear.

"He's in Connecticut," she said. "He graduated from Hampton last year and got a job offer up there."

"Where's your girl?"

"She's home."

I then squeezed her even tighter to let her know that it wasn't an issue.

We finished dancing and joined our peoples at the table. "I would really like if you came over for a drink or something later," I said.

"I don't think so. I enjoyed your company and conversation, but no more. Thank you anyway," she said in the sweetest tone.

My pager went off. There was an unfamiliar number followed by 911-911. I asked myself, "Who in the hell is this paging me 911?" before I realized it was probably one of those simple-ass 'ho's. I knew it wasn't Black because we had a strict family code to let each other know something was wrong or to call straight back. I ignored it and continued talking to Monique. I gave her my number and let her know I wanted to take her to lunch the following day.

The unfamiliar number came across my pager again followed by 911. It was about 1:00 a.m, *Who in the hell is this being stupid?* I thought. "Excuse me. I'll be right back," I said.

"Who is that?" Dog asked.

"It's her saying time to bring it on in," Monique said, smiling.

"Yeah, right. Somebody paged me four times with 911," I said to Big G, leaving the table.

I left out the club, and Big G followed.

Somebody was on the phone, and so we stood there looking out the glass doors. Two police cars came flying by with sirens blasting and lights flashing.

"They going to get somebody ass," G said.

"Because niggahs don't know how to act," I said, as the girl hung up the phone. "How could I forget my phone anyway?" I wondered, dialing the number.

"Hello," the voice said loud and quickly.

"Who is this?" I asked with an attitude.

"It's Lo, man. It's Black. They got him," he said, yelling.

"What the fuck you talking about?" I yelled, not understanding.

"Come to the condos. Hurry up!"

"Something's up with my brother at the condo," I said to G, hanging up the phone.

I jumped in the Lex. While flying down the Boulevard, I'm praying, "God, please don't let nothing be wrong with my brother! Please, God. Please!"

I pulled into the complex and tried to get by the condo. People were everywhere. I saw about five Virginia Beach police cars, two unmarked cars, a rescue squad and three ambulances. I jumped out the Lexus and rushed through the crowd. All I saw was two bodies, with white sheets pulled over them, lying in front of Black's crib.

"Oh, my god," I yelled. "Jesus, no. Please."

I felt a pain in my heart and stomach that hit so hard it dropped me to my knees. My breath got short, and my eyes filled with tears. I thought I was going to pass out.

Lo came and grabbed me and helped me up.

"What happened?" I asked, gasping.

"I don't know. Niggahs rolled up and just started spraying on all three of them," Lo said.

"Three," I said, surprised.

I looked up in the doorway and saw black jeans and black Timberlands, with two paramedics bent down over the body. I ran over to see Black lying there with blood coming from his shoulder and two small holes in his chest. His body lay limp, and his eyes were open but not moving. They were picking him up on the stretcher.

"What's with my brother?" I asked.

"We still have a pulse, but it's very weak. That's all I can tell you right now," one paramedic said.

I looked down into my brother's open eyes, not knowing if he could hear me or not. "Hold on, man. I love you. I can't make it out here without you. Please hold on."

They put him in the ambulance.

"Where you taking him?" I yelled.

"Norfolk General!"

"What's up, Dee?" Big G asked.

"Black was shot three times. It's real bad. Niggah ain't moving," I said, my eyes tearing uncontrollably. "Lo, go get my mom and bring her to Norfolk General."

I was in the emergency room when my mom, crying hysterically, came in with her buttoned down nightgown and slippers. She ran into my arms, and I just held her with tears rolling down my face.

"Doctor said he was shot three times, and he's in

surgery now. They're trying to get two bullets out. One in the shoulder went all the way through."

It was 7:00 when the doctor came out. "Ma'am, your son is in ICU. I've done all I can do. We just have to wait."

She hugged me, and I just held her. Lo looked at me with teary eyes and just walked outside. Boot followed him. Auntie came and sat Moms down. Dog and G came over to where I was standing.

"He's strong, man. He'll pull through. Black got mad heart, niggah," G said. "If he ain't dead by now, he ain't going no fuckin' where. He fought all through the night. That's showing you he ain't trying to leave."

I stood there praying, "God let this be true, please let this be true."

It was 2:00 p.m. the following day, and everybody had left except for Lo, G, and myself. I sat there with a sick feeling, thinking my head was going to explode. I was thinking I'd rather die than feel like this.

"Hey, little brother."

I looked up.

"Where's my other little brother?" he asked, holding back the tears that filled his eyes as we hugged each other.

I felt as if some of the weight had been lifted off me.

"Have the detectives talked to you?" Junie asked.

"Naw, why?" I asked.

"They didn't find nothing in the house, did they?" he asked.

"Not that I know of."

"Okay. I already called Tia and Shereena and told them that the detectives were up here and to chill, that we'll call them. We don't need the Feds following them to the other houses and shit coming up.

All of a sudden Tia came through the door crying and fussing because we didn't call her earlier. He must have been crazy if he thought she wasn't going to come.

Three days had passed, and I hadn't moved. It was about 3:00 in the morning. Me and Tia was sitting there in silence. I had my head in my hands, still praying. I'd heard of fasting to give of yourself while God answered your prayers, and that's what I had been doing for several days.

I felt a tap on my shoulder.

"Sir, he just woke up," the nurse said. "The doctors are in with him right now, and he'll be out in a minute to talk with you all."

Junie was at Black's house out Larkspur. That was the first call I made, then my mom's house, and finished with Lo and Shereena. Shereena didn't come up because Junie had talked to her, but she had my pager hot as hell.

We asked to see him, and the doctor only allowed Junie and me. He was looking very weak when we went in. He opened his eyes, and I just stood there with nothing to say and stared into his eyes.

Junie leaned down and kissed him and broke down crying. "I'm not here all the time, but you two mean the world to me, man. The world," Junie said.

"Man, you scared me. You really scared me," I said. "I've been here for days waiting on you to open your eyes."

"We're going to put him in a room in about twelve hours," the doctor said. "We have to keep a close watch on him until then."

We all left out and went back to the waiting room. About this time Lo came in and started walking back.

"Hey, Lo, you can't go back now. You gotta wait until he's in the room," Tia said.

"Fuck that shit," he yelled. Then he turned to where everybody was, and with tears in his eyes he said, "If anybody try to stop me from seeing my cousin, I swear to God, they'll be in ICU! I mean that shit!" Then he turned and walked away.

I followed him inside.

He touched Black's hand. When Black opened his eyes, Lo just fell to his knees by his bedside and started bawling like a baby.

I put my arms around him and helped him to his feet.

He stared at Black for a moment, speechless, and then leaned over and whispered in his ear, "If the DT come talk to you, they didn't find shit in the crib," he said. "Your man Derrick was thinking, even after seeing you get shot. He took the drugs and money, bagged it up and took off out the back. I got it at my crib."

I saw Black force a slight smile and try to squeeze his hand. Then he closed his eyes again.

We all left out. I could go home now, shower, eat, and rest with some peace of mind. I just had to get back by 3:00 a.m.

Three days later Black was talking a little bit, but you could barely hear him. Now, I was running again, coming by to make my daily visits, but Moms was up there from the time visiting hours started until they told her she had to leave.

The doctors and nurses were glad to see Black leave with all the commotion he was causing at the hospital. He had visitors like you wouldn't believe—guys and girls.

The hospital staff even had to call the police, one day when Shereena stopped by while Tia was there.

Tia didn't know Shereena but had heard of her somehow. As soon as Shereena entered Black's room, Tia jumped on her ass. Shereena never backed down, and they were going at it, pregnant and all.

Boot and Junie broke them up.

Tia stormed out mad as hell. She even told Black if he wasn't laid up, she would have tried his ass that day.

Shereena was pissed to no end, but she looked at Black and told him, "We have some serious talking to do, but this isn't the time nor place."

The doctor came in with the release papers for Black to sign. He went straight to my mom's house. He knew going there meant that he would be waited on hand and foot—Moms didn't play when it came to her boys.

CHAPTER 9

"Miami Connect"

Several weeks had passed, and Black was coming around pretty good. At first he seemed to be a different person, but then I saw Lo taking care of certain things that I knew only Black could be telling him to handle. Lo had shut down his spot in Newpointe also, the day after the incident with Black. He knew that once Black was back to his normal self he would start making moves again.

I had stopped at my mom's house to drop off a cellular for Black.

"I need this joint here," he said. "Now I can make some contacts."

"I heard that shit," I said. "E's Cue will be opening real soon. I want to launder as much paper through the door as possible, pump it right into the corporation. I'll pay taxes on it and make it all legit so you can retire from this shit. You had me fucked up, man."

"I got blasted and I'm still here. That's God's way of letting me know I was getting too comfortable.

They caught me slipping. But I'm still here. Now listen to me," he said.

"Do what you just said about pumping money through the corporation. Open another corporation for renovating houses and do the same. I'm getting ready to go on the low, low. I want you to get rid of that shit in Campus East. Tell Freddie Mac find some shit on the water off Shore Drive. I'm talking some fly-ass Miami-type shit. Get me two more ID's made and give one to Lo. I want you to go get a 740 BMW. Make sure you keep it plain, no rims, nothing but some tint. We need two garages, and I want to be in this house like yesterday. Call that kid from Miami and set something up. When you open the business, give me the key to the back warehouse. You should have no reason to go back there. Yeah, make sure I have plush carpet in my shit before I move in, along with fresh paint, and a new ADT system."

"Yes, sir, master," I said laughing.

"Shut up, niggah. And handle that shit for me."

Freddie Mac woke me up the following morning. He told me was up late, setting up appointments for two waterfront properties and two new construction condos. I met him, and we went to check them out. When I saw the houses I was quick to make a decision, but he insisted that I look at the condos first.

We went deep into the beach area near Shore Drive and Great Neck Road. We arrived at a security gate for which you had to have a code to enter the complex. We drove around and entered a garage large enough for two cars.

Most of the buildings were three stories, and I knew Black couldn't fuck with the stairs. The first floor had a very large bedroom, big enough to put furniture in with a full bath and a Jacuzzi tub. We got on an elevator in the house and went to the second floor, where we stepped off onto white and gray marble, which lead to an all-white kitchen, with new white appliances. On the other side of the bar's counter top was an enormous family room with a fireplace and cathedral ceilings, which went all the way past the third floor.

The third floor had a loft with two master suites and full baths with Jacuzzi tubs large enough for four. The back of the condo, from the second floor to the ceiling, was all glass with a balcony-like deck that had a waterfront view of the Chesapeake Bay Bridge.

I bounced up and down on the plush carpet. This was the finest home I had ever seen. "What they asking?"

"Three hundred and eight-nine thousand," he said. "This is new construction, and the builder won't budge."

"How long it's been on the market?"

"Three months."

"That's too long," I said. "I think the builder's anxious. Let's write it up and offer three hundred and thirty thousand. When you drop off the offer, give them fifty thousand up front and get my goddamn key."

After closing on the house three weeks later and having my key in hand, I took Black over there.

"I thought the doctor said I was still alive, niggah. I must be dead, because this shit is heaven. I am in heaven. How the fuck a niggah get an elevator in his house? That's why I didn't die. God had better shit in store for me. Look. Go to Haynes, lay this shit out, and tell them to deliver all my shit tomorrow, no matter what it cost."

When I went to the condo for the delivery of the furniture, I had already picked up the 740 BMW from Casey BMW in Newport News. Now that my corporations were legit, I could now handle business over the phone, show up with cashier's checks, and drive off the lot. When the garage door opened, I saw the back of a 560SEC Mercedes Benz. Black was on his second life. He was definitely a ghetto celebrity. It was his time to shine.

GRAND OPENING of E's Cue. There were sixteen Brunswick Gold Crowns III ready to be broken in, with beautiful light fixtures for perfect vision; fifteen video games lined the walls; menu to whet your appetite; a 60" screen for everyone's viewing pleasure, with Bose speakers in the upper corners for the Harman/Karmon system to pump sounds for your listening pleasure.

People were checking out balls and staying on the tables for hours. We had a big buffet, and the first hour of pool was free. The place was real busy, and the shopping center was getting a lot of publicity.

I was advertising on 103JAMZ and 92.1. The guys from The Bridge, the night club at the corner, was also advertising, but the hype was the barber shop in the shopping center, Clippers. They had 103JAMZ broadcasting live from the shop for their grand opening.

People were really astonished when the notorious "Men At Large" stopped in and played pool for several hours. My business was on its way. Finally I was on to something I could build, to produce legit money to carry my peoples.

In the warehouse in the back, Lo was handling business with RJ's peoples. I was in the front kicking it with RJ, while his soldiers went to the back. One was a tall, thin, dark-skinned kid with gold fronts, and the other was a big, dark-skinned kid with gold across the bottom of his mouth. They had a book bag and went to the side door, where Bo greeted them. They came in and put the shit on the table. Lo had Bo and three more soldiers that he had throughout the warehouse. Seven kilos of cocaine were exchanged for one hundred thousand. Everything was lovely. RJ's soldiers pulled around the front of the building, where we gave each other a pound before he broke out.

Lo's soldiers stayed in the warehouse, while he and Bo rolled out to go cook up the cocaine and turn it into crack—the drug that sold in the world I lived in.

Hours later they returned with it broken down, weighed out, and packaged perfectly.

He called Black himself, and people started dropping by to see Lo, leaving with half-kilos and whole kilos of coke. Boot even came by and got two kilos for himself.

Lo gathered up all the money and took it to Black. This system was perfect. Black had it where he never sat on shit a whole day, and it was on the street no sooner than it changed hands.

Lo was now handling everything for Black. Black had promised that nobody would see him until he got some kind of outlook on who had tried to assassinate him. Lo felt it was those New Jersey kids and swore on Mommy's grave that if he ever saw them niggahs again—he wouldn't give a fuck where he was—he was going to start blasting on the spot.

Mommy was our grandmother, and when one of us said, "Swear on her grave," it was stronger than swearing to God. Black, on the other hand, thought that it could've been some hungry-ass young boys just wanting to rob a niggah or one of those jealous-ass niggahs in the hood that he just wouldn't fuck with. All he knew was that he wasn't fuckin' with a lot niggahs no more and he wasn't going to trust a single soul.

Lo was very comfortable, but he was missing that money that came through the condos. He told Black that he had quite a few heads out Lake Edward and a few out Bayside Arms that were begging for him to serve them, but he was laying low. He had Bo making plenty of money, but he was still too young in the game to handle a whole brick.

Black told Lo to get rid of the apartment out Mayfair and serve kids at the spot in Stony Point, behind the McDonald's, but the kids he wasn't use to fucking with, to score at the McDonald's.

In no time Lo set up shop and had the young hustlers coming out Stony Point. Because it wasn't close or convenient for most of them, Lo knew he had to come up with low prices and a bomb-ass product to keep niggahs coming to him.

Lo was leaving Norfolk General and ran into two young boys he hadn't seen in a while. They knew Lo was on and wanted to get down with him, but never knew how to come at him.

Derrick and Dante were cousins who lived in Aragona Village, not too far from Lake Edward. They were originally from Bowling Park, a project in Norfolk. Derrick came to live with Dante's family after his mom's boyfriend stabbed her several times, killing her in front of him, before taking his own life.

They ended up hanging out Lake Edward on a daily. When Lo started hustling, they were trying to do the same. But it was all about the connections, and Lo had Black's help and guidance. So he blew up pretty fast.

Lo figured with his help he could blow these guys up along with him. After running into them, they were telling him they wanted to get their own crib. Lo thought they were stupid because, if his peoples had a house and money, he wouldn't think about hustling. He would've stayed in school and handled his business.

They said if it was all that, they would too, but their stepdad was an asshole. They were tired of him coming home and bugging out on them. Their mom wasn't trying to leave because she said she didn't want to go back to the projects. It was either move out or fuck around and get locked up over their step-dad.

Lo knew the story too well and couldn't help every young kid that he came across. But these little nig-gahs had heart, and he had seen them grind with him side by side.

Lo figured the timing was right to put the little niggahs on. It turned out to be a power move; in just a short period of time, they proved to be troopers, es-pecially Derrick.

Lo finally decided to put them out Stony Point. He asked Derrick and Dante if they were ready to make some real money in their own spot, which ex-cited the young soldiers. He put them in the house and told them they could bring one other partner in to work with them. Lo knew the more heads in the spot, the lesser the chances of niggahs running up in the crib.

Lo never went back to the townhouse after that. Bo was the man that everyone was going to be dealing with, and the niggahs on the block hustling—and even the ones who just hung out at the park—knew Bo wasn't anybody to fuck with, under no circumstances.

It was Friday night, and I was working the sports

bar. I usually worked weekends, and always, whenever business was being handled in the back. Boot and Lo came in, both wearing denim outfits. Boot was wearing black Guess jeans, Guess T-shirt, a black Guess jean jacket, and black cowboy boots. Boot was always dressed as if he was ready to head to the club. He was never a trendy person, but today he did have a nice rope hanging down just below his throat, similar to a choker. Lo was wearing stone-washed Levi set with his picture on the leg. Someone had drawn a picture of him and colored it in. The shit was phat. When he walked in the office and the back of his coat was revealed to me, it fucked me up.

He had bought a SAAB 900 and took it to Lawson's Rim and Paint Shop on the Boulevard and got it painted a candy apple red, just like that money-maker who had gotten killed, with the pretty-ass Jaguar. He had deep-dish hammers that would blind you if you stared too hard. He had the artist draw his car on the back of his jacket and color it in detail and the rims and windows colored with jewels.

I stood there in amazement. It was some shit I never thought possible. "What the hell?" I said.

"This shit phat as hell, ain't it?" he asked.

"You ain't lying. Where you get that shit done? When you were in New York?" I asked.

"Naw, these niggahs from New York opened a shop on Princess Anne Road across from Booker T. Washington High School. I think the shop is called Shirt Kings," he said. "I was up that way on Reservoir buying weed, when I saw it. I stopped off, and there was a book in there with all kind of shit. I'm getting me one more to bust out of town with the Acura on that bitch. Know what?—You need to go up there and put up some fliers because a lot of niggahs was just hanging out."

"I'll do that shit," I said. "Know what? We should get a weed spot out here and put it right in the apartments."

"You don't know," he said, giving me a pound. "I told Black that shit, and he said the money was too slow. He told me the only way to make real money with weed is if you get pounds for about three hundred and sell them for eleven or twelve hundred."

"Where a niggah gonna find that shit for three hundred?" I asked.

"Nowhere around this bitch. You have to go to Texas, Arizona, some goddamn where."

"Boot gonna open up a spot out The Lake," I said laughing.

Lo started smiling, knowing I was out my mind.

"Yeah, you motherfuckers better laugh. I ain't selling shit out Lake Edward. That bitch hot as hell. I don't even go out there no more. Leave that shit to Lo and Black," Boot said in a very serious tone. You knew he wasn't playing.

"You going to The Bridge tonight?" he asked.

"Hell, yeah!" I said. "R. Kelly and Public Announcement got a show tonight. My niggahs getting ready to come off, and that's going to bring more niggahs in this bitch."

Smalls, the owner of the club came in. "What up, gods?" he said real loud and excited.

We had gotten tight only after a few weeks, both of us being new business owners. I told Boot, along with the other two people we had hired, that Smalls and Lite were to never pay if they came in to play pool. He in turn introduced me to his security and bartenders. I was never to get searched, stand in line, and drinks would be on the house.

Most of the time I didn't drink anyway. Before the club would get jumping, Smalls and I would sit in the club and kick it, while sipping on Hennessy and downing Heinekens.

"What's up, son?" I asked.

"I hope this show comes off like I'm expecting," he said.

"It should. Ever since we went to Norfolk State basketball game that shit been phat every week," I came back, boosting his hopes.

"Remember that shit, kid!" he yelled. "I thought we might get a small crowd, and after the game, by the time I got here, niggahs was lined up. The parking lot was full. That shit wasn't no joke."

"From the club past the Food Lion," I added, "all down the side street leading into the neighborhood. I had every table in this bitch taken, and people were standing inside and out waiting for one."

"We ain't have no fuckin' control. Police was all out this bitch. Niggahs were bumrushing the doors. That shit was off the hook, son," he said, getting serious, "but I need the weekends too, not just Thursdays."

"Have more rap shows and let niggahs come in with sneakers on. Fuck that dressing up shit," Lo said.

"That will make that shit come off," I said. "You have David's in Portsmouth that's dress up, Club EnVogue that's dress up, and Mr. Magic's that just opened across the street that's twenty-five and older, with the people over there rocking suit and ties, them old heads."

"Come as you are," Lo said laughing. "That's the shit that will make you rich—sneakers; Timberlands; and jeans."

Smalls left to go prepare for R. Kelly. He told me to page him and put in a code if I was coming down there so he would open the back door. He had made prior arrangements with whoever was throwing the show. They had the door; he had the bar.

Later that night Boot, Lo, and myself were still in
there chilling making sure that, with the show going
on, the crowd didn't get out of hand like last time.

The Bridge was packed, and they had stopped letting people inside. All the guys and girls who couldn't
get in were coming in E's Cue, playing pool. People
who came to see who came out and to attend the parking lot party were all inside playing pool. Whoever
couldn't get in the club and was waiting on a table
were hanging out in the parking lot, checking out
girls dancing to the sounds in the players' cars and
checking out the hustlers driving through, showing
off their new fly shit.

Several of the "ghetto celebrities" who were trying
to show off their money had it spread out on the Ce-
Lo. Every time they would start loitering in front of
the sports bar, I would go ask them to move. It would
stop for a second then the crowd would reassemble
before I could get back in the door.

I remember going back out to the crowd with an
attitude, but the amount of cash lying on the sidewalk slowed my approach. "Yo, Gods! This can't be
going on out here. Don't disrespect my shit and
make the man shut me down," I said.

"All right, son, I'm the bank. Just give me a chance
to roll Cee-lo on these niggahs, and they will be carrying their broke ass."

I had to look twice at the guy talking. He looked
like the guy who had that phat-ass SAAB, and I stuck
my hand out and gave him a pound. It was good to
see the player was doing well, even though his acci-
dent left him confined to a wheelchair. I did notice
he was making money because, even in the wheelchair, he was still dressed in the fly shit from head to
toe, representing Big Willie style.

"Look out for me, partner. This my shit and this how I'm living," I said as I walked back inside.

"Are they clearing the front?" Boot asked.

"Yeah, niggahs got cash stacked all up on the sidewalk. I'm going to check again in a few."

"Don't worry about it," Lo said. "I'm leaving in a minute, and if it's still money on the sidewalk, me and my niggah in my waist taking it all. That will learn them motherfuckers something. Believe that shit."

I prayed to myself, "Lord, please let them niggahs move." I knew he was serious.

Three young boys came in, two were dressed in the fly shit and rocking small gold chains, the other had on an old Polo shirt, older jeans, and some old Timberlands. They asked for a table, but none was available. So they went to play video games for a while until a table was ready.

The guy with the old gear came back up to the counter. "What's your name, man?" he asked.

"Why you know me?" I asked.

"Your name Dee, right?"

"Who are you, son?" I asked directly, the kindness in my voice gone now.

Lo was standing behind the counter at the end, and I saw him put his hand on the nickel-plated nine that sat in his waist. Ever since Black got shot, all of us had become more cautious. We thought the world was out to get us, but we still had a business to run.

"I'm Carlos. Tammy's brother," he said.

I stood with a confused look on my face.

"Tammy that use to fuck with Prince," he said.

"Yeah, but ummm—" I started thinking. Tammy had gotten killed, but I didn't want to come out and say that.

"That niggah had my sister killed from prison. He

put thirty thousand on her head, and somebody collected," he said.

I was right. She had gone to the club and never came home. They found her two days later shot in the head at the Econo Lodge on Tidewater Drive, near Burger King. They always said it was a hit.

"I heard that niggah got mad time," I said, "like thirty years."

"Yeah, he'll be gone for a while," he said. "I used to swing with your brother before I left. I had to do a three-year bid in South Hampton. Just got home Wednesday. Been looking for Black."

"He's in California," Lo said. "I remember you. Next time I talk to him, I'll let him know you home. You got a number?"

"Not right now. Tell him I'm at my mom's, and her phone ain't on. We scrambling right now. But I got to put a bug in his ear. He really need to see me."

"It might be a while. If it's all that, talk to us," Lo said.

Big G had walked in, so I asked him to watch the front while we went in the office, sparked up a White Owl, and listened to what this kid had to say.

"Check this shit out. Black got a cousin name Lo," he said. The guy didn't even know that was Lo sitting in his face. "Lo swing with a niggah name Jay. Jay got a cousin name Dink that live out Lake Edward. I was locked up with Dink. Dink and Jay used to talk all the time, and Jay would let him know what was going on in the street. He told Dink about two condos behind here and that niggahs was stacking mad paper in them. Then he told Dink how him and Lo fucked up some New Jersey kids.

"See, Dink supposed to be coming home in September, so he told Jay to get with some of their family and hit Black's spot. He figured they would get at least thirty thousand. And if he took out Black, when he came home, shit would be open for him and then they would take care of Lo. So Jay wouldn't have to play second to a bitch niggah. At first, Jay wasn't for it, but Dink convinced him that everybody would think those New Jersey kids did it."

Me and Lo looked at each other.

"Look, man, if you running game, this shit can turn out real bad for you. I'm for real. No bullshit," I said.

"This shit is on the up-and-up. Don't even play me like that," he said.

"Once you talk to Black, you'll know what's up, he know a niggah real. We go back. Also tell him, 'I'm hurting, moms hurting, and I need some work.' "

"Come through here tomorrow and check me, son. We'll see what's up," I said.

The guy left, and Lo and I sat there staring at each other. Lo said that him and Jay hadn't been swinging real tight since that shit happened with those kids from Jersey. Bo was swinging hard and handling his business.

Lo had to talk to Black. He didn't know if this shit was true or not. Maybe he just didn't want to believe it. He still believed the Jersey kids did it, but I believed Dink and Jay had to get theirs. I believed the man was being real.

We called Black. He said that Mark had told him some similar shit, but this made it a little more solid. He said Carlos was a trooper and that they done some dirt before he got locked up. So there was no reason to doubt him. Dink and Jay would get theirs in time.

Black was real calm, telling us just play as if we never heard anything, and that their time was coming. Then, he told Lo to hit Carlos off with a big eight and give him some cash to get his pager and mom's phone turned back on.

Tia and Shereena had their babies a month apart. Tia was rushed to Bayside Hospital, when her water broke. Her mom called the crib, and she paged me. I called Black, and he waited at the condo patiently.

I went over to the hospital, and her entire family was there. I knew then she would be all right. Her family was down-to-earth people and seemed to understand that Black was away in California handling business that couldn't be put off. They knew Tia was going to be well taken care of.

Black had already bought her a nice townhouse. She was driving a phat-ass Acura Legend, and she had money to get the things she needed. All Black asked was that she took care of his little queen. No job, no worries. Just take care of the little queen, Kanesia.

When Shereena's water broke, she was with her girlfriend who called her mother and paged me. I called Black.

He said to let him know what was going on. He was determined to stay on the low until he received more insight on his assassination attempt. He kept saying, "Out of sight, out of mind." He wanted police to not associate him with Lake Edward, and it seemed to be working. But Lo and Bo were becoming well known up in the hood. Black even told Lo to chill from out there unless he was handling business that couldn't be avoided.

I called Tara. Her mom had our daughter, so she was able to meet me at Chesapeake General. Shereena's girlfriend had somebody else's car, so she had to leave, and her mother wasn't home.

When we got to the hospital, she was lying there in labor with no one to hold her hand, except for the beautiful nurses that I would later see on a social basis. When she saw us, even with all the discomfort she was experiencing, she was still able to crack a smile.

I called Black to let him know her condition.

"How is she?" he asked.

"Doing Okay," I said. "She was glad to see me and Tara."

"Why? Who's there?" he asked.

"Nobody. You know her sister's in Jacksonville with that Navy kid, and her mom's not home. Tara's in there with her now."

"I'm going to call her mom's house again. I'll hit you in a few."

I went to go check on her. They were still waiting for her to dilate a little more, so I stepped back out.

About thirty minutes had passed, and I was pacing the hall like an expectant father. Then I looked up, and there was Junie and Black.

"When you get here?" I asked excitedly.

"Early this morning. Thought you were coming by," he said.

"I was on my way when she paged me."

"What room she in?" Black asked.

"Come on, I'll show you."

When Black came in, through all the pain, discomfort, and all the changes her body was going through, she found the strength to throw her arms around him and give him a hug, tears streaming down her face.

We all left out when the doctor came in. We were outside for two hours, when Black came out.

"Check out my little niggah," he said.

We went inside to see the cutest little dark-skinned baby with a full head of hair. He stood there staring down at his little man then stared at Junie and me. "He gots to have it better than we did; he has too."

Tara stayed awhile, after my brothers and I left.

Junie was anxious to know why we stopped fuckin' with the kids from Hampton. Jacqueline's brother had told him we hadn't called his peoples in months. We let him know that Florida didn't have a drought and the product was better. He was good to us and shit ran real smooth, but we were talking about the money—fuck all the other bullshit!

During all my running I found time to stop at Shirt Kings and drop off some flyers. I told the kid about the work he did for my cousin, and he remembered instantly. There were several guys chilling in the store, all with northern accents, and wearing fly gear and jewels, looking like big ballers. There were about four girls there, all looking like they just stepped out of *Black Tail* magazine, plus a couple of the guys I had met before or had seen in my sports bar, or in The Bridge. The kid who owned Shirt Kings, I knew him from taking pictures in the club. I was told that he freaked his own backdrops, but I never imagined him having skills of that level.

The girls had left out. They were so fine and carried themselves in such a way, you could tell that they knew they were tight. *Any guy would be glad to lock one of these bitches down.* I went outside to scream at one of them. Three of the girls were climbing into a car in front, leaving one of the girls on the sidewalk just standing there.

"What's your name?"

"Shante," she said with the northern accent, but it was more to the proper side, as if she was from Massachusetts or farther north.

"What's yours?"

"Dee," I said, while turning to her friends in the

car, making commotion. My eyes glanced back at Shante's small breasts and tight waist. She had an ass like a fuckin' mule. My dick was throbbing through my fly shit.

"We're going to Female Adventure over by Military Circle Mall. If Sugar bring you the money, tell her to drop you off so you can get your nails done," one of the girls yelled out the car window.

"You want to get your nails done?" I asked, loud enough to catch the attention of the girls in the car.

"Yes. But my girl owe me money and hasn't brought it yet. They have appointments, so they can't wait any longer," Shante said.

I reached in my pocket and pulled out a knot and peeled off a fifty, after sliding a couple hundreds out the way. I could see her eyes on the paper, and I could feel the bitches in the car staring. "Here you go. Handle your business," I said.

"You going to just give me fifty dollars?" she asked.

"Yes. All I ask is one thing—when you finish, I want you to come by my sports bar over by The Bridge and show me how my money was spent."

"Sure," she replied.

"We'll all come by and show you," one of the girls yelled from the car.

I went by the condo to check on Black and Junie. Black was having the same color marble put down in the foyer and in the fireplace. We decided to leave and go get a bite to eat.

Once we reached Henry's on Shore Drive, Junie wanted to talk more about those Miami niggahs. He let us know that the money might flow because Jacqueline's brother had his shit organized and wasn't about a lot of bullshit. He said that he was going to talk to him and wanted to know if Black would consider fuckin' with his people again if he could get him to come back down. I knew Junie just wanted to keep an eye on things from his end. He felt safe with Jacqueline's people.

We sat, ate, drank, and had many discussions about other business ventures. He also threw out the idea for me to try and get the celebrities to stop at E's Cue whenever The Bridge had a concert or a show. He said that he was also going to try and get in touch with a few organizations to try and promote leasing out the sports bar for different functions. We all had different inputs on how the business should be run, but everybody's opinion was respected. We all had the same objective and that was to make money.

We went back to the house, where the workers had finished up for the day. Junie decided that he was going to call some girls from down the bottom (Florida) that he'd met at the strip club. He was planning to fly them in for the weekend.

Black was all for it. He was thinking of having a get-together for his new neighbors. Many of them had come by and introduced themselves. They weren't nosy; they were just being friendly. Black told them he was a producer in the rap music industry. That always threw people off. They didn't know anything about rap, but they knew that producers in the music business made plenty of money.

Junie decided to bring the girls in Sunday, and we were going to set up a fabulous dinner party with the white folks.

I got the money that I was supposed to deposit, the money I was supposed to lock in the safe, and the money I was to give to Tia and Shereena. Both of these girls had everything to make their lives comfortable, but they didn't have access to any of the money.

Black dished it to them as he saw fit. He said that it

wouldn't be long and he was going to be back on the scene with a new approach. He wanted to take the spotlight off Lo. Black's knew E's Cue opening a few months earlier meant that he was safe, but he would feel much better when he got things going in the other direction. He was also dwelling on the fact that Jay was still running around after the shit he pulled. With Lo running the house in Stony Point, he just didn't feel good about Jay walking around. He kept saying he had some real shit for their ass.

I got back to E's Cue, and we weren't real busy. Boot had the idea to fix food, charge five dollars a head, and let them shoot pool all they wanted to on Friday night. That wasn't a bad idea, but I didn't want to charge people until I pulled them all in first. Boot and I was sitting and talking, when Shante walked in. She now looked like she belonged on the front of *Essence*. We talked for a minute, and Boot screamed at her girl.

I found out that she lived in Runaway Bay apartments, off Bonney Road. She was married, but going through a divorce. Her husband resided in Columbia, SC, only giving them a chance to talk every couple weeks because of their son. Her son was with his father for two weeks, and she had a little time on her hands. She had been separated for a year and said she was real cautious about starting a new relationship. I told her that I had a little girl, but her moms and me were having mad problems. I explained that I had been with her for years and because some of my money was made under the table, I had most of my shit in her name: houses, cars, and even bank accounts. I let her know that I really wanted out, but couldn't chance losing everything I'd worked so hard for. I also told her that I wasn't looking for a girl, but a friend I could talk to, lean on and turn to when I got really stressed. I explained to her that I spent most of my time working and doing relaxing things by myself, like bowling, pool, poetry, and sitting in hot tubs, sipping on Moët.

Shante seemed to be really enjoying my conversation, and I was definitely enjoying hers. She let me know that she enjoyed everything I did and even had a book of poetry, but most niggahs didn't get into it. The more this young lady talked, the more I realized that she wasn't a young ignorant bitch, that she was a woman who had a lot going on and was looking for someone to love and give attention also. I was that someone to receive the attention, but I received all the love I needed from Tara—she gave me plenty of that. I asked if she would mess her nails up if she went bowling. She assured me that the nails would not stand in her way of beating me.

Meanwhile, her girl was making herself comfortable. She was throwing Boot hints to let him know he could fuck her, but as usual Boot was playing it off. She kept talking about how tight his body was and he could easily be a male stripper. Boot kept saying he had respect for himself and wanted to save his body for one woman and hadn't found her yet. All this did was make her more persistent. He leaned over the table to finish his game, while she sat down on the stool ready to play.

Me and Shante broke out. I decided to take her up on her challenge. We bowled several games over at Pinboys on Little Creek Rd. The entire time we bowled, we kept staring at each other. Then the touching started between turns. As the strikes started coming, so did the hugs. She began to talk in a soft tone, which led to me getting closer so I could hear. The closer I got, the fresher I got.

"What are your plans when you leave here?" I asked.

"Probably just go home, take a hot bath, and call it a night," she said.

I read into it. Her vibes were saying that's what she was going to do, not what she wanted to do. "I was going to sit in the hot tub for a while. Will you join me?"

"Sure. That sounds nice."

"Well, I'm going to stop and get me some champagne; then we'll get your bathing suit," I said, praying that it wouldn't be on long.

After picking up a few things, we went to the Courtyard by Marriott, where we changed and found our way to the hot tub. On our way down she was very close, very affectionate, and it was moving a niggah to no end. We got to the Jacuzzi, popped open the champagne, and started sipping.

Before long we were hugged up, our hands exploring each other's body thoroughly. I rubbed her breasts and eased my hands down until they rested between her legs. As I pushed my hand inside her bathing suit, she eased her legs open, and I easily slipped a finger inside of her as she let out a sigh of hot air onto my neck. As I moved my finger around, she hugged me and started kissing on my neck and ear. I started grinding against her body to get a feel of her.

She eased her hand down and began to massage my dick. I grabbed my condom, slid it on, then pulled her suit to the side. Not giving a fuck if somebody walked in on us on not, I eased inside of her as she spread her legs to accept me.

I was pushing hard and fast for about fifteen minutes, when I realized I couldn't feel shit. Because of her body juices, and all the moisture, I was about to fuck myself to death. So in one quick stroke, I acted like I came out and I grabbed it and slid back in. Then I did it again. The next time I did it, I pulled off the rubber and slid back in.

Goddamn. What a difference!

Before, I couldn't feel shit but now I was feeling her a little more. Yet, the water was still keeping me from feeling the warmth of her body, of only her body. I knew that at the rate I was fuckin' I had to be good—at least that's what I thought.

After a little while longer, I was tired as hell. The steam from the hot tub had drained me, and I couldn't seem to cum. I wanted to feel her, even though I was about to die from exhaustion. We went back to the room and sat on the couch. She poured us some Moët, and I sparked a blunt. She then got both of us out of the wet clothes.

Shante began to kiss my neck real slow then nibbled and allowed her tongue to enter my ear. She was in no hurry, and her actions were showing it.

Eventually she reached my chest and began to lick my nipples in a slow circular motion.

I felt like screaming, but instead I let her know how good it felt.

She began to ease farther down, kissing and massaging my pelvic region with her tongue. It tickled so much that I prayed she'd stop, but never asked her to. She slowly eased to my inner thigh and, in one swift motion, licked and sucked my balls with such finesse, I almost lost it.

She began to suck my manhood with such expertise that for a moment I thought I was in love. She then went to my balls again with a flick of her tongue, and I jumped. Raising my legs, she licked my ass. I jumped again as if I had gotten stuck with a pin, but she pulled me down to keep me from bucking and began to explore my ass, sticking her tongue in and out.

I began to moan like a little bitch. I never wanted her to stop.

She then jumped on top of me and rode me until I came, only to get a cloth, wipe my dick, then suck it until it was rock-hard again. She lay back and opened her legs, giving me a clear view of what I was about to get. She pulled me on top of her, and I stroked as if it was the best piece of ass I'd ever been in.

She turned around and allowed me to hit it from the back until she moaned in ecstasy.

She asked me if I wanted to go in her ass, something I had never experienced. I was down.

She then leaned back, opened her legs, and guided my dick into her tight ass. The snug feeling was very exciting. I came in a matter of minutes and collapsed on her.

She turned over, took me into her arms, and hugged me real tight, as if to say, "I'm never letting you go."

"I hope this wasn't a one-time thing, Dee. If things don't work out, please don't let it stop us from being friends."

After the way she had just served this dick, she didn't have a thing to worry about.

CHAPTER 10

"Payback"

The following day I was at the sports bar, cooling. Boot and I had started taking pool seriously. Playing for fun was out of the question. We had even paid for lessons from one of the best gamblers in the state of Virginia. We were arguing about a shot, as usual, when my man Muhammed pulled up. We walked outside to check out his new, bright red Suzuki sports bike, built for racing.

"What's up, man?" he asked.

"You, niggah. I see who making all the money," I said.

Muhammed was a true baller. I had met him through Black. When Black worked the corner and was trying to blow, Muhammed looked out sometimes. Black said he was cool as shit, but his product was real weak and the fiends didn't care for it too much. Muhammed, on the other hand, said that it sold and the niggahs in Norfolk had no complaints.

Black learned a lot from him. The things Muhammed had acquired through his endeavors Black also wanted for himself. When Black had a Tempo and was living with Tia and her mother, Muhammed had a Toyota 4Runner, new Acura, a ninety-thousand-dollar house in Rosemont Forest, and a bitch for every day of the week. Even after Black blew up and surpassed Muhammed, they remained friends—that was unusual in our hood, jealousy being a downside of the game. They never did much business together, unless their peoples just weren't straight.

Muhammed's family was pretty tight and very seldom ventured outside of each other. Houdini, his cousin, was from Norview, a real rowdy section of Norfolk. He started dabbling in cocaine strictly for his family, and he made a connect and put all his peoples on. His main source of money was heroin— somehow he had made a connect when he was fifteen and working for this Asian man at his restaurant. By the time he turned eighteen, he was rich and never looked back. Every hustler knew who he was. His name was well known, but he never flaunted his riches. Whenever he was seen, he was always draped in the fly shit, but never drove anything that was considered flashy or expensive.

Muhammed and Black had met through a mutual friend, Ace. Ace lived in Lake Edward but grew up in Norview. He hung out with Muhammed and was Houdini's bodyguard. I got real tight with Muhammed through Black—Muhammed loved to club; I loved to club—but Black never cared too much for clubs or even the desire to visit one.

"Let's ride, niggah," he said. "You can't fuck with this Katana."

"Niggah, please. Give me a minute and let me run to the crib. It'll take me fifteen minutes to get home and five minutes to get back," I said walking to my car.

I got back in what felt like five minutes. I turned into the parking lot, and Muhammed and Boot, amongst others, were looking around to see where the loud noise was coming from. I decided to bring her up, so Muhammed would know he couldn't fuck with it.

"What's up, niggah?" I said, taking off my helmet.

"That wheelie was nice. I gots to get that shit," he said, giving me a pound. "Why is that shit so loud?"

"Because she's ready to fuckin' run, niggah. I got a stage three jet kit on this bitch, with a Muzzy pipe, timing advancer, Keihn filter, and I had the heads shaved. She will come up in third. Can't no 750 fuck with her, and she'll run with any 900."

"That black bitch is sweet. Where you get it chromed at?" he asked.

"Newport News. White boy do all my work. He know his shit."

Two more guys came up on bikes, Cat and Ed. We all broke out and headed to Portsmouth to check out Magic City, a strip club that we all liked to frequent.

We were all sitting around sipping Heinekens and watching these beautiful bitches dance around half-naked or mostly naked. I had been in the Penthouse in Washington, DC, where the girls were completely nude, just like Atlanta's Magic City. These girls weren't naked, but they were fine as they come, with bodies to kill. We sat there passing the girls fives and tens on stage. Muhammed, with a stack of twenties, had girls fighting to dance for him.

My mind had been going back and forth about Shante. I wanted to talk to her so bad but, not wanting to seem pressed, didn't call. It wasn't long before I felt my pager vibrating. I peeped the number, and the code read 26. A smile shot across my face instantly.

I called back, "Who is this?" like I didn't know. But that's what players do.

"It's Shante," the sweet voice responded.

"Oh, how are you?"

"I'm doing fine. Waiting to see you," she said.

"I'm taking care of some business right now, but I should be done in about an hour."

"Okay. Have you eaten?" she asked.

"No," I answered.

"Then I'll see you in an hour," she said.

We chilled for a few, then left and went to the Flame, another strip club around the corner. It wasn't long before I had to burst. She had gotten into my head since the night before, and I had nothing else on my mind except getting with her.

When I arrived at her apartment, she had the lights low and a candle on the table burning to the soft, mellow sounds of Kenny G in the background. She was wearing a white silk teddy, with a long silk robe that hung open, showing off her sexy-ass body. She told me to sit down at the table as she placed a salad and glass of White Zinfandel in front of me. When she leaned over, I could smell the sweet aroma of the Victoria's Secret fragrances, which made me want to lick her from head to toe.

After the salad, she placed a steak smothered with onions and seasoned to perfection, along with a baked potato in front of me. I realized then that she didn't only have skills in the bedroom, but also other places as well.

Once we finished a perfect dinner, we sat on the couch and listened to the smooth sounds of Kenny

G's, "Silhouette." She began to give me a repeat of
the night before, which put my ass straight to sleep—
I was hers for the night.

For the next couple weeks, I spent almost every
evening with Shante. She was an extraordinary woman.
I realized she was a woman that was looking for someone to love, and she definitely had mad love to give. I
enjoyed her company and her conversation, but love
was never in the picture.

After the first night I spent with her, I thought that
possibly she could be a girl that I could keep on the
side, chill with—even spoil. But a guy only does that
for his girl or a girl that he feels he's the only one
she's being intimate with or giving all that special attention to.

At first I thought Shante was a gift, a woman that
had as much freak in her as I did in me.

Over the next few nights some things caught my
attention. Shante's phone would ring all times of the
night. A few times, after several rings and many return calls, there would be loud, hard knocks at the
door. She then would act as if it meant nothing. I, on
the other hand, realized that the treatment she was
giving me, which had me about to lose my mind, had
already made other niggahs lose theirs.

One day I was chilling over at her house when
there was a knock at the door. Usually she would ignore it, but today was different. When she opened
the door, two of the most gorgeous women I'd ever
seen, stood in the doorway. After many hugs and
kisses they all sat down.

Shante introduced me, and they passed me hugs
as if I was their man, letting me know that any friend
of hers was a friend of theirs. Two passionate kisses
followed from each gorgeous girl. Damn, I wished all
girls had this same attitude. Both young ladies were

from New York, and when they began to talk and express themselves in different ways, their accent and personality had me turned on to no end.

When Shante answered the door she was wearing just a T-shirt and thong. China and Shawn went in the room and made themselves comfortable. When they returned, Shawn was wearing a long silk nightgown with spaghetti straps and no panties. I could see right through it. Her breasts weren't that large, but she had ass for days. China was wearing a short tank top, her breasts bursting out, and bikini panties. I sat there knowing in my mind that these girls didn't think I didn't want no pussy. They had me fucked up.

They were talking and catching up. Listening to their conversation, I found out that somebody had flown these girls in for the weekend.

After about an hour, I heard a knock. China jumped up and peeked out. She got excited. When she opened the door, a tall, slim, dark-skinned guy walked in. There was no mistaking that he was a true player. The Nautica gear that hung from his body, the fresh Jordans, and the jewels that he rocked let me and the hookers in the room know that the kid had bank.

We all started talking and joking. I sparked up some weed and got shit popping. He suggested we get some champagne, and everyone agreed. He asked if I wanted to ride. I figured, why not—sometimes it's good to know people, and plus I wanted the scoop on the bitches in the room, including Shante. The guy pulled China in the kitchen, and they began to talk in a tone so no one could hear.

Shante called me in the room to let me know a little bit about this kid. She let me know the niggah name was Peter and he was from Up Top. He ran with some real niggahs. She said that he had done a lot of people wrong in Norfolk by taking their money with the intention of going Up Top and scoring, but never did. A lot of niggahs wanted to deal with him, but his brother Unique was a major player and well connected. Peter had a reputation, but his brother was known from New York to Miami and was nobody you would ever want to fuck with. That left Peter untouchable.

They had a house in Hampton—she had been there once with China. It was like something out of *Miami Vice*, as they both had to be blindfolded before even going there.

Me and Peter jumped in his new red 300ZX to go get champagne.

"You from here?" he asked.

"Been here so long, kid, you can say that," I answered.

"The girl said you and your peoples have a sports bar."

"Yeah, up on Newtown Road."

"You and your peoples handle a lot of business?" he asked.

"We do our share. Our bitches and seeds live well," I responded.

"I heard that shit, god. I just want to get back to those bitches, and make them put on a show, and freak. Then I'm going to take China red ass back to this room down the beach with a Jacuzzi and fuck the shit out of her," he said with a wide-ass smile.

I thought we were going to Farm Fresh to get some Moët. We hit the interstate going downtown Norfolk and ended up by Waterside, at an Italian restaurant, La Galleria. We walked in, and the manager greeted him by his name. He purchased four bottles of Cristal at two hundred and seventy-five dollars a bottle. He pulled eleven hundred bones off the fat roll he had in his pocket and didn't sweat it. I knew I was fucking around with a niggah from the big leagues.

When we got back to the apartment, I began rolling up instantly. Peter started popping bottles, and it was on. Once the girls were laid back and re-laxed, Peter said, "I'll give you five hundred, Shawn, if you eat Shante pussy."

I almost choked on the blunt, hearing that come out this niggah mouth.

"And I'll give you five hundred, Shante, for letting her," he finished.

The girls agreed, taking off the little they had on, and Shawn began to eat Shante's pussy right in front of us. This shit was new to me.

"You can get yours, China," he said. "Go eat Shawn from the back."

He paid these bitches to put on a show for us, which lasted about two hours or until they all came twice.

Peter told China to get dressed, gave me a pound, and the two took off, leaving me with the other two girls.

The show had me horny as hell. I pulled Shante towards me, hoping we could get down.

She eased over and took off my shirt. She fell to her knees and removed my pants.

As I stepped out of my Polo boxers, she quickly slipped her wet, warm mouth onto my dick. Shawn slowly eased over and started licking my chest. My en-tire body was stimulated from head to toe, while they both fucked and sucked me until I was on the floor, panting like a bitch. I was so glad that the lights were out because I was all smiles—from ear to ear. I couldn't wait to tell Big G and Black about this shit.

* * *

Things were still booming with the telephones
and fake ID's. Many of the kids from New York that
hung out in Shirt Kings were now hanging in E's
Cue. All the big ballers that I always saw hanging
around town were now hanging in my shit and giving
me my props. I was now well known. Everywhere I
went, heads would be coming up showing me love. I
wasn't nationally known, but in my world I was the
shit. I always tried to catch real niggahs' names and
faces, never wanting to disrespect anyone—because
you never know.

I started spending more time in the sports bar.
There was a lot of activity going on in there, and I
needed to be alert. We were still fucking with RJ and
his peoples, who had started meeting niggahs up at
E's Cue. Muhammed's and Houdini's family also
started meeting niggahs up there to make transactions.

This one guy I met at Shirt Kings, Rock, medium-
built, brown-skinned, with a baldhead, and drove a
big Lincoln was in E's Cue every day, but he was also
in Shirt Kings every day. Once we started talking I realized he was pretty chill. I noticed that he always had
bitches with him, usually two at a time. After a while,
I came to find out that he wasn't just fuckin' these
bitches, but that they also worked for him. They were
always fly as hell, but these pretty bitches were out to
get theirs—fuck the dick; they were out for the paper.

Rock told me that his peoples were coming in
from New York, uptown. I was under the impression
that the niggahs I saw him with at Shirt Kings and
The Bridge was his peoples, but they were just soldiers who had come down from "Harlem World" to
make paper in our town. All this time I was thinking
that Rock was the man, but he let me know that the
scale went higher than him. He wanted to set up a

time for all of us to sit and talk, his people wanting to open the same type of sports bar in Harlem.

This particular Saturday was hype. All the pool tables were taken. Tupac, a well-known rap artist, was supposed to do a show at The Bridge, and word had gotten out that he loved to play pool and was going to stop in E's Cue for a couple hours before his appearance. It was a regular routine now. Whenever there was a show, the celebrities always stopped at E's Cue first.

Rock came in with his peoples, and he introduced these niggahs—Buc and El—who I didn't know. I assumed these kids from uptown had to be paid because, like Houdini, they also had a bodyguard. This kid was a light-skinned, real thick-ass motherfucker. Girls were amazed at the niggah's hard, cut physique. This reminded them of Mike Tyson—except this pretty motherfucker went by the name Big Wolf. Rock told me later that the girls loved him, but niggahs despised him uptown. He was known for being a vicious son of a bitch.

We all went into my office, where we talked business: Norfolk, Uptown, investments. They even turned me on to some shit about promoting shows. They had a production company, Butt Naked Production. And like my corporation, it was making a name. They asked me about getting down with their team, but their prices were nothing like RJ's.

They did, however, turn me on to something for which I would forever be so grateful. They had a shop in New York that designed cars. They took me out to the Lincoln and showed me all the secret compartments and a set-up for the Lincoln to drop oil if someone was chasing them. They also told me about bulletproof cars and other shit that could be done if it was in demand and the money was there. I quickly let them know money wasn't an object to me as long as they had what I wanted and it wasn't no bullshit. I sat there thinking these niggahs had to be large, but was sure Black could still hold his own with any niggah.

Later that evening Boot, Big G, Lo, Bo, and myself were hanging in the Sports Bar. Black had said, whenever there's a show at the club, he wanted everybody to be in the spot because niggahs came out the woodwork and sometimes didn't know how to act. Everyone was there for security purposes, but it wasn't like work, because all the big money-makers came out to shine and the bitches were out to see what they could catch.

I was in front at the register, when a kid told me that a guy came in smoking a blunt. I immediately came from behind the counter, followed by Boot, who was definitely ready to catch wreck. As soon as I saw the young man's face, the anger disappeared, and I caught myself. "What's up, Tupac?"

"Nothing, partner," he said.

"Glad you could stop through, but the blunt got to go. You in Virginia Beach now, and they don't give a fuck who they lock up. Besides, they looking for a reason to shut my shit down anyway."

"Shit. I know how they roll. No problem," he said, putting it out and placing it behind his ear.

"Niggahs can get some pictures?" I asked.

"No doubt," he said willingly.

After a few snaps he grabbed some balls and started playing with some kids he came in with.

I saw someone pull in front in the fire lane, with rental tags on a new Camry. Because the blinds were halfway down, I could only see from the neck down.

As the guy approached the door I saw the Tommy Hilfilger jeans shorts, Tommy T-shirt, and Timberlands. Shining and loud as hell was a long Cuban Lynx chain with a phat-ass medallion and matching bracelet. He was rocking a gold Rolex that definitely took him to Big Willie status.

He entered, giving me a clear view. I was shocked as hell, not being able to recognize my own little brother. He had dropped some pounds since the shooting. Niggahs from the hood began to give him dap and show him mad love. Tupac stood there wondering who this niggah was, shining like the sun. He had to understand national celebrities come and go, but ghetto celebrities' reputations ride on forever.

I took Black over and introduced him.

They gave each other pounds and began to converse. They clicked instantly, because Black had blunts behind both of his ears. They walked back in the office and kicked it for a few. When they returned, the office was like a smokescreen, and both their eyes were real low.

We snapped a few more pictures, and Tupac left to go do his show.

Black was getting ready to leave, and we all walked outside. He introduced us to two girls he had with him. Monya was driving him, a Latino bitch from New York, bad as shit. She had a very stern look on her face as if she didn't want anyone to even attempt to try to talk to her. Sarah was the other girl. She was black and Cuban. Calling her fine was an understatement. She said she was from Miami, and had a real pleasant, "let's party" attitude, but she only spoke to Black and Monya.

Black let us know that both of them bitches had some bomb pussy, that they came here to work and, fine as they looked, were very, very dangerous. Black told Lo to take a ride with him and that they'd be back later. Later never came.

* * *

I had been shooting pool a lot lately, trying to hone my skills. Sometimes I would lock up at night and, after making my nightly deposits, come back and shoot, sip Hennessy, and play CD's until the wee hours of the morning. My game had picked up to where the kids coming in wouldn't play me for money, so I had to venture out to other spots to find money games.

This particular night I was at Guy and Gals, a pool hall on the corner of Witchduck Road. and the Boulevard. I was gambling with some white boys, when Dink came in with Jay and started playing on the other side. On my way out I stopped by their table to check with my two-timing friends.

"What you niggahs doing here?" I asked. "My spot still open."

"Naw, we just wanted a change of pace," Jay said.

"I just came home and there's a few people I'm not trying to see right now," Dink replied.

"I heard that. Y'all niggahs take care. I'll catch up."

I knew the only niggah they didn't want to see was Black. It was hard even talking to those kids and not wanting to blast them right in the pool hall, but that wasn't my job. My job was proprietor, player, launderer and salesman, not hired gun. Black had someone for that. Of course he took a personal interest in this job because his life was almost taken.

I went straight to E's Cue and paged Black. He had already heard Dink was home. Lo had seen them out Lake Edward and was having words with the two kids.

Black sent a fiend with Monya and Sarah to the Courtyard to get a room. He took a key and gave the girls one. Monya and Sarah then went up to the pool hall and got a table near Dink and Jay. They were trying to play pool. They knew the basics but had no real skills.

They called the waitress over to order drinks, but before they could order, Dink intercepted, "Can we get your drinks for you, if y'all don't mind us playing a couple games?"

"As long as y'all not waiting on anybody," Jay added.

"Naw, it's all right. We can't really play," Sarah said.

"We can't either, but we can all still have fun trying," Dink said. "Where you girls from?"

"Maryland. We just came down to enjoy the beach for a minute," Monya said.

"Where y'all staying?"

"Courtyard."

"Where the weed at out here?" Sarah asked.

"We got the weed. Why—what's up?" Dink said.

They all ended up playing and drinking for a while before leaving and going back to the hotel.

After smoking a few blunts, Sarah began to dance around seductively. The guys thought they had gotten the girls fucked up. Monya started fucking with Jay, suggesting they go into the shower.

Sarah had started rubbing her ass on Dink's dick. He was having the time of his life—or so he thought. Sarah told Dink she had to make a call to let some other girls know they were going to be running late.

When she came back, she took out Dink's dick and began to massage it. She undressed him and began to kiss and lick him all over. Monya had undressed and started the shower. Jay was in there wrapped in a towel, anticipating the fucking he was going to give to this Maryland girl he'd only known for a couple hours.

Sarah had climbed on top of Dink and began to
ride him like the stud he thought he was. He got so
loud it gave her an excuse to turn up the TV so his
peoples couldn't hear them. When Sarah climbed
back on top of him, he closed his eyes and just enjoyed the love that he was getting.

Jay had Monya bent over with her hands on the
wall, the shower pouring on both of them, as he
pounded like there was no tomorrow.

Both guys were so far gone that they never heard
the squeaking of the door as Black, Lo, and Boot entered the room. Black came in, eased to the bedside,
and quickly put his cold steel against Dink's head.
Dink was startled but quickly calmed down, once he
caught a glimpse of the chrome .44 Magnum.

Sarah jumped up, threw on her shit and pulled
out her .45.

By this time Boot and Lo had made their way into
the bathroom. In one quick motion Boot pulled
back the curtain and snatched Jay by his neck so hard
he slipped and burst his head on the toilet. Boot
pulled his naked ass by his chin into the other room.

Jay started confessing, laying all the blame on
Dink, but the stuttering stopped when Monya's 9mm
got stuffed in his mouth.

"Dink, we started out together on the same corner, scraping and scrambling. How the fuck it come
to this?" Black asked.

Dink opened his mouth to say something, and
Sarah pulled her trigger, frowning as his brains hit
the headboard. When Black followed by pulling the
trigger on the .44, the rest of his face exploded beyond recognition.

Monya then fired two times, putting Jay to rest.
They were now a memory.

The day after was a sad one for Lake Edward. Lo and Black stopped over and gave Jay's mom a card with some money in it. It was the money they took out the dead niggah's pocket. Lo even went to Jay's funeral.

CHAPTER 11

"Greekfest"

It was Labor Day weekend and we were hanging out at Foreman Field to see Norfolk State football game. We actually went to pass out flyers to promote the sports bar. Smalls was out there with Lite, passing out flyers promoting House of Pain, who was doing a show at The Bridge that night.

After the game the crowd gathered at 7-Eleven by Norfolk State. Big G and I was right in the midst of things. He had his Maxima backed up in front of 7-Eleven and the sounds banging off the hook. He stood out, but real niggahs were beginning to swamp the parking lot quickly. All around us, nothing but expensive foreign cars, young black men pulling up on motorcycles of all kinds. Just a gathering of black people having a good time.

During this Laborfest weekend, I sat in 7-Eleven parking lot, remembering how things used to be, and how drastically it had changed. I remember for so many years this weekend was called Greekfest, when every young black college student and every hustler from Massachusetts to Florida came to Virginia Beach. They would come and have picnics in parks with DJs, sororities and fraternities step shows, and the bomb-ass beach parties. People would be on the strip at the oceanfront, and it would be like a car show and bass off. Brothers from the boroughs up north to the counties down south; girls from Morgan and Howard, to the fly bitches from Spelman and FAMU, were migrating to the strip. The shops on Atlantic Avenue were swamped with people shopping and gathering souvenirs to carry back home.

Everybody else began to hang on Pacific Avenue where it was just miles and miles of traffic, but nobody had a problem. It gave Big Willies a chance to show off their money on four wheels. Kids from up North had the Benzs, BMWs, Corvettes, Audis; but the boys from down South were pushing Sevilles, "El Dogs," with sounds to rock the hotels. Things seemed perfect.

Then in '89 all hell broke loose. The city felt that all the other years were a fluke and that blacks were coming to terrorize the city. Virginia Beach decided to bring in the National Guard, state police and beach patrol for extra security. When they tried to abuse their authority, blacks weren't having it. They began to retaliate. I remember one guy having the trunk to his Pathfinder open, pumping Sybil's, "Don't Make Me Over," and the crowds were in the street dancing and having a good time as they'd done every year prior to '89.

Out of nowhere the National Guard began to push its way in, and the confusion started. One kid with New Jersey tags popped his trunk to reveal six 12-inch woofers. He began to pump Public Enemy's "Fight the Power," and the crowd got hype. Bottles began to fly, windows began to break, the looting began, and the beach suffered. The police came and started making people leave. Greekfest was no more. They changed it to Laborfest, and it was never the same.

Big G and I decided to go to E's Cue. We knew that was where people would end up, because of the show. By the time we reached the spot, the parking lot was full, and the line was down the walkway. Everlast, from the group, House of Pain, was still in E's Cue playing pool. We went inside and took pictures.

Rock and crew came in the spot. I introduced Rock to Black and Boot. Rock hollered at Black, trying to get him to get down with him. Little did he know, Black was already on, in a very strong way.

RJ came in and was talking to Rock. He had still never met Black.

When I went into the club, I noticed that RJ also knew a lot of kids from Norfolk. He was serving a lot of people. I found out that he and his peoples were blowing up. The prices that they were bringing from Miami made New York kids buy from them. They were meeting New York prices without the drive.

When I told Black about this, he knew if everybody else was getting down with him, it wouldn't be long before he heated himself up. Black figured it was time to see if Jacqueline's brother had come out of his drought.

Black called me early one morning. He wanted me to meet him at Tia's house. I got over there, and he had about thirty guns in the living room and three kilos. We got everything up and took it to the sports bar, stashing the shit in the ceilings. One of the kids that he had served at Tia's house several times had gotten busted. He didn't know if the niggah's mouth had a slow leak or what, but he couldn't take the chance.

A few days later his boy called Tia's house, telling Black that he was locked with a guy that was down with Rock and his people. He found out that Rock was just one of the major players, that there were about six more moving just as much weight, if not more. They had a real tight clique, and all the niggahs were about making paper.

They had came down and locked up quite a few areas, first setting up shop beside Shirt Kings. In just a short period of time, they had locked up Huntersville, where Tracey got locked up. (He had bodies all over the city, and it finally caught up with him. He was looking at the chair, but in the end got life.)

Moton Park, Bowling Park and even the club on Princess Anne, Casablanca, were being held down by the same niggahs. They had other niggahs serving people out Grandy Park and Ingleside. These young boys were definitely making moves. They tried to move into Park Place. That's when they ran into problems. The Jamaicans weren't having it. Quite a few Jamaicans had come in and was working Park Place, Tidewater Park, Youngs Park and many of the other projects off Monticello in the downtown area. He told Black that he wouldn't advise rolling with them, but they were good people to know.

Rock began to do most of his business out of E's Cue. He would come in early in the day and get a table. He always had a girl with him for business purposes. Niggahs would come, and he'd walk outside or go in the bathroom, but the girl would always serve the kids. By him being around all the time, we all got kind of tight. He always said that the bitches wanted money, but just wanted to beg for it. He was going to make them earn every penny he dished out. If they wanted it, they were going to earn it like him—in the ruff.

Over the next several months business took off. The Bridge had brought a lot of notoriety to E's Cue. I had slowed down a lot due to unfortunate issues. It was said that Black had set up a hit out Park Place, resulting in some kilos being taken and cash coming up missing. Word was floating that Black or his brother would be worth forty thousand dead. Black said we were all going to roll in cliques from now on.

It seemed like all the businesses that were being opened were being run by young black entrepreneurs. We had the sports bar, and Black had opened up a hair salon in Greenbriar. Young boys had the Bridge going, and Shirt Kings, with the new airbrush graffiti trend, were doing quite well. Club EnVogue had shut down. The word was that it was going to be bought and re-opened by the kids from that uptown clique. The Iranian man from Mr. Magics across the street was coming every week, trying to promote his twenty-five and older club, which was now twenty-one and over, but you still had to be dressed.

The Inner Circle was a reggae club in Newport News. They didn't get much business. Some Jamaicans came up with the idea to put one on our side of the water on Brambleton Avenue. The Blue Light. This restaurant/club took off from day one. The first time I stopped there was one night after I had left David's. When me and Small's arrived at David's about 12:30, all the New York and Shirt King players had a table to the left, as soon as you came through the door. They had empty Moët bottles stacked on the table and were still ordering more.

At the bar to the left, Miami and Portsmouth niggahs had mad Moët bottles stacked on their table. Directly in front of the bar, Houdini and Muhammed hung out with LL and Lou, two hustlers from Tidewater Park. They had more Moët and Dom P. bottles spread out over two tables, and promised to buy out the bar before the night was over. It was like a signal to the bitches—there was money at every table.

I joined the New York and Shirt King kids. Smalls bought two bottles of Moët, and I got a bottle of Dom P. We sat and drank until the champagne was hard to swallow. We got shots of Hennessy to smooth out the champagne then drank some more.

By the time we left, we were feeling too nice. I saw Tara's cousin. She was all in some niggah's face, fucked up, and trying to show out for her friends like she really knew a niggah.

By me hanging out so much in the past, and now being the owner of E's Cue, pussy was being thrown at me. Some I took, but most I threw away. I had become very picky about who I fucked.

With forty thousand on your head, any bitch would set you up. Besides, I was now looked at as a major player and had a reputation to hold up.

Tara's cousin asked me where I was going when I left the club. When I told her I was heading for The Blue Light, she wanted to hang out awhile. "Can I ride with you?" she asked. "I'll find a ride from there."

"Sure," I said. "But I'm getting ready to roll out. What's up?"

We're in the car, and she leans her seat back, her beautiful, long, yellow legs sticking out from under her short, tight-fitting dress that rises to just below her panties.

"Dee, where your friends? I mean some decent niggahs. I see the way you look out for Tara. I saw that DKNY sweat suit and sneakers. That shit was fly as hell. I need somebody in my life that I can count on and enjoy life with."

I had bought that sweat suit a couple days before,

when Black and I went to Baltimore. Tara was supposed to be out of town for the weekend with her parents in Lynchburg. I saw her pack the sweat suit away the night before. So her cousin could have only seen it today.

"When did you see Tara?" I asked.

"Earlier at . . . this morning before they left," she continued.

"What's her mom's number?" I asked.

"I can't think of it," she said.

"Look. I'll give you fifty dollars, and I won't tell her you gave it to me. Actually I'm not even going to say anything. I'm just trying to see if she's there," I said, resting my hand on her thigh. "You know a niggah tries his hardest to give her the world, and if she can't appreciate what I have to offer, then I can focus my attention elsewhere. Can you understand?" I asked, knowing I had her.

"Okay, I'll dial it for you," she said, dialing the number on the cellular as I held the phone.

"Hello," the voice answered.

I hung up the phone. I got upset instantly. *Why would this girl lie to me?* I think I had it figured.

"I don't feel like driving back out the beach. I'm going to go get me a room and smoke until I pass out. Do you want me to drop you off at the club?"

"You can," she replied . . . "unless you feel up for some company."

I went and got a suite at the Howard Johnson. We smoked and kicked for about an hour, when I received a page from Black. He didn't want shit, but I played like he did, so I could jet out for a few. I couldn't get into her, with Tara heavy on a niggah's mind.

I left and went straight to Tara's mom's house. I parked down the street, so she couldn't see my car. After ringing the bell, I put my ear against the door, so I could hear the steps squeak if someone came down.

Sure enough, the stairs began to squeak. As I leaned over, I noticed the burgundy Lexus coupe with Connecticut plates, sitting on chrome and parked on the other side of the street.

The thought of another niggah in the crib began to make the rage swell inside of me. I heard someone step up to the peephole.

"Open the door, Tara."

Nothing happened.

"Don't make a niggah come up in that bitch because your peoples will be buying a new door. Open the fuckin' door. Do you think I'm playing with you?" I kicked in the door.

She stood there in a short T-shirt screaming. This brown-skinned niggah with a long, gold chain, no shirt, sagging jeans and untied Timberlands was standing there, looking as if he'd just thrown them on.

I caught her with an open-hand slap that took her off her feet and slammed her into the wall. I then followed up with a straight jab to her forehead that laid her ass out.

Turning to him, I swung, catching him on the jaw. As I swung, he faded with the punch and before I knew it, I had blows being thrown at me. We were throwing blow for blow. All I knew was that I was in front of the door and he had to get past me to get out.

I thought I was in his ass but, looking back, I have to give the northern kid props—he was nice with his hands.

He busted out the door, jumped in the Lex, and was out.

When I went back to her, she was coming to, still

on the ground, crying with a bloody nose, and holding her jaw.

"What the fuck were you thinking?" I yelled. "You better get your trifling ass over to the crib and pick up your shit because it will be in trash bags on the fuckin' corner. I don't believe you did this shit to me. How trifling can a bitch be? We'll see if he take your stankin' ass in and put a roof over your fuckin' head."

I jumped in the 740 BMW and sped off, stopping at the corner to get myself together. My leg was still jumping from the incident, and my heart was hurting from the pain. I grabbed my heart as if to catch my breath but realized the pain wasn't going away. Then the tears began to fall. I sat there trying to pull myself together. I couldn't believe that my girl could do something like this.

The red and blue flashing lights brought me back to reality—two Norfolk police cars were pulling in front of her house. I eased off and shot down the street towards the hotel. When I got to the hotel room, her cousin had undressed and was lying across the bed with just her thong and bra.

My pager started going off. It was Tara.

I sparked a blunt and tried to pull my head together. Tara had done what I'd said no girl would ever do to me. She had me fucked up.

Tara blew my pager up all night. I laid there beside her cousin, and she kept putting her ass on my dick, trying to get me excited. But I couldn't fuck the finest bitch. My heart was hurting.

I dropped her off and gave Tara a call back. For some reason I wanted to hear what the fuck she had to say.

"Hello," she answered.

"What the fuck you blowing up my shit for? What could you possibly want?"

"I'm sorry," she said crying. "The police came by here—one of the neighbors called. They made me take out a warrant . . . they made me. I think I have a concussion, and my jaw is fractured."

"I don't give a fuck. You better thank God your ass is still living," I said and hung up.

I stayed on the low through the weekend.

I had talked to my mom about the incident; she wanted me to turn myself in and not give them the opportunity to pick me up in the streets.

So Monday morning I went downtown to the precinct and turned myself in. I knew it was for the best, because I didn't want them coming to the sports bar and starting confusion. The last thing I needed was to bring more attention to E's Cue, with all the shit that was going on.

Tara's mom had told her that she should get a restraining order against me because now I was supposed to be crazy and unpredictable.

They processed me and put me on a fifteen-hundred-dollar bond. They allowed me to leave on my own recognizance, just because I didn't make them look for me.

I was in the sports bar, when Black walked in. He told me Tara was outside and didn't want to come in. She wanted me to come outside and talk to her.

It had been a week, and I had barely eaten, had no appetite, and was still feeling sick. I wanted to go outside and hug her, take her in my arms and let her know she was forgiven. But she had done the unthinkable, and I couldn't get past it.

I went outside, where she stood crying, telling me how sorry she was. But I wasn't hearing it. How could she give what belongs to me to another niggah?

She went on and on about me giving her everything but time. She brought up times when she begged me to stay home, even when she cried for my attention, and I still had to run. She talked about before the baby I took her everywhere, but now we have to pack up everything before going anywhere. That I find it easier to jump up and bounce by myself, but it left her feeling lonely.

I was listening to her, but I wasn't hearing it. All I knew was, if I ever got rid of this feeling, not another bitch was ever going to get me open like this again.

I went back in E's Cue, where Black was in the office on the phone.

"You remember Boo?" he asked. "The niggah I ran track with when we broke the national record?"

"Yeah," I answered.

"He gave me a call and told me he was making moves in Richmond. He built him a little click, and they running shit from Petersburg to DC and Maryland."

"I thought Richmond niggahs scored from niggahs in DC or Philly. They got more going than Norfolk," I said.

"I don't know. I was giving him some prices, and he thought they were lovely. Him and his crew, they're ready to buy two ki's. Thing is, they want me to bring it there."

"What you going to do?" I asked.

"I'm thinking on it," he said, pulling out some weed and blunts.

"If you know the niggah straight, call him and tell him that you'll be in Richmond in an hour and as soon as you get there you are going to page him. Don't give that niggah a lot of time. Tell him his time is limited. And if he don't show on your time, burst. Because you can get two adjoining rooms, let them 'ho's carry it up, while you and Lo follow, serve them niggahs and get that paper."

"You right. I don't know why I feel funny about this. I guess I know a lot of niggahs out here tripping. This girl I'm knocking off said she was at a party with mad heads and heard kids talking about, they wished a niggah had lost his life, and that my time was coming. The same niggahs I see at the rec, smiling in my face, giving a niggah props, but waiting to see a niggah lying in a pool of blood," he said, shaking his head in disbelief, but understanding the game.

"Yo, son, these niggahs jealous. That's why we have to hold our own and let shit go, always keeping our eyes open, and never taking a chance. Think about it. It's not like you really need those niggahs' money, so you do have a choice. Fuck them."

When we came out, Smalls and Lite were playing pool.

"What's up, kid?" Lite asked.

"Nothing, son. Just trying to keep the lights on," I said.

Black had kept walking out the door. If he didn't know you, he didn't have much to say, and as I didn't introduce him, he knew that they weren't too important.

"I know you coming to the club tomorrow," Smalls said.

"No doubt, son. You know a niggah ain't gonna miss Guru."

"Gang Starr be ripping shit. Right, son?" Lite said, giving me a pound.

We all kicked it for a while then they invited me down to the club to drink. I couldn't roll because I was supposed to meet with Freddie Mac to check on some investment properties.

I knew I needed to do something because sitting around with Tara on my mind was about to drive me insane. I sat and thought about all the girls I was kicking it with, and not one of them did I trust enough or even care a little about to make my girl.

I had heard a long time ago that the way to get over a woman was to get another one and throw yourself into her. I had dated some nice girls, bad as they come, but all these money-hungry bitches couldn't get my love, only this dick. That was all I had for them.

My style was changing. Instead of all the fly-ass girls that I wanted so badly to fuck, now I wanted someone who carried herself like a lady. One with style, class, and a future.

CHAPTER 12

"Cee-lo"

After checking on some investment properties, I came back to E's Cue to write checks to go with the offers I'd decided to give a try. Instead of renovating some properties, I wanted to get some rental properties. I made an offer on one of Dick Kelly's four-unit buildings in Ocean View, and two of Man Jac's properties, off Chesapeake Boulevard. in Norview. I knew from living in Virginia for so long that these properties would rent with no problem. After finishing up my business with Freddie Mac, I jumped in my Corvette and ran to the house.

On my way there I realized three things: that I had to get a closer spot; that I needed a new car—driving the truck every day wasn't the answer, and the Vette had gotten me two tickets too many; and that I needed a girl, one to call my own and show mad love too. One that is always there. Not one you have to call and see if her time is free.

I arrived at the house and finished putting Tara's shit in trash bags. As I did it, the feeling in the pit of my stomach was still there, and I still didn't have an appetite, but I knew I was going to be all right. I took the silk sheets off the bed—getting them was her idea—and removed the silk pillowcases we had gotten them so her hair wouldn't slide and mess up. I threw that shit in a bag then headed for the bathroom to get hair curlers, flat irons, and hand dryers. I took two trips and gathered up all her clothes and shoes then laid them in the back of the truck. I came back in and stood looking around, trying to figure out if I forgot anything. I changed the code on the alarm system then called a locksmith.

While talking on the phone, I walked back upstairs to the bathroom and looked at her toothbrush and picked it up. All of a sudden my world came tumbling down, feeling like someone shot an arrow through my window and got me. I knew then I was damaged and the next bitch would definitely have to be about her work. I knew that I would miss her to no end, but she fucked up the trust. Once that was gone, our relationship would have been pure hell.

After getting all the baby things off the loft, I drove it over to her mom's. I wasn't supposed to be around there, but I knew she wanted her shit.

Tara stood outside, as I carried everything in the house.

After my last trip, I came back out and handed her a grand, letting her know that was for her to find her a spot to live and that my daughter would be like her roommate. I'd take care of her half of everything, and if my child needed anything, all she had to do was just give me a call.

She stood there with her eyes filled with tears, as I walked by and jumped in the Range. It was hard for me not to stare as I drove off, but I knew it was for the best. I knew things had to get right in my head because, when I made the decision to give her a baby, I was aware that we would be connected forever. Forever now seemed like a long time.

On my way back to the house, I decided to stop at Haynes for a comfortable set to decorate my loft. I then set up an appointment to get my walls measured, so I could put mirrors all around. Off the first floor bedroom I had planned to build a deck and put in a Jacuzzi; I was already making plans for the new bachelor.

When I returned to E's Cue, I saw Lo's car parked on the side and RJ shooting pool. I knew they were in the back handling business.

I sat there talking to RJ, when this gray Acura Legend pulled up. I had seen this Acura up here every day. These same kids would come in smelling as if they just came from a session of unlimited blunts and play pool for hours. That made me money. I had seen them at Kempsville Skating Rink, when Norfolk State had their parties up there. They would go to the DJ stand and get on the mike and rip it. They were always ready to battle with anybody who came their way, and whoever stepped up always fell to their wrath. They seemed to be real chill with a laid-back type of attitude. It didn't seem like they hustled. But they were always around hustlers and hustlers knew them.

"Give us our regular table," one of them said.

"Naw. Give us two," said the other.

"I'll give you three if you spark that 'ism,' " I said laughing, as I handed them some balls.

"You niggahs be getting nice every day."

"Every day high, son," one of them said. "Every day high."

"Can you play this tape?" one of the kids asked. "It's some shit we did called 'Money and the Murder.' "

When I played the tape, a beat came on that I thought was tight as shit. Then the lyrics kicked in: "Money and the murder, money and the murder, shit you never seen, shit you never heard of . . ."

I continued to let it play.

After a few minutes I walked over to their table. "This shit is nice, kid. "What's the group called?"

"Lost Boyz. That's us. I'm Mr. Cheeks, and this is Freaky Tah. The rest of the crew coming in behind us.

"Why don't you all do me a commercial to run on 103 JAMZ or 92.1?"

"That's no problem, son, but it will cost you about fifteen hundred," one of the other guys said as he pulled a stick off the wall.

"Shit. Who you think you are—NWA, Ice Cube and the boys?" I asked jokingly.

"Naw, but we are professional, and one day niggahs will blow," he said.

"I heard that shit," I said.

After a couple of hours passed, I paged Black to see what was up. Instead of calling, he came strolling in with his eyes low and smelling of weed, his boy Carlos by his side. Carlos didn't look anything like he did the first day we met. Now he was in new shit from head to toe. He was rocking a nice herringbone and gold watch, and driving a new rental. You could always tell when niggahs had paper—they would get a rental in a heartbeat.

"Remember me?" he asked, giving me a pound.

"Yeah," I said. "Carlos, right?"

"Yeah. Black said you had skills with the stick," he said smiling.

"Little bit."

I knew he was just making conversation and was feeling good. He had just got home from lockdown and was hanging with Black. If you hung with Black, you were making money. He knew it, and so did everybody else.

Black had run in the back and was talking to Lo. He came back and called me in the office. "I'm getting ready to run to Richmond," he said. "You remember Carlos, right?"

"Not really," I answered.

"Me and that niggah played stickup kids together. We used to get fiends' cars and go out Norfolk, Portsmouth, and down the beach, robbing niggahs. You remember when I was getting those guns, shotguns, TVs, and stereos, when we lived out Lake Edward? Me and that niggah were running up in niggahs' spots. He's a real trooper. I was talking to him, and he was saying his peoples been put out three times since he been locked up. But they straight now, and he don't plan on getting locked again."

"You don't have to convince me that the niggah real. As long as he's all right with you, he's all right with me. If he fuck up and you get caught up in some shit, I'll do that niggah myself," I said.

"He's all right. Check this—them 'ho's rolling, and me and Carlos is rolling tail. I'll hit you as soon as I get back."

When they left, I saw the girls in front, in a Nissan Sentra. All I could do was pray, "Lord, take care of my little brother." I knew this was going to be a long night.

I began to think about the murder count in Richmond and DC. Washington was ridiculous. How in the hell could the president let his hometown get so fucked up? Norfolk had its share of homicides, but Richmond was definitely up there.

"What's up, black man?" Lo asked, trying to talk like the Muslims that he'd seen selling *The Final Call* and incense on the corner of Newtown and the Boulevard, or up on Brambleton by Norfolk State.

"Chilling, cousin. I thought you were rolling with Black." I said.

"He figured him and his man could handle it. Plus, he said if something went wrong, he wanted me here to keep this paper going. I know if anything do go wrong, two to the head of Carlos. He will have to meet Allah! No question. Last night I saw your man's brother up here."

"Who?" I asked with a confused look on my face.

"Teddy Riley brother, them Wrecks 'n' Effect kids."

"For real. I heard Teddy think he got game. Niggahs say he got a pool table up in the studio. I'm gonna catch him one day and put some of that big producing-money in my pocket. I'll give that niggah the eight ball," I said, giving Lo a pound and smiling.

My cousin knew my game was tight, and I'd play a motherfucker for anything.

"I'm going to check out this condo in Cypress Point. I need me a spot out this way."

"Buying that bitch?" he asked.

"No. Rent it because you and Black be done did some shit and have me moving again," I said laughing. I loved my peoples, but they had a knack for getting in some shit. "I need me a new load, some nice-ass, phat shit, but I want to look like a businessman, not that thug-ass look."

"I know this kid from Maryland. He stay out Chesterfield Heights. Him and his people pump out Ingleside Projects," Lo said. "The kids he was scoring from got knocked off, and his shit been slow. He has a Q45 he only want fifteen thousand for."

"Call him and tell him to be here tomorrow at twelve. I'll buy that bitch. What color is it?"

"Beige. That dark, tan-like shit. You'll like it." He

got quiet and began to stare outside. "Don't turn around, but check out this bitch coming inside."

"Hello," she said.

I turned around to see Monique. "How are you?" I asked.

"Fine. And how are you?" she asked softly.

"I'm doing much better now," I said smiling.

"So what brings you this way?" I asked.

"Sheila and I went to the Naro Theater downtown in Ghent."

"I've been to the Cafe's down there, but never the theaters."

"I just stopped by to say hello. I've been in before, but you're never here."

"Yeah, right. Nobody told me shit," I said.

"Honest. I've been by," she said with a smile.

I began to stare at her beautiful skin, short cut, and nice body, which wasn't as tight as the other bitches I'd been fucking around with lately. But she had some class to her, and the way she was presenting herself turned me on to no end. She wore a wrap-around skirt, sheer stockings, heels, and a sheer blouse, where I could see the lace that outlined her bra. When she smiled, she had the most beautiful white teeth. Made me want to kiss her right then.

"So have you had dinner?" I asked.

"No, I haven't."

I had asked Lo to lock up when he was leaving. I told her we would come back for her car, as we walked over to my Corvette. I don't usually open doors and shit, but I felt that it wasn't a bad time to start.

We rode down Shore Drive to Bay Billiards, a very upscale pool hall. They already had their alcohol license, a stocked bar, sit-down restaurant, and twenty-five pool tables. We went inside and sat down at the bar, where she ordered a glass of wine, and I got myself a Heineken.

"So how does the long-distance relationship work?" I asked.

"It works. I'm not complaining," she said.

"But you're reaching out. You're saying, 'Dee, I have a man, but I need hugs and affection more often than I'm getting them,' " I said with a slight grin.

"You're crazy. But really all I want is a friend, someone easy to talk to. Is that you, Dee?"

"We'll find out," I said as we stared into each other's eyes. "Why do I want to kiss you so bad?"

She didn't respond to my comment, so I figured I'd leave it alone until later.

"You know your friend been calling Sheila," she said.

"Yeah, he told me that he'd been talking to her."

"That seem like so long ago that we met," she said. "Oh, I meant to tell you I was sorry to hear what happened with your brother. When you left I told my friends that I woulda gone with you."

"For real?" I asked. "I heard that."

On the way home I threw in some Christopher Williams, "Not a Perfect Man," and went straight to track two, "Learning to Love Again."

As I drove she moved closer to me and took her left hand and gently caressed my neck. She then took her right hand and held mine as she gently rubbed them together.

I realized then that there is nothing in the world as great as a woman's touch. She had me going. All I wanted to do was hold her in my arms. She was going to take me to a new level. She wanted to allow herself to ease into my head, but my mind was definitely too strong.

Our conversation flowed to current events, events in the world that affected us directly and indirectly. It was a big change from talking about which niggah in Norfolk was blowing up, what bitch done fuck another bitch niggah, what kind of hair she was going to buy Saturday, or what nail she had to get fixed.

"So how long you been at Hampton?"

"I'm in graduate school. I got my bachelor's in psychology from VCU, but now I've changed it . . . and don't ask."

"I'm not going there tonight," I said. "Look, Monique, it's late, and I wouldn't feel good you driving home alone. So why don't I carry you home and bring you back to your car in the morning?"

"I would appreciate that," she said, smiling as to let me know I wasn't slick.

I let the slow soothing sounds of Christopher Williams take us to Hampton. By the time we reached her place the tenth track was playing, "Down on My Knees," and I felt her melting. We went into her little apartment, a nice little one bedroom.

"We're going to stay out here tonight," she said, opening up a little sofa bed.

She poured herself a glass of wine and went to change. When she returned, I had gotten a soda out of the refrigerator and was lying in my boxers and "wife-beater." She came out wearing green pajamas. The bottom had buttons and a tie string; the top had about ten buttons. I could see that she still had on her bra.

I sat there thinking, *Either she plans to undress again, or pussy ain't in the plan tonight.*

As soon as we lay down I drew closer to her. I worked my way through the ten buttons up to her bra. Working my way past the draw string, I eased my hand into her panties. I massaged her body as she wiggled and swarmed, but she didn't allow the panties to come off.

Then I decided to give her the test. I reached up, hugged her, and got the arousal smell of her body off my hand. It made me want her so bad that I eased down, and as far as those panties came, my tongue was able to reach.

She threw her head back and just enjoyed the pleasure I was giving her. The panties came down on the thigh but never came off. She wouldn't break that night.

The next day she was off, but paged me as soon as she got out of class. "You still coming over?" she asked excitedly.

"Yes. Let me finish up my business, so I don't have to rush back."

I didn't want to seem pressed, so I arrived about three hours later. She was there waiting patiently and looking better than the previous day.

We decided to get a movie, and for her relaxation, I picked up a bottle of Alizé.

We had dinner at Fisherman's Wharf seafood restaurant that sat at the edge of the Hampton tunnel. I could tell she was enjoying the atmosphere of the place and the style I was throwing at her. She ordered a Baileys and coffee, something I had never had, but came to enjoy. After dinner we ordered Grand Marnier for after-dinner drinks.

After arriving back at her place, we watched a movie. I tried a few moves that didn't work but was allowed to show all types of affection.

Later we woke to a snowy television.

It was Friday, and she had called me three times before noon that day. I enjoyed Monique's company all week long. She was the only female that was relieving some of the things that were on my mind. I didn't mind—this attention felt good. I felt good about being at her place because no one ever came through, except for her two girlfriends. And her phone never rang after nine. It seemed like she was a person that kept to herself, all about school and work. I couldn't believe that nobody was hitting that ass. I couldn't believe it.

"How long do you think you'll be?" she asked.

"Boot just came in, so I shouldn't be an hour," I said.

Black came in with Boot. He was still upset about the state troopers pulling him over coming back from Richmond and taking sixty thousand. They told him he could go to the Federal Bureau and claim the money if he wanted to get it back. He decided it would be safer to chalk it down as a loss.

"I'm supposed to get with Rock and his team. They're going to let me know where to get the bulletproof load from, with the oil slick and the secret compartments. If I had that shit, I would have been straight for last time."

"Do that shit, but I'm out of here," I said, pushing the door.

I jumped in my new Q45 and headed to Hampton. When I stepped out of my shit, I glanced down at myself and knew my shit was on—Russell shit was no joke—Phat Farm jeans, Phat Farm shirt, Polo T-shirt, boxers and socks, new Timbs, and rocking Black's new Cuban lynx gold chain.

"Hey, baby!" she said, leaning over and giving me a kiss. "What's up?"

"I have a taste for some crab legs. Let's hit Red Lobster," I said.

When we arrived, there was no need for a menu. Black and I, usually accompanied by two bitches, would hit either Red Lobster or Darryl's on a daily for lunch.

"Crab legs, clam chowder, seafood fettuccini, then some more crab legs, and a jumbo Long Island Ice Tea."

"I would like a shrimp platter," Monique added.

"Don't forget my biscuits," I said.

Monique began to laugh.

"What the hell you laughing at?"

"No. I'm laughing at the way you said that. Those biscuits are good. They better not forget them."

Having her company was great. She looked so beautiful sitting across from me.

After dinner and some great conversation, we made it back to her place. We sat and talked then began to get a little cozy. She quickly pulled away and went into the kitchen, returning with a piece of paper.

"What's that?" I asked.

"A contract. And I already signed it. This states that under no circumstances are we to fall in love. We will always hold respect for one another at all times, especially if the other is with their friend. What we do is all fun, no seriousness. AGREED."

I thought this girl was tripping, but what the hell, I agreed and signed. At the bottom it said: No matter what, good or bad, husband or wife, kids and divorces, we will always be friends, and nothing and no one will ever come between our special friendship.

As I looked over the contract she had drawn up, she walked in the bathroom and began to run some bath water. She returned, telling me to undress and come into the bathroom. She slowly washed me from head to toe.

This shit was definitely fuckin' me up. I had never had a woman show me attention in this way, but I was enjoying the hell out of it. I quickly let her know that she was starting something, but I felt she knew because all she did was smiled.

She dried me off, handed me the towel, and walked in the room.

I went into the living room and sat down to my drink on the counter, waiting for her to come out and set up our little cot on the floor. But to my surprise I turned to find her standing outside the doorway with a red lace nightie, like she'd stepped out of the Victoria's Secret catalog. At that time I knew she was worthy of no one's touch but mine.

All of a sudden there was a loud knock on the door. Different from the soft knock of her girlfriends. She didn't move as the knocking continued.

"Monique, Monique," the man's voice sounded off through the thin wooden door. Then I heard him run down the stairs, and he was gone.

"Are you sleeping out here? Because I'm sleeping in my bed tonight," she said.

I got up and went into the bedroom. We held each other close, and it felt like she was made for my arms and my arms only. We began to kiss, and before I knew it, I was on top of her, moving slowly in and out. We made love for hours off and on until we fell into a deep sleep.

About four in the morning we were awakened by the same loud knock and voice I'd heard the night before. She didn't move as we lay there until the knocks and the voice disappeared.

"What's up?" I asked.

"Nothing," she said.

I sat up, looking at her silhouette. "Look, goddamn, I'm going to ask you again—what's up?" I asked for the second time, sharpening my tone.

"I used to talk to him a while back. I don't know why he's coming by. I haven't talked to him in months."

"Tell you what—I'm going to give you a chance to

handle your business, but if he come by again and I'm here I'm going to answer the door. If something's up, I'm going to straighten his ass, then yours. Your man I will respect, because you threw it at me from the beginning. Outside of that, you're mine, and I'll handle that shit just like you my girl. Do you understand?"

"Yes," she said in the softest, sweetest voice. Then she cuddled into my arms and laid her head on my chest and fell back to sleep.

The next morning she was in the shower, when I looked in her closet and checked the size of her clothes and shoes. I yelled to her that I would return in a few minutes and ran out to Coliseum Mall. I stopped at Hecht's and picked her up an outfit and shoes. But I couldn't leave out without grabbing a phat-ass Nautica shirt for myself.

I returned to the crib and sat the things on the couch. After putting lotion on her beautiful body and laying her down once more, we took another long shower together.

When I gave her the outfit and shoes, she was all smiles.

"You dress all your women?"

"No. Only the ones I feel something for, and you are definitely a special friend. Feel like spending the day with me and taking a ride to DC?"

"Sure. I'll go anywhere with you, baby," she said with a smirk, giving me a kiss on the cheek.

We went to Cracker Barrels for breakfast. Afterwards I decided to show her she was fuckin' with a real niggah.

Before getting into the car she handed me a key—"This is if you want to surprise me and I'm not home. You can still get in."

"Sounds good. But sometimes, baby, I already be on this side," I said, taking her key.

"Really? Where at?" she asked.

"You'll see," I said. I kept driving and turned into the Oyster Point section and into the driveway of my phat shit, or Black's shit.

"Damn, this is a nice place," she said. "Who lives here?"

"I do sometimes. I bought it for investment property but haven't been able to rent it out yet."

We walked inside, and by her facial expression, I could tell she was in love. The island in the kitchen, the marble foyer and fireplace, but the Italian leather would fuck with anybody's head who wasn't used to it.

"Dee, I am impressed. I dream of having a beautiful home like this one day," she said.

"And you will. You taking the necessary steps to get right now."

"True," she said, still exploring the picture-perfect house.

I hit the garage door opener, so I could pull the Q45 in the garage. "Come on out, so I can set the alarm."

When I pulled out the garage with the Porsche 911, she stood there looking fucked up. She knew she was fuckin' with a real niggah, no doubt. She just didn't know how fuckin' real my little brother was.

She got in, and we hit 264, headed to Washington, DC.

She didn't say a word for about thirty minutes then out of nowhere asked, "What do you do?"

"I own a sports bar."

"No. How did you get your sports bar?"

Usually I don't play "bitches questioning me," but

I was looking at her in a different light and wanted to be straight up. But being honest could get Black in some shit, and nothing in the world was worth that.

"Through real estate investments. I play real hard, but I work even harder, Okay. Are you all right now, baby?"

"Yes, Dee, I'm all right."

I leaned over, gave her a kiss, then ran that Porsche like a bat out of hell, straight into Georgetown. Then ran her ass back, only to slow down around the Richmond area. Niggahs was always getting knocked off, running shit from DC to Richmond. I wasn't running "dirty," but I didn't have time for the bullshit.

When we returned, she confessed that she was scared as hell and had never gone that fast before in her life. I just laughed, but I didn't think I had either.

The next several months were very profitable. In over a year's time, we had two corporations holding assets worth over four hundred thousand and over two hundred thousand in three safes. The sports bar was the city's new hangout. We were pulling people from P-town, Hampton, and Norfolk, and New York kids who had come in town to politic were meeting niggahs there on a daily. I realized that I was introducing pool to a lot of kids in the area, and for that I always kept a crowd.

One night I had just got back to E's Cue from the condo in Cypress Point. This young girl who attended Norfolk State lived behind the sports bar in Newpointe Condos. She had been coming in quite often, and we always found time to throw jokes at one another. This particular night I needed to run to the condo, and she came along. I sparked a blunt on the way and found out that she got down.

We ended up stopping at Ming Wah in the shopping center for a bite to eat, then the crib. I sparked another L and began to massage her shoulder and rub her back. Surprisingly, I got a response that I wasn't even expecting—she closed her eyes, relaxed her shoulders, and opened the door for me to continue. We got down and afterwards headed back to the bar.

Black was coming in with some girl, as I was leaving. I knew I'd see him back at the spot.

When we walked in the place was packed. The kids who called themselves the Lost Boyz had two tables, RJ and his peoples had two tables, Rock peoples— Buc and El—had two tables, and Houdini and Muhammed had a table.

This Jamaican kid named Big D had four tables. He had brought several niggahs from Tidewater Park in with him. He had moved from Brooklyn into the projects and was making young niggahs rich. Two of his main workers he put on were LL and Tite; they were on the table shooting pool with him. LL and Tite were known throughout Norfolk since they were in high school. They blew up slowly. Then out of nowhere, the cream began to flow.

Not far from these kids was the guy in the wheelchair. He was always shaking dice and ready to gamble. I noticed that, whenever I saw him, he was always with two guys. One was this small kid from the islands. I didn't know him, but I'd heard him talk several times and couldn't understand shit he was saying. He was a little niggah, quick to step into somebody shit. I never seen no one fuck with him, but I heard he was quick to pull his shit, just like my cousin Lo. And the niggah had paper.

Black came in carrying boxes of bathroom cleaner. I went into the office, where he was pulling weed out of the boxes. He had bought three pounds from Rock for fifteen hundred and had it all bagged in ounces. He said he was going to sell ounces for hundred apiece and come off lovely.

"Niggahs going to pay hundred apiece for an *O*?" I asked.

"Yeah, if they want it. If they don't, fuck 'em," he said. "Selling *O's* will keep down the flow of traffic. Whenever niggahs can come and get shit and not have to go look for it, they'll be back."

Just then Muhammed knocked at the door. "Yo, Black, niggahs want to know if you want to house a Cee-lo game?"

"How much house usually get?" Black asked.

"Usually five percent."

Black looked at me, confused. He didn't really know the game, but I knew that five percent was five percent of the bank.

"Give us a few. I'll be out in a second," I added.

After talking with Black, he realized that we would come off, as long as the bank stayed phat.

"Everything sounds good, but if the man come up in our shit, we'll be shut down. Not to mention, if any of those niggahs got drugs, guns, or whatever, they're going to drop that shit on the floor or the pockets of the pool tables," I mentioned.

"Shit, if the man come in this bitch, we got more shit to worry about than that. You forget about the guns in the back, drugs in the ceiling, and this shit sitting in front of you. Shit. I don't know. Fuck it, niggah. We can't get paid being paranoid. Yo, check this thought—house gets ten percent, or fuck them niggahs—they ain't feeding our peoples."

I told Muhammed, and they agreed. They didn't like it, but they agreed.

After closing up I pulled the shades down. The

guys who weren't playing had to go. Their presence made the players uncomfortable, and I wanted them to bring out all the cash and bet it up. I took paper towels and stuffed it in the pockets of the pool table. As I double-checked the doors, I realized that only Acuras, Lexuses, Infinitis, Beamers, and Benz were parked in the lot.

One of the guys asked if they could spark a blunt. I told him, as long as he passed it along. Other kids were mad because they didn't have weed. Needless to say, we ended up selling about nine ounces.

The guy in the wheelchair started the bank off with five hundred, and it wasn't an hour and the bank was four thousand. RJ took a thousand; Houdini took a thousand; Muhammed took a thousand; and so did Big D.

The bank came out and rolled trips. House got four hundred off the roll.

Another hour passed and house had twelve hundred. The next thirty minutes house had accumulated three grand, watching the bank rise and fall, but house percent stayed the same.

Going into the third hour, the bank was about eight thousand. The kid in the wheelchair was losing; he decided to only bet a thousand, and LL and Tite was betting together and put up three thousand. Rock boy, El, took the other four gran', bank rolled an ace, and house got nothing.

By five in the morning, house had over five gran', and shit was getting hype. Niggahs had started arguing over petty shit. RJ, Houdini, Muhammed, El, and Big D were the only ones left playing. Houdini had sent his bodyguard to his Maxima to get a bag of loot. Rock had run to the Lincoln and got mad stacks of paper for El.

All within thirty minutes the bank rose to fourteen

thousand, with El holding the bank. RJ took four thousand, as Houdini, Muhammed got two, and Big D got ends. Bank rolled four, and bets started flying on "four better."

After everyone rolled, the bank was up twenty gran'. Houdini stuck the bank and lost. Bank rose to forty gran'; RJ, Big D, and Muhammed each took ten. The bank rolled an ace and was left with ten gran'. Big D stuck that and became the bank, holding twenty gran'. Muhammed took ten, and so did RJ.

RJ lost and quit, leaving only Muhammed and Big D. They played back and forth for a few until Muhammed had the bank up to twenty-three thou'.

Big D kept trying to bet low, until Muhammed argued the fact, "Niggah, you ain't gonna nickel and dime the fuckin' bank—bet it up or quit."

"This my goddamn money. Not a motherfucker is going to tell me how to fuckin' bet my shit. *Bloodclaat!*" Big D said.

We could barely understand his thick Jamaican accent. The arguing began, and each one began to involve their peoples.

Houdini yelled, "That shit is on house—what is the fuckin' house rules?"

"Got to bet at least five gran'. That's a quarter bank. House rest!" I said quickly.

"Fuck that shit," Big D yelled. "I'm going to end all this bullshit and break all you broke-ass niggahs." Then came the words that all niggahs who play Ceelo love to hear, except for the bank: "Stick that shit, niggah. I'm leaving with forty-six G's tonight."

Things got quiet. Muhammed shook the dice and threw them.

"I got those," Big D yelled.

The call was good, and everyone watched the triple

fives hit the pool table. Niggahs fell on the ground in agony. Big D smiled at the fact that he caught that roll.

Muhammed began to shake the dice again in complete silence, and then he let them go. "Four-five-six," Muhammed yelled as the dice stopped rolling.

"How the fuck a niggah roll Cee-lo following goddamn trips?" Big D yelled as he stormed out the sports bar.

Everyone followed.

Muhammed threw me three gran' on the way out the door, either showing respect for the house, or because house fell in his favor when they were arguing. He never said; I never asked. But we both knew we didn't owe each other anything.

One night, five hours, we had made over ten G's. This instantly became an everyweek thing. At first I wondered why they didn't just play on the corner or at someone's house, but they needed that neutral party to put down the law when shit became heated. And shit heats up every time.

It didn't take long before Black got hooked on the game. None of them really knew Black, except for Muhammed. And after playing with Black for weeks, they still didn't know him, but they respected his pocket.

Black didn't care for RJ's style. He said that RJ and Big D had some shit with them. From that point on I made sure Boot was up there too, never knowing when some shit might spark off.

One particular night the game had gotten real intense. RJ and Black had words over a gran'. Black stood ground, and RJ said he wasn't going to beef over a thousand dollars that wasn't shit to him.

That same night one of the New York kids stuck the bank, with Black holding it. Bank was four thousand. After the point was seen, the kid yelled, "No bet."

Black let the kid know that it was too late. Words were exchanged, and Black told the guy that, if he didn't have the money, he should just say so and shit would be left alone.

The kid told Black that if he had it he still wouldn't pay him.

A few pool cues were broke, a few stools were thrown, then several blows. Seconds later, I was pulling Black out the niggah ass. The kid folded up and whimpered like a bitch.

The next day we had niggahs deep in E's Cue. Boot, Bo, and myself was inside, strapped. Black and Lo had the big guns and were in the back with bullet-proofs on, waiting for some shit to happen, and excited about it. That evening about six men—two in suits—came in, introducing themselves as detectives.

I was like, "This kid done sent fucking DTs to my shit. All the shit I had going on inside this place, and he sends the police to my shit."

I stopped at the Blue Light on Brambleton that night, all the kids asking what the fuck happened at my spot. Beef travels fast. He had told kids that me and Black beat him down. But I straighten that shit and let niggahs know he sent the man to my shit, and Black beat that niggah ass by himself. We never seen the niggah no more. He was now a fuckin' outcast for breaking the number one rule—Never involve the police.

CHAPTER 13

"Big-time Politics"

Jacqueline's brother came out of his drought, and Black instantly cut RJ off. Lo didn't mind because now Black had his shit back. He didn't have to score no more; all he had to do was get it when it came into the warehouse. Black got real tight with Rock. Rock and his crew even invited Black to swing with them to the Soul Train Music Awards. They ended up getting silk suits made, and running Up Top to get jewels and ice for the occasion. When he came back, he had gotten an iced-out Rolex and a necklace of the same design with an iced-out medallion on the end.

Rock had turned him on to Rande'z. He dealt in selling luxury cars with many hidden assets. Rande'z had a 600 SEL that was almost finished. I Federal Expressed him a check for forty grand out of B&D Corp; all Black had to do was bring his Lex in as a trade. He told me to call the Marriott in Atlanta, on Peachtree, and make reservations for Jack the Rapper, that was coming up. I had heard of it but had never been. He said without a doubt in his mind that he was going to have his 600 to shine in the ATL. Rock and his peoples, Butt Naked Production, were having a pool party set for that Saturday night in the Marriott and E's Cue had VIP.

I was supposed to meet Monique at the condo by 8:00 p.m. We were going to have dinner at Alexander by the Bay, a restaurant that sat on the water of Chesapeake Bay, on Shore Drive.

We had been seeing each other for months, and her boyfriend had only been in town once, to stay for the weekend. Before he'd come in town, she was telling me that she was going to have to break the contract or leave me alone. She was starting to break her number one rule and fall in love. I felt that she was really attracted to me, and she kept being with me every day, talking to me non-stop about everything, making love to me at least five times a week and sometimes twice a day.

I knew, with her man many miles away, it was just a matter of time before she broke. The thing was, I didn't have a girl, didn't want a girl, but had given all my attention to her. I felt she was mine. She acted like she was mine, but I wasn't in love.

After dinner I decided I wanted to do something different, so we got a room at the Virginia Beach Resort. The evening fell perfectly. We began to really open up to one another. As we weren't in a relationship, it was easier for us to express ourselves.

Over the months, she had taken the time to explore every inch of my body, learning it inside out. She knew exactly what excited me, what turned me on, and how to make me cum, even when I tried to hold back.

We woke up in each other's arms, and with just one movement of her ass, I was hard again. I reached down and raised her right leg a little, easing in from the back. She moved and matched my every rhythm. She then rolled me over and rode the pony until she came, her body shaking in my arms.

She rolled back, and, as I turned on top of her, opened her legs, threw her head and hands back, and let me enjoy her love. When she felt she was going to cum again, she lifted her head to my chest, took her arms and hugged me under my shoulders so tight as to let no air get between us. Then she pushed her knees out and her ass up to give me every bit of that wet pussy.

In seconds, we came together.

She squeezed me tight and began to cry. "I know I'm breaking the contract," she said crying, "but I love you, Dee." She just hugged me real tight as if she was never going to let me go.

We ate breakfast and talked for hours, conversation between us never seeming to be a problem. It was like we had just met and had a thousand things to talk about. While sitting there I began to stare into her eyes and go deep into thought. She was my friend, my lover, and I had yet to find a woman to match up to her credentials. She was like mine; but she wasn't. Another niggah could come in and take it all away at any time.

We left Thursday, headed for Atlanta for Jack the Rapper, all of us rolling down 85 South like a convoy of Big Willies. Big G and I were leading the pack in the 740iL. Black and Boot was behind us in the new 600SEL, no rims, just thirty-five percent tint. Lo was four deep in the new burgundy GS300 sitting on chrome, with thirty-five percent tint. Derrick, Dante, and Bo had Lo car smoked up from VA to ATL. Big G and I rolled eight blunts and had over a half-ounce packed away in the trunk.

We arrived in Atlanta around 1:30 a.m. When we

pulled around on Peachtree, to the Marriott, the streets were full, and niggahs were definitely staring at the fleet of luxury that whipped by.

"Goddamn," G said, "I like this shit here."

"No joke. This weekend is going to be the shit."

"We can act the motherfuckin' fool out here. Niggahs don't know us. All they know is that major players from VA have arrived."

"Peep the motherfuckin' tags, niggah! Peep the motherfuckin' tags!" niggahs yelled, getting hype.

"Big G knew we were making plenty of paper and he knew all that I was doing and some of what Black and Lo was into. He knew he was rolling with major players in the game, but he didn't know he was also rolling with hard-core killers. I remembered his reaction, when I told him that Black and I had forty gran' on our head. He just said that he better start packing his shit because, as much as he was with us, if anything kicked off he'd definitely be caught in the crossfire. From that point on I knew that he wasn't only my partner, but my motherfuckin' niggah 'til the end.

We parked the cars in front and got out to go check in. Mad niggahs were outside trying to get into the hotel. Only thing was without a pass, you were "ass out." Several shows were going on and many stars were inside, so you had to be registered in the hotel to get inside.

"This shit is off the hook," Lo said. "Check these niggahs out, squatting on these out-of-state tags. Hope I didn't come all the way down South to straighten a niggah."

We all began to laugh as if it was a joke, but we knew it could become a reality in a split second if any niggah showed out. Just then Rock and Big Wolf came outside and began to show us mad love. We all talked for a few, and they informed us that the International Hair Show was going on across the street in the Hyatt, wall-to-wall bitches everywhere. We went inside and checked then sneaked passes out to Derrick and Dante. Since we only had two rooms, we worked it out so that there were three guests in each.

Once inside you were at the party, and Norfolk was definitely in the fuckin' house. We started running into kids from Tidewater Park, Park Place, and mad niggahs from Kappatal Kuts. You could feel the difference, because at the crib we would just speak and keep going, if that. But being out of town, everybody was representing VA, Norfolk niggahs, and that made us all on the same team. Everybody was hollering at bitches and smoking blunts, passing the budda to niggahs you didn't even know but had seen in Military Circle one time or another.

The next day we woke up to the weed in the air. Lo knocked on our door to find out what time we were trying to eat. Lo and his peoples were in a room and G, Black, Boot and myself were in another. Everybody stretched across the beds, on the floor, in the chair. No one cared; we were there to have a good time.

After eating we headed to the infamous Underground that we had heard so much about. The downtown crowd reminded me of Freaknic: Everybody hanging out, and girls running around with everything exposed, making niggahs with fifty-thousand-dollar cars beg for ass.

The malls were impressive; several of the top designers had stores in Atlanta, not just bits of clothing in the stores. We did very little shopping, because our objective was to see which of these bitches was down for going back to the Marriott.

Later we ended up at Magic City to check out the strippers. We knew we weren't in VA, when we saw

butt-naked bitches all up in our face. This was a lot
different from the crib, and I realized that we could
go broke fuckin' around in this place. We were
throwing cash around like we were buying pussy.

All of us had paid a crackhead bitch to suck niggahs' dick at one time or another. But we considered
ourselves players, and players don't just outright buy
pussy; we get it in a roundabout way.

When we reached the hotel, it was chaotic. We had
to park in a nearby parking lot. Peachtree, between
the Hyatt and the Marriott, was packed, and people
were not trying to move. We found our way through
the crowd; then I saw what appeared to be a familiar
face. I thought I knew her but could not figure out
where. Then it hit.

"Monya," I said.

She began to look around. "Hey, how are you?"
she asked.

"Great, baby. Great," I said smiling, catching the
attention of her four friends. They were five deep
and all of them were looking like dimes. Their shit
was well put-together, and they had on gear revealing
every curve of their goddess-like physiques.

"Black and Lo here with you?" Sarah asked.

"Yeah, they're over there going in the hotel."

"You know I gots to see my boo," Monya said.

"Oh, Dee, this is Chantel, Gloria, and Gwen."

Gloria and Gwen were sisters that had come in
from Cleveland. They flew in to meet Monya and
Sarah in Atlanta. Chantel was from Detroit but now
lived in Charlotte. She had graduated from Howard
University in DC, but was now working in Charlotte,
NC. She had driven down to meet her crew.

"Nice to meet you all. What's your name again?—
Chantel? I like that," I said, staring directly into her
eyes to let her know of my interest.

Chantel stood about 5' 4", with a flawless pecan-brown complexion and long braids. She was dressed sexy, but not revealing. The short skirt she wore showed her sexy brown legs, and her sleeveless button top was open to her cleavage. She had the most beautiful breasts, which I could see through her champagne-colored lace bra. This made me wonder if she had on panties to match.

We wandered towards the front door of the hotel. Black was inside but quickly came out when he saw us.

"What's up, girl?" he asked, grabbing Monya and hugging her, then Sarah.

"Nothing, boo," Monya said.

"Why you didn't call us and let us know you were coming down?" Sarah asked.

"This was some old spur-of-the-moment shit," Lo said, interrupting. "Where y'all staying?"

"We're over at the Sheraton. It's sold out over there, but everybody seems to be hanging over here," Gwen said.

"Because this is where the motherfuckin' party at," G blurted.

We started laughing.

"You right, big man, but we can't get in the motherfuckin' party," Monya said.

"Roll with us, baby," Black said, walking towards the door.

We had a few problems, but fast talking and a few twenties got them inside, where everybody wanted to be. Lo and his crew went into the conference room, where a show was going on. Gloria, Gwen and Sarah followed them. The rest of us stood out, talking and checking out the surroundings.

Then we saw Jam Master Jay strolling through the crowd, searching for talent and whatever else caught his interest. We all went upstairs to the restaurant for drinks.

I sat at the bar next to Chantel, still wanting to know if she had on champagne panties to match her bra. The thought of it had a niggah turned on. There were mad bitches around me, but this bitch had all my interest. Conversation moved slowly. And she was answering my questions short and direct, as if she wasn't really pressed to talk. But my name was Dee, and my brother was Black. Bitches don't turn us away, or maybe somebody didn't tell her.

"Dee, tell me something, will you?" Chantel asked. "Why are you focusing all your attention over here, with all these attractive women here? Why me?"

"Why not you?" I asked. "I came here to have a good time, to get away from all the headaches of my business in VA. All day I run non-stop, with all kinds of shit to do and my brain being worked overtime. And you may not believe me, but I have no one to help me relax and re-group for the following day. So that stress just continues to roll over."

"Yeah, right," she said and began sipping her cranberry and Absolut.

"I'm serious. Then I come here, and I meet such a sweet, attractive woman, and she's not trying to be my friend. Now tell me, why is that? Do you have a man that's so insecure he can't handle us being friends?"

"Actually, I haven't had a man in my life for seven months."

"Seven months since you been with a man, or seven months since one has played a part in your life?"

"Both," she said quickly. "And, to let you know, when I'm in a relationship, the last thing my man has to worry about is feeling insecure. I make sure of that. I was in a relationship for three years, when I graduated from Howard. I had job offers in DC and in Charlotte. I decided to go to Charlotte because my man wanted to go there. We weren't there six months, and he had gotten another bitch pregnant. You tell me—how trifling can a niggah get?"

"Hold up. Don't classify us all in the same category. We aren't all bad. Give me a chance, and maybe I can build up the good guys' credibility," I said, taking her hand.

She seemed real sweet, so I changed the conversation. I didn't want her to start thinking about past shit and fuck up my groove.

We were all disturbed by the confusion going on in the corner. Treach of Naughty by Nature was beefing with YZ, and it looked as if shit might get out of hand. Other people started gathering to see what was going on, but where we from, if niggahs start, arguing, you look and see if it's your peoples. And if it's not, it's time to be out.

We left and were going down the stairs, when we saw another crowd of people, as if some more shit was going on. We realized that it was three young ladies singing for Michael Bivens of New Edition.

"Look at these bitches singing for Michael Bivins," G said.

"All on that niggah dick. Fuck him," Boot said.

"They might get a record deal," Monya added.

"Got to have faith in these hookers," Black said. "Bitches have to have something positive in their life to believe in, no doubt."

After they finished, the crowd began to applaud. They weren't professionals, but they definitely had skills.

The girls went their own way, and we went back to the room. The hallways were packed, people laid out everywhere. They knew once they left they weren't getting back in the hotel. We figured we had time to spark a few *L*'s before the pool party.

There was a knock at the door. Lo entered the room with five bitches he'd met downstairs, five free-loading bitches ready to smoke. We rolled a couple extra blunts. And just as we thought, they talked a good game but couldn't hang with the big dogs. They were local girls going to Spellman. They gave us the run-down on the clubs to check out, but we had no interest in clubbing, while surrounded by some of the finest bitches on the East Coast right in the hotel.

We left Dante, Lo, and G in the room with three of the girls, while we went to check out the pool party. When we arrived, we felt eyes fall on the crew. Tommy and Polo swim trunks, gold chains iced-out, hanging from our necks, and the females were definitely on our dick. The girls were running around in bikinis and thongs. Even the one-piece French cut shits were off the hook.

I'd never seen so many bitches in my life. Niggahs were like kids let loose in a candy store, with plenty of money to buy whatever the fuck they wanted. The party had just got going, when niggahs started beef-ing. It ended after a little scuffle and some kids flash-ing their steel.

Everyone went back downstairs, where they had a DJ rocking in the conference room. The hotel itself became a club.

I got with Chantel and talked her into going to the room. We relaxed awhile, and I tried my hardest to get her to give into me and share her love or just let a niggah hit. Either way I would have been satisfied.

After pulling shit from everywhere and giving her some of my best shit, I realized that it wasn't going to happen. We exchanged numbers, and she swore up and down that I wasn't going to call. Little did she know, I had peeped the fact that she had her shit established and carried herself like a real woman. She reminded me of Jacqueline, and that was something I could handle.

The next day we were packing things in the car, when we ran into Rock and El.

"The pool party was nice, kid," I said.

"Yeah, until simple motherfuckers fucked it up as usual," El added.

"Leaving now?" Rock asked.

"Yeah, got to get on back to Norfolk, son. Got shit to check on," I explained.

"Check this shit out, Black," Rock said.

Then El cut in and began to talk to Black on the low, "I want you to be safe, god. You remind me of myself when I got started in the game too many years ago. Flashy cars, jewelry, shit like that. That's all good, but when you're at the crib, fuck that shit. I got a crib in New York and a beach house in VA. I drive a 740, and I got the big Benz shit. But I'm getting ready to retire from the business.

"I'm talking to you now because I'm through with Norfolk. When I came to Norfolk I brought a strong clique, but now I'm jetting. Some of my niggahs are staying, but me, my man and Rock, we're out. Listen, I been locked before, and word to my mother, it will never happen again. You have to be careful. You niggahs think Norfolk big because it has a lot going on and money is there. But it's small compared to Harlem or Brooklyn. Niggahs get jealous and run their mouths like bitches—and that's the shit that gets you caught up. Be careful and be safe," he said before walking off.

"Listen to him, fellows," Rock said to Black and me. "That kid got mad knowledge of this game, and he's been around. He's good at making judgment calls. He told us that niggahs in Norfolk are living real foul and it was time to go."

"When you all plan on breaking out?" I asked.

"We already gone, son. We packed all our shit before coming here. Norfolk is in the past. Here is the kid's number in Hampton. I'm gonna let him know you're good peoples, so he'll straighten you on the weed tip. You niggahs, take care. Peace and love, baby."

CHAPTER 14

"Bad Vibes"

We arrived in Norfolk, our pagers blowing off the hook. We dropped niggahs off at the sports bar then put the cars up. I took Lo's Acura. Lo and Black took off.

As soon as I got in, I called Chantel. I knew she wasn't home yet, but I just wanted to let her know that she was on my mind, coming back. I wanted her to know that I wanted to hear from her real soon and that she had to come to Virginia Beach to spend a weekend. I thought of flying her to Norfolk on a Friday, showing her a nice time here then getting up Saturday, flying to New York for a little shopping, dinner at Sylvia's, and back to 39th and Broadway, on the king size at the Marriott Marquis, downtown Manhattan, suite 1112. Then she'd know she was fuckin' with a real niggah, not a fake-ass player.

After getting a drink and rolling a blunt, I picked up the phone to call Monique. She quickly let me know that her man was in town, but was leaving in a couple hours.

I actually got an attitude, but I dealt with it. I had strong feelings for her, and this boyfriend shit was getting ready to end. I knew I was giving her much more time and had her head and heart. Now it was time for him to say, "Big Dee is taking over."

I called Shante, who was all upset because her child support hadn't come through and her light bill was due the following day. I had been fucking this girl for a while now and had never given her more than a hundred dollars. After going all weekend with no ass—just freaking 'ho's—I had to have it. I called her back to let her know I would be over in a few and we would go to the bank to get a hundred twenty in the morning. I planned to forget my ID and only have fifty dollars in my pocket.

After leaving the next day, I figured her lights weren't in anymore danger of going off than I was of going broke.

I was in the pool, with two steaks on the grill, when Black came in and said, "What's up, fool?"

"Not a thing, kid."

"You here by yourself?"

"Yeah, fuck those bitches," I said, getting out of the pool. "That's how I feel today."

"Who is the other steak for, fool?"

"Me, niggah. I'm starving."

"I'm going to throw some corn on, but one of those shits is mine."

We went into the game room and started playing pool. He gave me a rundown on how shit was going.

I let him know exactly how much money I had cleaned up and what was being put away so we could retire one day. "I had to lower the cost on the phones. A lot of the kids from Up Top are doing the same thing now, so I had to come down to compete. I definitely see the difference," I said.

"What about the IDs?" he asked.

"That's still all good. Niggahs don't have connects like that."

"Why? Do you need some paper?"

"Naw, I'm straight. But I do want to trade in the Range to get something cheaper and bigger."

"What's that?"

"Land Cruiser—I like those big motherfuckers," I said.

"Why don't you trade in the 'Vette with it? You don't hardly drive it anyway."

"You right. Plus I got the Porsche."

"Shit. That's my baby, niggah," he said laughing. "Oh yeah, why the fuck you leave that shit on *E*? Keep gas in that shit. I don't need trash getting in the tank. The crib we have in Ghent, get rid of that shit. We don't need it."

"You hear about that kid who got shot at The Bridge this past weekend?" I asked.

"They're going to close that bitch down. Just a month ago, kids were shooting in the parking lot."

"As long as they keep that shit away from E's Cue," I said.

"Don't hot up our shit. Goddamn, I forgot to ask you. Those kids I fuck with from Hampton are having a party at the Radisson in Hampton this Saturday. They asked if I wanted to come check it out, semi-formal. Bring a hooker if you want, but bitches are going to be there. What's up?"

"I'm down. Who is going with you?"

"Shereena, probably, I ain't fuckin' with Tia like that no more. That reminds me—Monique came by the spot looking for you. She said will you please call her. She said she been trying to catch up with you for three days."

"She will be all right. Tired of the drama that bitch bringing,"

"I talked to Monya. She said her girl really likes you."

"Shit. She don't like me but so much—she didn't fuck a niggah."

"Naw, actually she wanted to get with you. But Monya said she didn't want to play herself."

"Just because she fuck a niggah doesn't mean she ain't shit; it's what she does afterwards—ain't none of these bitches shit."

"From what they tell me, the hooker has been through some shit, but the girl is real chill. The bitch got a good job, don't hang out a lot, and she plays fair. She called her crew and told them you left some sweet shit on her machine. You ain't slick, fool," Black said.

"Maybe I'll call her to tell her to come this weekend. Take her to that shit them Hampton niggahs planning and see how she likes it."

We sat around and kicked it until late. After a few drinks and a couple of L's, the next time I opened my eyes, the Preview Channel was watching me, and the sun was coming up.

Black broke out to take care of some business and never came back. I fell back to sleep.

When I woke up it was 10:30 a.m., and I had to open the spot up at 11:00 a.m. I jumped in the shower to handle my shit real quick. I threw on the new Guess work jeans, red Tommy Hilfilger T-shirt, and the old faithful Timberlands. I jumped in the Range Rover and headed out.

I reached the sports bar, and Lite and Smalls were out front.

"What's up, son?" Lite asked.

"Nothing, kid. What's going on?"

"Motherfuckin' crackers done put a lock on our shit," Smalls said.

"What?"

"Paper was taped to the door, talking about some tax shit. Lite got to go down to the courthouse to see what the fuck is going on."

"If they're trying to find out where the paper came from to open this shit, I ain't fuckin' with it," Lite added quickly.

"Let's just go see, son. If that's it then we out of VA, kid. Crackers got too much shit with them here anyway. Just mad shit been happening since we been here," Smalls said.

They came inside and made some calls. I wanted to know what was going on just in case I was faced with that shit. They left intending to come back later.

I was setting things up, when Monique came in with a very serious look on her face. She was upset because I hadn't returned her pages since I called her this past weekend.

"Hello, lady. How are you?"

"I'm fine. The question is, 'how are you?' "

"So what's the problem?" she asked. "I've paged you and even tried to catch up with you. Let me know something."

"I've been busy. A niggah's work load increases from time to time."

"Am I going to see you later? I'm missing you," she said in the softest, sweetest, whining tone.

I couldn't do shit but give in.

Then she had to get back to class. She had come all the way across the Water just to make amends with me. She cared, and I knew she did. Knowing another kid could come in at anytime and hit what was mine didn't sit right with me anymore. Either, he had to go or I had to go. It was beginning to fuck with me.

* * *

I tried calling Chantel, but she was at work. I left a message, and she called back soon after.

"Hello," I said, answering the phone.

"Yes. May I speak to Dee?"

"This him. Who this?

"Chantel. How are you?"

"Fine, baby. And yourself?" I replied, excitement in my voice.

"I'm Okay. Same old things, different day."

"Look here. I want you to come here this week-end. Some of my peoples having a little something, and I would like for you to be on my arm. It's a semi-formal affair."

"Dee, I will be honest with you. I would love to, but my car needs two new tires. I don't have any extra money to come there or to get anything for a formal function. Your timing is a little off. Maybe another weekend," she said.

"By 3:00 p.m., there will be some money at Western Union. Get your tires, some gas, and when you get here, I'll introduce you to Hampton Roads. We have six malls, all within twenty minutes of my house. We'll find you something. And if we can't, we have a thousand boutiques at the Beach and Downtown Norfolk. So you have no excuse."

"You're right," she said.

"So I'll see you tomorrow evening?" I asked.

"Look for me about 8:30 p.m. tomorrow evening."

Before I could hang up the phone, Smalls came in beefing about them locking his club's doors. The city explained the tax laws to them and said they were under investigation. They had to come up with W-2 forms for the previous years. Lite said he wasn't fuckin' with it and the club could stay closed as far as he was concerned. He couldn't chance it.

The doors never opened back up, and the same crowd began to hang over at David's in Portsmouth. David's had started getting Biz Markie to DJ on Sundays and was a little more lenient with the dress code.

One night, some kids began to bum rush the door and tore it off the hinges. The security got a little rugged and roughed up some kids. Moments later the kids rolled down High Street and began letting off in niggahs. Glass shattered, two security guys lay dead, and one innocent young lady was hit. She was confined to a wheelchair for the rest of her life. David's was no more. The city shut it down and boarded the doors.

The club across from the sports bar that used to be for suit-and-tie niggahs was now changing their crowd. The owner of the club came over to the sports bar and hung up flyers, letting the crowd know he was changing things. He realized that Bob Fields, the man that owned Broadway, had the twenty-five-year-old and older crowd locked down.

The only way to make money was to get The Bridge crowd and David's crowd.

Ray, the operator of Mr. Magic's, was trying to change his club into the new hip-hop club of Tidewater. There hadn't been too many hip-hop clubs, and his timing was perfect. The Bridge was closed, and there was nowhere for young niggahs making money to hang out and shine.

I started networking with the owner of all the clubs so they would advertise E's Cue to help me put it on the map. It worked because business was still flowing and money was still stacking.

I was getting ready to go wire Chantel some paper, when Black and Lo pulled up in the Honda. I knew then that they were getting ready to handle business or had just finished.

They both jumped out. I could tell by their facial expressions they weren't in the mood for joking and playing.

"I should've pulled that niggah wig back when I saw him at the Blue Light," Lo said.

"I don't give a fuck. Wherever I see those niggahs, I'm blasting," Black said. "How the fuck is that bitch niggah going to tell my girl's mom that my time is over? Derrick and his brothers lived out the way all that time. They move to Jersey and think they going to make moves here and fuck up my cheddar. I be goddamn."

"Check this shit out, Black," Lo said. "I'm going to give the order that if anybody come out the Lake trying to sell and they not on our team, I'll pay two G's to the niggah who does the most damage."

"I got half of that," Black said. "Make sure you put that word out today."

Evidently Derrick Bowles and his brother were back in town and had made connects in Jersey with some major players. Derrick was my age and had three brothers. One a year under him had been in all kinds of shit. The niggah didn't give a fuck, as a kid, about anything or anybody. Word was, he had never changed.

The other two were Ronald and Reggie, twins. These two had been put out of the school system real early and had been in and out of detention homes since age eleven. These two cats were inseparable. You would very rarely see one without the other.

Together the brothers had built a reputation for not being fucked with.

Black didn't give two fucks about their family because we had our own. Black also knew that those niggahs had heart. Only thing was, with those Jersey niggahs backing them, they had a strong-ass clique.

After wiring the money, I decided to ride by Kline Toyota and run some numbers. The Toyota dealer off the Boulevard was talking straight out his ass. I guess he took me as a big-time hustler who didn't give a fuck about spending money. I splurged a lot and bought a lot of shit I didn't really need. I watched my dollars, and you got it if I wanted you to have it. But you weren't going to beat me for it.

At Kline, I met a real chill sales lady named Melody. She not only looked out, but she taught me a few things and became a close business associate. I ended up trading in the 'Vette and the Range for a pretty burgundy Land Cruiser. I left the lot and went straight to Street Sounds on Monticello Avenue, downtown.

I knew my man Kenny Bug would have the Land banging so hard niggahs would hear it over at the naval shipyard. He ran an Alpine CD player, with an Alpine pre-amp, with two Punch amps, pushing four twelve-inch JL Audio twelves. I was standing outside waiting for Monique to scoop me up to hang, while Kenny finished up my shit. I knew it was going to be a while.

This girl and guy came walking by that looked so familiar to me. They were looking real bad, and I knew I didn't fuck with no crackheads. As I stared I realized it was Cheri and Tevin, two kids that came out of school a year before I did.

I remembered Cheri as a cute-ass girl with a loud fuckin' mouth. When she was in the tenth grade, she

had the body of a woman. Not just any woman, but a
woman who had a couple kids and big-ass titties that
drooped. She was always known to fuck quick, not
having the best reputation. Now that I thought about
it, she probably just needed a stronger bra. Her ass
was phat as hell, but she carried herself in a way that
guys screamed at her on the low, not in front of their
crew.

Tevin was one of those guys that was supposed to
be all that. Captain of the football team, basketball
and track star, he was what the girls in school wanted.
Now here he was, with this other trifling-ass bitch,
roaming through Norfolk, trying to find out where
their next hit was coming from.

"Hey, Dee," Cheri said smiling.

I stood there staring at her without saying a word.

"What's happening, man?" Tevin asked, as if we
were friends.

I looked at him with disgust.

"Can we get a ride out Burton Station, man?" he
asked.

"I'm not driving. I'm waiting on a ride myself," I
said.

"Loan me ten dollars, Dee," Cheri said.

"Fuck I look like? I'm supposed to just give you ten
dollars? Come on," I said, going into the bathroom
on the side.

She came in, and I let her suck my dick until cum
was dripping down her chin and chest.

I felt bad afterwards because I should've been trying to help her instead of shifting on her. In school,
she didn't fuck with me and acted like a niggah wasn't
shit. Some things you never forget, and payback is a
bitch.

I arrived back at E's Cue, where it looked like a
party was going on. I went inside and allowed Monique

to sit behind the counter with me. Ce-Ce and her crew came in. Her girl came up talking as if Monique wasn't even there. I didn't care too much for the disrespect, but what could I say. I was realizing that being a ghetto celebrity had its benefits, but it also had its problems. It kept girls coming my way, and sex was never a problem. But so much drama. Bitches running their mouth, niggahs jealous because of the 'ho's I was fuckin', and that kept shit going. I remember girls coming in, asking me if I was going with or fuckin' girls that I didn't even fuckin' know. Many times shit got back to Tara, and it would have us going at it in the crib. She would fall into it and then the girl who told her would be trying to fuck me the next night. I thought niggahs was "trife," but bitches ain't no joke.

Things were settling down, and I had started cleaning up before closing. Out of nowhere Derrick and this big-ass, cock-deisel niggah name Bear came through the door swinging my shit so hard it made a loud, thundering noise. Everybody stopped playing pool and focused their attention on the shit that was going on. I rushed over to the door before they could go any further.

"Where the fuck Black at?" Derrick asked in a loud, strong voice.

"Where the fuck you think you at, son?" I said, stepping closer, staring into his eyes, and not being intimidated.

"I don't give a fuck where I'm at, niggah," he said. "Tell him I heard the order he put on the street, and my cousin over at Bayside Hospital fighting for his life with his motherfuckin' head split the fuck open. So you tell—"

"No, I ain't relaying shit, but you can get the hell up out of my shit with all this confusion—fuck your

goddamn cousin. Don't fuck around and get—"
Bear stepped up, towering over me like a polar bear.
"Fuck around and get what, niggah? Get what?" he
said loudly, his voice bouncing off the walls.

I was shook for a split second as he caught me off-
guard. By him standing much taller than me, it was
easy to catch him under his jaw and try to tear his
head off his shoulders. And so I did. When his head
went back it slammed into the door, and I took a step
to the side and caught Derrick with a headbutt across
his nose. As they both fell back I pulled my nine and
threw one in the chamber.

I don't know if I would have shot them or not
since I never had the chance to find out. They burst
out of there, almost tearing my door off the hinges. I
finished up and closed the place.

Monique and I left for the condo. I paged Black as
soon as I got in to let him know what had happened.
He said he was going to handle that shit.

Monique and I got up the next morning and went
to breakfast. We spent most of the day together until
she dropped me off at my truck. I told her I was
going to be tied up for the next couple of days and
would call her Monday.

Kenny Bug had done more than I expected. He
had my truck ready to go to a bass off. I got inside
and knew I had to make a few stops and show off my
new shit.

My first stop was Shirt Kings, but when I got there,
they were closed down. They had shut down right
after The Bridge had closed. I guess they were all tied
together.

My next stop was Kappatal Kuts. Kappatal Kuts
had moved from Park Avenue to Brambleton Avenue

in the plaza. In this little plaza was a 7-Eleven, a liquor store, a beeper shop, a nail shop, a hair salon and a barbershop. Because it was right next to Norfolk State University, the complex was always packed. It became a new hangout, not only for the college students, but also for all the players in town. It brought a lot of traffic, and you could get whatever you wanted within one block.

I pulled up and felt the eyes on the pretty new Land with the sounds of Wu-Tang banging. I jumped out the truck, letting the black Wallabees hit the concrete, rocking the Nautica khakis and T-shirt, gold and silver Tag Heuer, and white gold chain and medallion with matching bracelet, just a little extra shit to set off the look.

I ran inside and let Ken-Ken hook up the fade. My original barber had got caught up in some shit and was away for a minute. Ken-Ken hooked it up, and the waves I was rocking going sideways were making bitches seasick. Most kids had gone to boxes, but a lot of kids had the 360. My steez was to the side. That got the bitches attention, and that's all that mattered.

By the time I pulled in front of the sports bar, Black was in the front with Muhammed and Carlos. He told me not to even turn my shit off. He threw me the keys to the Beamer and said he'd catch up with me later.

I was outside talking to Bo, when Lo pulled up in the GS300 with chrome BBSs, and the windows tinted.

"What's up, kid?"

"I don't fuck with you, niggah," he said. "Why you didn't put them niggahs to rest the other night? All you had to say was they tried to rob you and you did what you had to do," he finished, throwing his hands up as if he didn't give a fuck.

"The spot was packed, and plus they took the fuck off."

"I would've chased the bitches across the parking lot and pumped mad holes in they ass," Bo said. "Word to my mother, son. I ain't bullshitting."

"Let them bring they ass back up this motherfucker. We'll show you how that shit is done," he said, giving his man a pound.

We had just finished talking, when Chantel pulled up.

"Who that bitch?" Lo asked. "Oh shit. That's the bitch from Atlanta."

"She live in Charlotte. Came up to check a niggah for the weekend," I said.

"Hope you handle your bitches better than you handle them niggahs punking you. Let niggahs come in yo shit and take it over," he said, laughing with Bo. They walked inside as Chantel approached.

"Hello, baby. Glad you made it here safely," I said softly, leaning towards her.

"Thank you. Good to see you again," she said, giving me a hug.

"Come on inside a second then we'll go drop your car off."

Once inside she was sitting behind the counter with me.

I must have received five calls within ten minutes. One was Tara fussing about me not watching my daughter for the weekend. I had told her the day before I had plans, but she seemed to want to throw some drama in my life.

She had started talking to some other niggah in Norfolk, from what I'd heard. He was supposed to be nickel and diming it. But one day she dropped off my daughter and was driving a black Beamer, M3, chrome sparkling. I had seen the Beamer before, and word was the kid scored his shit from Mr. BMW from the Big Apple, a major player. So this niggah was stacking paper, not nickels and dimes. I had even called her apartment once and he answered the phone. So I knew some fuckin' was going on. It sent a funny feeling through me at first, but it quickly went away. I was over her. My daughter was our only connection.

"You seem to be a popular man," Chantel said.

"No. Just friends trying to hang out," I replied.

"I hear you. Just friends? I'm not going to have any problems with anyone, am I?" she asked.

I knew right then it was time to straighten her because smart-ass, arrogant bitches get their ass beat. I was the wrong one. "Look. What did I say?" She sat as if she didn't hear me.

"I'm talking to you," I said, looking her in the eye.

"They were just friends," she replied very softly.

"All right then. Don't contradict what I say. My word is everything, and I have no reason to lie to no one. I handle my business like a man, and getting you caught up in some shit is not handling my business. If I had someone here that meant that much, why would I ask you to come stay? It wouldn't happen. I'm not going to play you or myself in that manner. You understand?"

"Yes," she said softly again, as if she knew she'd said something wrong.

"Okay. Let's go," I said sternly, as if I was the man.

As she followed me to the crib, I wondered if I should go with the fun route or a romantic route. The type of woman she was coming across as, I figured I'd come with the seriousness, then with fun, so she'll know that I was exciting, too.

We arrived at my house in Glenwood. I had made everything so beautiful inside she swore a woman decorated it. I had a fish tank the length of the wall with all tropical fish.

She took off her shoes in my foyer and sighed as she stepped down on the off-white extra plush carpet. "This is beautiful. Please show me around."

I took her bags to my room. I figured taking the initiative was sometimes good.

"This is my dining area."

She took a long look at the big China cabinet that rested against the wall and the matching table sculpture with the clear glass that rested on top.

"This is my kitchen."

The color scheme was white and light beige tile, with a strip around the wall as wallpaper.

She glanced at the island, then the oven with the built-in microwave.

Everything was spotless.

She walked towards the fireplace and ran her hand ran across the beige marble to feel the texture. Chantel slowly strolled over to the French doors that led to the deck overlooking a beautiful 18-hole golf course.

"This is our bedroom."

She never objected, or she probably didn't catch what I said. I just kept thinking positive.

Her eyes wandered to the dark solid oak king-size bed that covered the wall and the two dressers. The young lady began to pat the king-size down comforter and pillows that would make her feel as if she was lying on clouds. She followed me as I walked over to the bathroom. She stood there staring without saying a word for what felt like ten minutes. I knew the

Jacuzzi, standup shower, and skylights had her attention.

Once upstairs on the loft, she glanced into the sunken master suite off the loft. It just took her breath. All she could do was relax on the plush leather and look at the big-screen Hitachi and the two-thousand-dollar paintings that hung above it.

I knew she was in love with my place. *But what about me?*

"I love your house. All I want to know is, can I have the picture?" she asked with the most beautiful smile and laugh. "I saw a very similar picture at an art show in Charlotte, which ran almost two thousand."

I just smiled and never said a word.

"Would you like something to drink?" I asked, going downstairs to the kitchen.

"Yes, please. There's no dog, is there?" she asked, pulling open the door to the garage. "You have a bike, I see."

"Yeah. You like to ride?"

"Yes, but I don't want to go real fast."

"Never, baby. Never that."

"Whose Infiniti?" she asked.

"Why?" I asked, laughing at her many questions. "Are you the police?"

"No," she said. "I just wanted to know."

"My brother's. He has my other car. Okay?"

"Okay. I was just asking. Didn't mean to pry into your business," she said, moving closer and rubbing my stomach.

"What would you like for dinner?"

"It's on you. What would you like?" she asked.

I stared into her eyes and smiled as if to suggest something.

"From the restaurant, Dee," she said smiling.

We ended up going to Three Ships Inn on Shore

Drive. I had to call ahead to make sure we could get in without reservations. I wanted to slow down the pace and pull her in close to me. I needed a romantic theme.

We were sitting at our candle-lit table. The atmosphere was perfect. There was also a fireplace that lit the room. I was thinking that I had made a great choice.

After dinner we ordered a glass of White Zinfandel for her and a Remy VSOP for myself. We discussed her career and other future plans.

One thing caught my attention. During our conversation, in all of her endeavors, she kept putting God first. That moved me. In spite of all the wrong I'd done, I always kept a relationship with God and wanted a woman in my life that acknowledged him as I did.

Afterwards we took a long walk on the beach. I parked down by the Sheraton, out of the way of the tourists. We walked along the boardwalk then took off our shoes and came back up on the beach. She began to get comfortable and hold on to me as if I was her man.

We got on the topic of relationships. I found out that she wanted to try again but was scared to give her heart to anyone. She let me know that she needed a close friend in her life, one to talk to and share things with.

I stopped and turned her to me, I let her know that I wanted her friendship. In addition to that I felt she had a lot of love to give. I needed and wanted the entire package. I put my arm around her waist and pulled her to me. We began to kiss. A long, wet, passionate one.

Kissing girls wasn't my thing, but she made me want to be affectionate with her, and it felt good.

As we pulled our lips away, she rested her body against mine and her head on my chest.

I just wrapped my arms around her and held her. "Are you tired?"

"Yes. I'm thinking about a hot bath and the bed," she said without lifting her head.

"Let me take you home."

When we reached the house, I went into the bedroom, asking her if she wanted the hot tub or bathtub.

She said, "the Jacuzzi would be wonderful."

"Can I join you?" I asked softly, like I was shy or something.

"Can you be a gentleman?"

"Always. Under all circumstances."

She went into the bathroom and returned wearing only a short robe. She laid it to the side and stepped in, not allowing me to get more than a glance.

I undressed and stepped in slowly, so she could get a good glimpse of my dick. I was proud of my dick size, and I knew I had a few skills.

We sat there listening to Mary J's new album, "What's the 411."

An hour had passed, and I was as relaxed as possible.

Before falling asleep, I got out and showered. I was on the loft playing an old Teddy Pendergrass CD, smoking a blunt, two drinks of Remy sitting on the table. She came up wearing a teal silk nightie and robe, sat right under me, and leaned back. We talked as we finished our drinks.

Our touching became more intense. The kisses became longer and wetter.

I stood up, took her hand, and guided her to the bedroom. I slowly pushed the robe down her arms and tossed it on the bed.

As I slid the straps off her shoulder, the nightie fell to the floor. Her large but firm breasts stared at me, her nipples inviting my lips.

I laid her back and began to slowly massage her breast, running my tongue across the nipples, just to feel her body jump. I made love to her with plans to move slowly then speed up the pace.

She opened her legs partially, not allowing me to lift them like I wanted to.

When I tried to turn her over, she resisted. Her body was so snug. And even though I didn't get to hit it the way I wanted, I still enjoyed her company.

She woke me up to hugs and kisses. I wondered how someone could wake up feeling so good and with so much energy.

We took the bike for a morning ride—I wanted her to see the outlets in Williamsburg.

When we came back we ventured downtown and found a dress at The Cage on 21st Street. We then went to The Cage on Atlantic Avenue at the oceanfront. We searched around and the sales lady found an outfit by Donna Karan. She went into the dressing room and returned wearing the short dress and matching sandals.

"How do you like it?" she asked.

"That shit looks good. And those open-toed sandals got me fucked up. That shit is sexy as hell."

"Did you see the price?" she asked softly.

"How much is it?"

"The dress is $375, and the shoes $205."

"Do you like it? Will you feel good wearing it later?"

"Yes," she said smiling.

"Then I want you to have it. I like to see you smile. I'll do anything to keep it there." I could see I had her fucked up.

Black called about 9:00 p.m. and told me to meet him in Hampton at the house so we could go to the party. He drove the Porsche, him and Shereena.

She wore a red evening dress by Dana Buchman that was quite short and had open holes on both sides, allowing you to see her bare skin from top to bottom.

Black wore a black Versace shirt with beige linen pants and black Cole Hahn's. I was rocking black Gucci pants, burgundy Gucci shirt, Gucci vest, and $1,200 gators that I had picked up from the Ralph Lauren store in Georgetown.

When we arrived and pulled up front for them to valet park the Porsche and Benz, there was nothing but beautiful foreign cars: Porsches; BMWs; Acuras; NXs; SL500 convertibles; SC400 Lexus coupes; Infinitis; Hummers; and four 600 SELs parked one behind the other. We knew there'd be major players in the party.

Once inside we sat and mingled with the kids Black had been dealing with. When another kid came over, we were introduced. He had to be someone important for us to meet him. I later found out he was the biggest niggah in their clique. Without him shit falls apart.

Throughout the night we met several brothers from all over. I gathered all of them were in the game, because they were shining like the sun. Several of the kids were dressed out-of-date, but I realized that they weren't from the East and the mid-west style they portrayed was their steez. It seemed outdated to me, but the tailor-made suits, the gators, and the ice they rocked made me realize that niggahs were making money everywhere.

Everyone seemed to be having a great time, and the attitude was just mad love being shown, especially from the kid hosting the party.

Jacqueline's brother, JB, came in. He had just had his red Ferrari valet parked. Four guys, Black, and himself walked off and entered a conference room. They all returned after about twenty minutes in a pretty good mood.

Shereena, Chantel, and I sat there eating shrimp, crab legs, and anything that you could possibly imagine. I had never been to a party like this. I realized that Black made money, but the majority of these guys made much more. They discussed major events they followed throughout the year, the different award shows they'd experienced, and I found out that some of them were backing some of the large record labels. I listened, trying to catch hints of things to invest in to make dirty money, clean money. That way Black's seeds and mine could live well in the years to come.

We danced and mingled, but as the night progressed, the sophistication wore off, and the hood began to come out, with the help of the champagne and liquor. The extravaganza became a house party. You could smell the "ism" in the air, niggahs were in the corner gambling, and the bitches were starting to get wide-open. Shereena and Chantel were mingling as well.

Every time Black and I stepped off, niggahs eased their way over to them. I was standing in an open doorway just chilling, and someone walked up behind me, a little too close for my liking, invading my personal space. I stepped up and turned. Realizing it was Jacqueline's brother, I relaxed a little—but not too much. I didn't really know this niggah. He wasn't my peoples.

"What's up, son?" he asked. "You enjoying this shit?"

"No doubt," I said real slow. I had been sipping Hennessy most of the night with Black, and the blunts we had prior to arriving had a niggah feeling real nice.

"I like the way you and your peoples handle your business, son. Good brother, bad brother, corporate brother and thug brother, mad love there. My brother's making mad noise in the music industry, and his shit is blowing up. Shit was all up in *The Source* last month. Making good investments and getting his name out there amongst the white folk.

"Guess what—he's blowing but bad brother, thug brother backing it all. That's family. Can't stop us, son," he said, giving me a pound.

"Your brother Junie, I have nothing but love for him. He's become my right hand and has the connects of a real don. I will do anything for him, kid; he's like my brother. He helped me expand my shit. I was trying to make moves to Detroit but didn't really know the city. Junie told me of a girl he'd met down South from Detroit. He left and went to Detroit.

"A week later he called me to come out for a few days. I meet him at the girl's cousin's house he went to go see. This bitch has a degree from one of those Ivy League schools. Partner in a big accounting firm making six digits, bitch had paper. I stayed for a few days, laying up in her phat-ass condo while she at work, but at the same time handling business. Only after a few days, niggahs had shit set up, and now niggahs know me in Detroit. Your peoples have skills. I don't give a fuck where we go, son, he can talk us into anything and out of anything. Whatever comes up, he gets the job done."

I'm standing there wondering why this niggah all

on my brother's dick. I didn't know Junie was swinging that close, but we learn new things every day.

"Right. Good to know he's straight even when he's
not around for me to keep my eye on him," I said,
letting him know that I got my mind on my brother
at all times.

"Family, son. We're all connected now, kid. Check
it. You be safe. I have to make these rounds," he said,
giving me a pound and stepping off.

Black strolled up feeling nice, but being just as ob-
servant as I was.

I realized, looking around, that you could classify
the kids in the party. Everybody there was stacking
cheddar to the point that their lives were quite comfortable, but the amount of running varied.

You had regular money-makers, ones who confined themselves to one area and never ventured out.
Then you had Big Willies like Black—niggahs who
had different areas locked down and many people
depending on them to come through to feed their
families.

Also in the party were your "dons." These niggahs
supplied everybody. No matter where you were, they
had a way of getting you your shipment. No matter
where your shop was, or how much weight you needed,
there was no limit to where these dons could touch.

"So what was JB talking about?" Black asked.
"Not too much. Just letting me know that he and
Junie are real tight, and he was down with family. I
didn't know he was tight as he was with Junie. I don't
care too much for that. What you think?"

"I knew. Junie had talked to me and said that he be traveling and chilling. He told me that he get things done and the niggah looks out," Black said.

"I don't mean no harm, but fuck that niggah. He may seem chill, but suppose something doesn't fall right. Junie may need us, and we may not be able to get there in time."

"I realize that too. But Junie said his hands never get dirty, so I'm rolling with it. And plus it's just a minute and all this shit is going to be behind us. True, big brother?" He asked as if he really wanted me to assure him.

"Fuck that niggah had to say in the room?" I asked.

"He was saying that there was a drought because of a big bust Up Top and that it would be good to chill for a minute. He was saying not to go venture out and fuck around with hot-ass niggahs."

"I agree. Better to be safe than sorry," I said. "Plus we have money coming in from the sports bar, real estate, and the hair shop out Greenbrier, which seems to be doing well. Shereena's doing a good job over there. In time she should have bitches out the door. I forgot to tell you that the building next door is vacant. If you open a nail shop, it would damn sure attract more heads."

"Yeah, but I don't want to spend without something coming in," Black said.

"Naw. Let the shop carry the nail spot until it comes off. Now is the time, but it's on you. Look, this is what you do—check the books and you'll see the numbers say do it. Then check the numbers on the computer at the crib and you'll really see now is the time," I said.

"If you feel real strong about it, do it. We just can't take any fuckin' losses right now. I can't afford it."

"Black, can I drop this bug in your ear?" said a voice from behind. It was the kid Black scored from in Hampton.

"I'm going to get the girls. I'll meet you by the front door, when you finish," I said.

I found Chantel and Shereena sitting and sipping champagne, engaged in a conversation, looking "oh so beautiful." I walked over and gave Chantel a light kiss on her cheek.

"Shereena wants a kiss, too. But all these kisses are for you, baby," I said, loud enough for Shereena to hear.

"Shut up, Dee. I ain't studying you. Where my baby at anyway?" she asked.

"He's coming. We're going to meet him up front. Y'all ready?"

We walked up front to wait on Black.

He came along moments later. "Waiting on me? Let's bounce, fools," he said.

We went back to the crib, deciding just to stay in Hampton. Nobody was pressed on that ride back to the Beach.

I was planning on climbing in the bed with Chantel and making love until I passed out.

We arrived at the house and went our separate ways. We climbed in bed, and she curled up next to me. I took her in my arms and, before I knew it, I was fast asleep.

The next morning we all got up and went to Cracker Barrels for breakfast. I felt it was going to be a good day. Black and Shereena went on back to the other side. They had to get the baby from Mom's crib before she left for church.

"Why did they take your car?" Chantel asked as we walked inside the house.

"That's her Beamer. Black bought it for her a while back. The truck is mine."

"You told me that y'all owned your own business . . . but those guys at the party, the beautiful extravagant homes, the expensive cars. Dee, be honest with me, Is that all y'all do? I ask, Dee, because I've been around hustlers most of my life. Between my brothers and cousins, I know the style that y'all niggahs bring, and I just need to know. Be real with me."

"Years ago I dipped and dabbed to get ahead but always knew that life had more to offer. I took the little money I had made and invested it and made some good decisions, and this is what God has blessed me with. So some things do pay off, as long as we're smart about how we go about things." I kept a straight face as I looked into her eyes. I knew that if I was rolling by myself, I would have been honest and told her, but I wasn't putting my brother's life or his business on the line for nobody.

"It seems to be paying off well. You and your brother have a very lavish lifestyle."

"No, just comfortable. That's all we want."

"That's all you want?" she asked smiling and moving closer to me.

"Why? You have something to add?"—I asked, putting my arms around her and kissing her with mad passion.

She just fell into my arms and allowed me to make love to her.

Very slowly, I did, paying attention to every part of her body.

The way she responded to my every action, the way she held me, the noises she made, it all made me feel like I would never need attention from another woman in my life.

We laid around until about 2:00 p.m. My pager kept going off, so I picked it up off the floor. It was one of my supervisors. They had a problem at the sports bar that needed my immediate attention. We then headed back across the bridge.

"What time were you thinking about leaving me?" I asked Chantel.

"Probably about six or seven—why?"

"After I take care of this shit, we can go for a swim and put a little something on the grill."

"Sounds nice, but I'm not too crazy about getting into beach water," she said.

"No, I'm talking about the pool at the house. Just hold tight. This shouldn't take long."

After handling shit at the sports bar, we went to my house and gathered her things. She then followed me over to Black's house. I knew we would be there until she decided to leave.

"Whose house is this?" she asked, going inside.

"Mine. I've been trying to sell it. I had it on the market before I bought the other one, but I haven't gotten the right offer yet," I said, trying to be nonchalant.

I showed her to my room so she could change while I tossed two ribs on the grill.

I turned when I heard the glass door slide open. Standing before me was one of the sexiest bitches I'd seen. She was wearing a black French cut bathing suit that tied behind her neck and came down to a V-shape in the front, which covered only the nipples on her large but firm breasts.

I walked towards her and kissed her gently on her forehead. "Let me change right quick."

I returned rocking the plaid Polo swim trunks, Polo T-shirt, and Polo sandals.

"Don't you look cute. You kill me, matching everything you put on," she said.

I just smiled as I removed my shirt and sandals. I knew my flavor was on, but she had it going on in a way that had me going and she didn't even know it. Or did she?

We dove inside the pool and began to mess around. From the first time she touched me, I was glad I was under water because my body got aroused and would not go down.

I leaned on the wall in the pool and watched her as she enjoyed herself. The smile and laughs that I got from her made me realize that I wanted her to be part of my life forever. She was different in many ways and that shit excited me.

After playing in the pool and eating, we showered and shared a glass of Dom. She began to talk and I listened.

Before I knew it, hours had passed, and I was not once bored. Not only was I not bored, but I did not want this woman to leave me. I was already looking forward to the next weekend she would spend with me.

We ended up making love again before she left. I enjoyed her tremendously, but I knew the next time she came in town, the condoms had to go. I ached to feel the wetness of her body and to cum inside her until I was drained and unable to move. I wanted that bad, feeling that she wasn't mine until we had our special moment like that.

She ended up leaving about 9:00 p.m. Even then it was a long good-bye. She asked if I would like to come to Charlotte the following weekend, but I let her know that I had business here that needed my attention. I could tell she understood, but a look of disappointment came over her face. She quickly changed her expression, when I told her that I wanted her to return to me the following weekend.

"Yes, Dee. I'll see you Friday evening," she said with a smile.

"Do you need anything? Anything at all?"

"No, you've done enough. You took care of my tires, got me an outfit, and showed me the best weekend I've seen in a long time. All I need is for you to continue showing me the respect and attention that you've given me since we met, and I'll be Okay."

"Never a problem there," I said.

We hugged, kissed, and she made her exit.

I had been running all day. I was sitting on the couch rolling up, when the ring of the phone disturbed me. It was Black checking to see what I was into.

All my peoples were at the sports bar, Lo, Boot, G, and Dog. I didn't even know he'd come home. I sparked the *L* and jumped in the Land. I knew the night had just begun, especially if I was getting ready to fuck with these niggahs.

Monique had gotten out of class early, made her way to the sports bar, and taped a letter to the door. I was there by myself. Black and Lo hadn't been hanging around much, and things were slow because of the so-called drought. They were just concentrating on moving the shit they had through the house out Stony Point with a hell of a markup. Once I got everything set up, I noticed the letter sitting on the counter. I knew she had some shit in it, because we hadn't been spending a lot of time together lately. I picked up the letter and sat down to read it.

My Dearest Dee,

We haven't spoken since Friday. Still, you remain on my mind non-stop. I know you've heard many times how very much I care and love you. I don't get tired of saying it, and you don't mind me saying it even more. I never dated anyone that required so much attention, until you. I remember us coming up with our contract. You told me that you needed a lot of attention and wanted it with no excuses, which has turned out to be all the time. [Smile] Lately that is what my life has been devoted to and I actually enjoy it. Whatever "it" may be.

Many times I know you don't want to talk, but just want someone to be there with you and for you. I am glad that someone is me. Then there are those times that you do want to talk, and that is usually strange hours of the night. We spent a lot of time together making many memories, but I seemed to have lost you after the other weekend. Those days I didn't hear from you, I swore that if you spoke to me again and let me get close to you again, I would never let you forget that I love you. I believe that's why I say it so often now and show you every chance I get. When we do converse, it is so stimulating to my mind, body, and soul. The sound of your voice brings me so close to you, you would not believe.

Although we haven't seen each other in a few days, I feel as close as if we talked an hour ago. I don't know what I would do if you told me we couldn't talk anymore. The connection we have is so unreal to me. There is electricity between the two of us that neither of us can hide or explain. If you look back at our relationship, there was not a lot of talking done when we were together. However, we spoke and heard one another clearly. When I come to the sports bar we make small talk, but I still remain there for hours with only a few words spoken. I have never become bored with our relationship. Frustrated, yes. Bored, no. I really believe that holding hands, hugging, and some type of physical contact is all that we need, to speak and hear one another. There's been times when a hug said so much, so loudly, and I know you too could feel it.

I hear people talk about making love to someone and crying. I always believed they were crying because it felt so good physically. However, I know something different. Those few special times that you made love to me, so much was said through our bodies, it was unbelievable. The way you pull me closer to you says, "I want you near me, so close that I should be inside you." The tender slow strokes say, "You can always feel secure with me. I will never hurt you." The contact of your chest against mine flesh against flesh, says, "You are a part of me, I feel your energy. Words are not necessary for us to communicate whether making love or just saying, "Thanks for being around or listening."

There are many memorable times of making love to you that you left me speechless, like the time I came to the condo out Cypress Point. I know your memory is shot from the weed smoke on the brain, so I'll tell you. I spent the night and had taken a shower, preparing to get to class. Black had gotten up early also, because he had to go to court for the money they took coming from Richmond. Anyway, before I could get dressed, you pulled me back to the bed. We hugged, caressed, and exhaled for a while. You proceeded to pull me down further into the bed before you mounted me. Before you entered me, you put your left arm underneath my shoulders and held my head so gently in the palm of your left hand. We were completely naked and the warmth of our bodies together was so peaceful. You held my head in your hand as you gently made love to my body and soul. You said things with your body that I could not put to words. Now, I may be seeing more into this than what you were actually doing, but this is my interpretation. [Smile] As I had an orgasm, tears flooded my eyes as I realized how much you enjoy making love to me, not my body, but me. Your body said it even if you never admitted to it. I had no control over my body this day. You controlled everything.

As I write this I can feel you all over again. Well, that was the most beautiful experience I have ever had. Thanks for loving me. I am going to say this for the last time . . . I WILL LOVE YOU UNTIL THE DAY I DIE AND LOOK TO SEE YOU AGAIN IN THE AFTERLIFE. I can't imagine my life without you in it; therefore, things will never change between us. Our encounters have been less frequent lately, but I will have no problem picking up where we left off.

Dee, I'm pregnant. I'm not sure of your reaction, but all I ask is that you continue to love me and never forget that a relationship like ours has a LIFETIME GUARANTEE.

Forever Yours, Monique

I sat there with the letter in my hand, not knowing what the fuck to think. We had to talk and we had to talk tonight. Even after the weekend with Chantel, Monique meant a lot to me, and everything in her letter was on point. I did love her and she would see just how much.

I called her and got an answering machine. I left a message for her, letting her know as soon as class was over to bring her ass to me. Work would be the only excuse. And, in that case, I would see her about 12:30 a.m. About 6:00 p.m. the sports bar had packed up. Several of the kids who had played Cee-lo several times wanted to get a game going early. I called Boot to come up there, so I could open the back and get this money housing. Everybody was there except for Houdini, Muhammed, Buc, and El, those two cats from Up Top.

Once in the back, I found out Houdini, the Big Willie from Norview, had got knocked off. The Feds had caught up with him. Not with drugs, but with several hundreds of thousands of dollars. Word was, he was getting ready to bring Norfolk out of the drought. The Dominican that was bringing the drugs into Norfolk got stopped in Jersey, but agreed to a deal real quick, as long as he kept going and set the guy up who was making the buy.

Houdini caught a raw deal. It was sad, but you have those who feel some things are justifiable. But whether you're living a good or bad life, every man is someone's father, son, or brother, and family is affected by their loved one's misfortunes.

The Cee-lo game only lasted 'til about 9:00 p.m. I didn't care, still making $2100 this night. These kids came to break a fool quick, no bullshitting.

By 11:00 p.m., the bar was near empty except, for two tables, the boys who called themselves the "Lost Boyz" and a couple on table nine. I started cleaning, knowing as soon as 12:00 a.m. hit I was going to burst to Hampton so Monique and I could have a talk. I heard the door open and who comes in—Monique.

"Hello, baby. I got your message," she said. "I came over so you wouldn't have to drive. When you said 12:30 a.m., I kind of figured you would have to close the shop tonight."

"Good to see you, lady," I said, smiling and giving her a hug. "Have a seat behind the counter until I finish a few things."

The last tables brought their balls up and paid. I figured I would close a few minutes early, since it was empty. Monique helped me count everything, and we put the money in the safe. I had parked in the back, so we set the alarm and jetted out the back door.

As soon as we stepped out the back door, somebody snatched her by her neck and slammed her to the concrete. She let out a partial scream as her body hit the ground. I reached for the gun that was in my waist, but by the time I touched it, I got hit in the head with an object that sent me into the wall, seeing nothing but darkness and stars.

When my vision began to come to, there were four niggahs in my sight.

I saw Derrick, Bear, and two more kids I had never seen before. One was slightly smaller than Bear, and the other was looking like he had just come home from doing a bid, all pumped up. They all had guns in their hands, except one guy. He had something, but I couldn't figure it out until I tried to stand and he touched me with it. It shocked me and sent me back to the ground.

"Sit the fuck down, niggah," he yelled, hitting me two more times.

My body went limp. I lay there shaking and burning. As I looked up, Bear took the butt of the shotgun he was holding and busted me in the forehead. It was hard trying to get my composure, with the blood running down my face into my eyes and burning them as if they were sprayed with pepper spray. I heard Monique letting out screams, in between her pleading and begging them to stop.

"Niggah, who in the hell did you think you were fuckin' with?" Bear asked. "I'm going to show you what happen to motherfuckers who go against the program. He raised the butt of the gun and came across my temple and eye.

Pain I never felt before in my life shot through my body. I collapsed back to the ground with my head on the concrete.

"Why a fine bitch like you want to fuck with these punk-ass niggahs?" the kid looking like he just got out said. "Hold that stankin'-ass bitch up," he added.

As two of the other guys lifted Monique to her feet, he came across her with a blow that damn near knocked her ass unconscious.

She fell headfirst to the ground near me. I could feel her hands on my body and could barely hear her cries. But it gave me strength enough to make an effort to get to my feet. When I lifted up to my knees, she fell into my arms.

Just then I felt a piercing blow of someone's boot in my side, which quickly made me release her. I saw Derrick grab Monique by her hair and snatched her to her feet, then picked her by her neck, only to slam her on the hood of the car. He lifted her skirt and reached down to unzip his jeans.

I don't know where the strength came from, but I got back to my feet and charged at him with all the strength I had. A couple blows to the side and couple hits with the stun gun, then a crashing blow to the back of the head with the butt of the shotgun dropped me again.

The anger, the will to want to help her, kept building inside, but my body had nothing left. My eyes began to tear, as I watched Derrick pull her panties to the side and run up in her as if he was a mad man.

She tried to fight, but her little strength was no match for him.

As he pounded in and out of her, grunting, she reached up, fighting and scratching, for him to stop.

He reached down and put his hands around her neck and, as he pounded inside of her, began to choke her until she gasped for air and her arms fell to her side. He continued to verbally abuse her as he stripped my girl of all her dignity.

"Aw, how you like that?—Stupid-ass bitch," he yelled as he came. "Fuck you, niggah," he said, turning to me, just before he planted his Timberland boot down on my face.

He was in a rage as he just kept kicking me, with the brick building being my only support. All I could hear was the cock-diesel niggah hollering he wanted to fuck next.

"I'm not putting up with all that fighting shit," he said, pulling Monique up and turning her over. He pulled her skirt up to her chest and ripped her panties off.

As she tried to fight with all the fight she had left, he grabbed her by her hair and beat her face into the hood of the car continuously . . . until her face was covered in blood. He pulled down his sweats and then situated her now limp body where he could do what he wanted. He spit on his hands and rubbed his dick just before shoving it into her anus.

She let out a half a scream, lifted her head, and then it hit the hood, face first, with no more movement, except for her body jumping as he slammed against her. Before he could finish, I heard the sounds of my alarm going off. The door must have never been secured. They all jumped.

"Shit," the guy pounding Monique yelled. "Take this, stinkin'-ass 'ho'."—he grabbed her body, picked it up over his head, and threw her against the brick wall beside me. I heard her head hit the wall with such a force, I wondered if she was still living. He then came charging at me with the shotgun, busting me in my head continuously in a mad rage.

I came back to the world two days later with a headache that no medication could handle. My family was all standing around. "Monique, Monique," was all I could find the strength to say. My jaw was broken, my ribs were fractured, my eye was badly damaged, and my head had sixty-four stitches.

Black leaned over to my ear and took my hand. "Them niggahs will die. Was it them?"

"Yeah, four of them," I said, straining. "Monique?"

"Monique's dead, son," Black said. "They messed her up real bad."

I only had one eye, so I couldn't cry. The pain I felt inside made me wish I was dead.

The detectives came in and cleared the room while they asked questions. They wanted to know if I saw who did it or if I knew the people.

I told them, "No. I came outside and got busted in the head and never saw or heard anything else." All I knew was they had to get theirs. If it took the rest of my life, they were going to pay.

I was in the hospital for a couple more days before going to mom's house. Black and Lo waited until I got home to tell me the rest.

The same night I got busted up, those Jersey kids had sent three niggahs to the house out Stoney Point and robbed the crib for the cash and the stash. They left Dante with half his brain lying on the floor. They had pushed Derrick to the back of the townhouse. He was about to lose his mind, and I knew how he was feeling.

They had caught Lo at 7-Eleven on Newtown Road and shot up the Lex and him. One shot caught him in the stomach and the other in the chest, but he was wearing his vest. They even rode by Tia's house where Black was and shot up her house while he was in there with the baby.

All I could say was, "These niggahs came correct." They were well organized, and they came deep. But they fucked up because family was still here, living and well.

Black called Chantel and told her what had happened—that I had been robbed leaving the sports bar and was beaten real bad because I wouldn't give up all the money. I thought she might cancel coming up for the weekend, but she let Black know she was still coming and would stay to take care of me until I could take care of myself.

And she did just that.

She met Boot at the sports bar, and he brought her around to the house.

Everything at this time was being run in a legit manner, because too many detectives and police were nosing around. Chantel took me home and waited on me hand and foot. Cooking, cleaning, bathing, changing bandages—she did it all. She had taken two weeks off her job, showing her concern and more so her love. She'd only met me twice. I knew what she was doing was straight from the heart.

I decided to go to Charlotte at her request. Already I was doing better. She insisted I get away from everything and come down there for a couple weeks. She had to get back to work but insisted she wasn't leaving me.

I went down for two weeks. Black made sure I had two 9mm. He said that she seemed real cool but we never know what skeletons might pop out of her closet, and I was in no condition to be catching wreck. The nines would be my bodyguards.

I spent two more weeks lounging in her beautiful condo. The furniture she had was Okay. It was something her man had left. He took the good shit, leaving her with just a full-size bed that was in her guestroom and a small, bullshit-ass 19" TV. I told her to put her bedroom set back in the guestroom, go to Helig and Meyers, and get us a king-size bed and the other shit to go with it that made up the set. I also bought a big-screen. I knew that this was going to be my new spot and wanted it as comfortable as possible.

I told her to call a locksmith and have the locks changed.

She had never bothered to change them since she and her man had separated. She said he wasn't coming by and he never did.

I let her know that I was one of those paranoid-ass niggahs. If he didn't know she had a new niggah in her life and just happened to come through that front door unannounced, I was going to unload one of those nines in a motherfucker's ass before I asked any questions.

She knew by my tone and the way I explained it that I was not bluffing, instantly calling the locksmith.

I spent the next couple of weeks looking at *The Young and the Restless, The Bold and the Beautiful, As the World Turns,* and *Guiding Light.*

* * *

By the time I returned home, business had slowed down at the sports bar. The Bridge clientele was not there, and I was getting the aftereffects. Barry, the same guy who owned the Royal Blue on Little Creek Road, had bought The Bridge and turned it into Stampedes, a country western nightclub, and they were not coming into E's Cue. The club across the street, Mr. Magic's, was starting to build a young clientele but had a ways to go.

I was sitting in E's Cue, when Black and Lo came in.

"What's up, man?" Black said, coming through the door.

"Shit. I'm all right," I said.

"Check this—remember the night of the party, right? They were saying JB doesn't believe in holding a niggah back. He wants any kids he fuck with to blow to the highest level. He was saying that from where we're sitting we should've been branched out and dominating all of these areas that a lot of mother-fuckers think is too small."

"Like where?" I asked.

"From Suffolk to South Hill," he added. "It's sup-posed to be money in Franklin, Emporia, and even Smithfield, and it's all open. Before I do anything, I'm going to handle my business right here in the hood first."

"I told you them niggahs can't operate without Big Head and Strong," Lo said. "And if we take out Derrick and the twins, Ronald and Reggie, the entire clique will fall."

"I want that big-ass motherfucker and the niggah that look like he just came home," I said. "I don't care where I see them motherfuckers at, word to my mother. It could be on the courthouse steps or in the middle of the fuckin' mall. Wherever the fuck it is, you'll see yellow tape surrounding the area."

"I think it's time, Black," Lo said. "This shit has lingered on long enough. Them niggahs still got soldiers pumping out Lake Edward, and all they do is come and collect. They got us, and they got us good. It's our time. The twins—I heard they be at the Blue Light, hanging with those dirty-ass Jamaican niggahs. Your boy Derrick live with his girl out Kempsville Lakes. I already peeped all this shit."

"What about them other niggahs?" I asked.

"They weren't from here. They came in just to do work," Black said. "But when we go up in the two houses they got out LE, whoever's there will pay for their mistake."

Just then Big G came through the door. "What's up, motherfuckers?"

"Are you ignorant all the time?" I asked.

"Hell, yeah," he yelled. "I got two bitches outside. What's up? They ready for the pool."

"What they look like?" Lo asked, putting his hand up and peeking out the door.

"The brown skin one, she's phat as shit. I can't wait to see that ass in a bathing suit," G said. "The red bitch is Hawaiian and Puerto Rican. Body is nice, but not like your girl. But she is fine as hell—fall-in-love fine."

Black peeped out the window, walked over to the door, and opened it. "Where them 'ho's from, son?" Black asked.

"I didn't ask. Met them at the car wash. We went to their spot over in Hillcrest Apartments. and smoked their shit. Then I mentioned the pool and them bitches freaked out. So let's go freak, niggah."

Black and Big G left me and Lo in the crib. He was catching me up on the latest shit in the street.

Two hours had passed by the time Black and G came back. They had talked the shorties into taking off their suits and skinny-dipping. They ended up hitting them 'ho's, saying the bitches were down for "the homey switch." Me and Lo thought they were bullshitting, until Black came in with the camcorder. Then we saw firsthand how wild them niggahs were acting. Big G was holding the diving board, his ass in the air. Them 'ho's found that shit amusing. When niggahs got money almost anything they do is funny, as long as the bitches don't feel threatened.

Black and Lo burst out. I sat there behind the counter and saw Monique's letter lying there. My hands shook, as I picked it up and read it again. It was so hard to read and hold back the tears. But it was only Big G there, and I knew my niggah understood.

"You miss that bitch, son?" G asked.

"Like you wouldn't believe," I said.

"She was a thorough-ass hooker and fine as shit."

"No doubt. She made me feel like I was all that at all times, son. Like a niggah was a fuckin' king. I really cared for her ass, and niggahs have no idea how her death continues to fuck with a niggah. I can't change the past. So I have to accept reality and the way life is. People come and go, but your life has to go on. I have to. I can't give up. But motherfuckers don't know how that shit fuck with me."

"I know it's hard, son. But I guarantee you, once our peoples handle that shit, you won't be over it, but you'll feel a hell of a lot better. Now what's up

with Ms. Charlotte? Motherfuckin' woman take off
work to take care of my peoples. What kind of shit is
that?"

"Chantel, she ain't no joke, son. She willing to give
her all, kid. It ain't much, but what she does have, it's
mine."

"Other words, she ain't one of those begging-ass
bitches," G said. "That's all a niggah ask for—that a
bitch carry her own and stop begging so goddamn
much."

"She got her shit together. Definitely wife material," I said.

"I know my niggah didn't say that word. Don't
make me stop fuckin' with you," G said laughing.

We sat there kicking it for a while. Time always got
away, whenever we sat around talking about old times
and new times while sipping on a bottle of Erk and
Jerk (E & J Brandy).

"Where everybody? Fam usually be done stopped
through by now," G said. "I got to stay up here with
my man, so niggahs don't beat his ass or bust him in
the goddamn head and shit," he said laughing.

"Fuck you, son," I said.

"You the one who said that if we seen you and a
bear fighting to help the bear," he said laughing.

"Well, that's if it's one bear. It was too many motherfuckin' bears this go-round. And plus, these bears
had shotguns and nines," I said laughing. "Smokey
packing gats now. I know a niggah better not start a
forest fire."

We were about drunk and damn near in tears
from our jokes.

Physically I was doing well. Everybody noticed the
difference in my attitude. I didn't have any love for
anybody, but my peoples. Family was everything;

everybody else was just there. And I felt everybody else was just out to harm me or get what the fuck they could get out of me. Mentally, the death of Monique and the fact that she could have been carrying my child, which could've made me marry her, was still really fucking with me.

I always smoked trees, but now it was more often than usual. Without the weed, so many things kept running through my head. I would sit around and worry about different shit. But after one blunt, I realized that some things you couldn't change and had to work with.

Me and G were about to leave the sports bar, when Dieta came strolling inside.

"Where Lo at?" she asked.

"I don't know. He ain't in my motherfuckin' pocket," G said.

"Where your mama at?" I asked. "I'm going over there. I'm going to be your stepdaddy."

"As long as you pay some fuckin' bills, I don't give a fuck. He told me to meet him. Where is his simple ass at? I got to get back home to my baby."

"Don't talk shit," I said. "I'll tell him then you know what the fuck is up."

"He ain't my motherfuckin' man," she said with an attitude.

"And," said G, "you act like that will stop him from going to your ass. Tell me—if he pull up right now, and I tell him you was talking shit, what he gonna do?—Tell me."

"Shut up," she said real low, knowing G had pulled her card. She wasn't scared of Lo, but she did know Black wouldn't hesitate going to her ass.

We were outside joking, when Carlos pulled up on a Suzuki GSXR sports bike. Before he could even park, Bo came around the corner driving with Lo and Derrick, Dante's brother. Dieta jumped in the car with them, and they were out.

Carlos was kicking it with me and G when we heard the pipes coming up Newtown Road.

Muhammed and Black came screaming around the corner on their bikes and never stopped. Carlos threw on his helmet, and they burst. Me and G decided to grab some drinks before heading in.

Afterwards, we were coming up Princess Anne Road past the Casablanca and Momentos, and noticed the full parking lot. I decided to stop for a while even though G never cared for these two clubs. He always said too much shit happened and things were bound to kick off with the crowd it attracted. I agreed with him. But sometimes you wanted to be in a club where people came to have a good-ass time, party, and not try to be cute for the niggah with the most money.

These clubs were side by side and packed every night. They were small clubs, but the dance floors were always packed. Guys didn't have to ask girls to dance, because girls stayed on the floor, ripping it with or without a niggah. Casablanca was non-stop hip-hop. Momentos was R&B and hip-hop, with a slightly older crowd. I had to admit that the crowd got rowdy every now and then, but you always caught the real and everyone knew it. That's why there was always a crowd.

I went into the Blanca, and the metal detector beeped, but because I was known and a regular, it wasn't a problem.

After checking out the crowd, I eased to the dance floor and hollered at one of the bitches dancing wild on the floor. I then went back by the pool tables to get a game. Niggahs were always ready to gamble. I played a few games peeking over the club to see if there was anything I wanted to holler at or fuck. Nothing caught my eye, so I eased out and slided to Momentos.

Outside, kids were standing around, smoking weed, hollering at bitches. Others were just loitering, seeing what confusion they could start. I gave a pound to the kids I knew and hugs to bitches I'd seen around or who knew me. For the niggahs I didn't know, no pounds, no speaking. Just eye-to-eye stare, then a turn of the head, just to show I was hard. This also let a niggah know: Yes, I seen you, but I don't fuck with niggahs I don't know.

Coming around the wrong way, speaking to everyone, playing yourself soft, could easily get your head busted or your pockets emptied by one of those niggahs loitering around. How could a place where so many people have lost their lives turn out to be so exciting?

I ended up going home alone, even though several caught my attention. I was being choosy with my selections this night.

The following morning I was awakened by the knocking at the front door. I eased to the door, so no one would hear me inside. I peeked through the peephole and saw men in black. Thinking it was the Mormons, I opened the door. The flash of badges quickly satisfied my curiosity.

After realizing I was the one they were looking for, they asked me a series of questions. "Where were you last night? What time did you leave the sports bar? Do you have an alibi for your whereabouts between 12:00 a.m. and 2:00 a.m.?" These questions were being thrown at me by two detectives.

"Sir, can I ask what all this is about?" I asked.

"We know about your incident a little over a

month ago," said one of the detectives. "According to you, it came off as a random robbery. But from other sources, we heard that your family was feuding with the late family over territory."

"What the hell are you talking about? I know nothing of a family feud. And I know nothing about territory. Y'all got me fucked up."

"We know your brother Black and about the rivalries that you all had."

"Sir, can you please tell me what all this is about? It's like you speaking a foreign language to me. Please stop talking in circles and share what's on your mind," I said.

"Last night a family was brutally murdered in Windsor Oaks, and we have two more bodies in Kempsville Lakes and a man fighting for his life in Norfolk General. Even if he lives, he'll never walk again, nor will he ever be able to take care of himself. He suffered head injuries much more severe than you did."

"I'm sorry for the family, but I can't help you in this matter. I don't know nothing about that shit."

"We'll be seeing you. Thank you for your time."

I brought in *The Virginian-Pilot* and the front page read: Two Families Slain in Virginia Beach off of Holland Road in a housing community called Windsor Oaks. Unknown assailants entered the home of the Curry family. Ronald and Reggie Curry were both found dead, shot execution-style, two shots to the back of the head, and castrated.

Sandra Curry, a 22-year-old sister, was found decapitated, one of the brothers' penis in her mouth. Her body was found in the bed nude, but her head was in the living room with the brothers.

Martha Curry, 62-year-old grandmother, was found tied to a wood-burning stove and badly burned, one of the brothers' private parts in her mouth.

In Kempville Lakes townhomes, Tonya Wilkens was found hanging in the garage with her hands and feet tied together. Takeisha Wilkens, her 10-month-old baby, was found suffocated to death and lying in the trunk of the car in the garage.

Derrick Curry was in Norfolk General fighting for his life. He was brutally beaten with a 2x4 and a crowbar, his knees busted beyond repair. His index and middle fingers on both hands were smashed flat. He was found in his kitchen floor, his head split open from massive blows and his body severely burned from the waist down.

"This man was suffering," I said to myself as I continued to read. It was sickening to read, but I read it three times. And even though I knew that this was a horrible act, I was still able to smile.

I went by my mom's after showering and getting dressed. I wanted to take in her mail, since she was out of town. Lo and Black had sent Moms and Auntie to visit their brother Arthur Jr. in Brooklyn.

Moms and Auntie were always excited about going to visit their brother. He was much older than they were and more like a father-figure than a brother. They had always spent summers with him in Brooklyn, where they met our fathers. Our father was from Norfolk, but he had family Up Top and was in Brooklyn running from the man when he met Moms. That's how we ended up back in Norfolk. Lo and their pops was born and raised Up Top. But Auntie realized that Brooklyn wasn't the place to raise kids, so she came to Norfolk with Mom.

Now all of us were grown. That gave them the opportunity to travel, and they did. After all the struggles they had been through, they deserved happiness, and now it was their time.

Black came in looking real serious. We just stood there looking at each other. I let him know that the detectives knocked on the door this morning.

"They knocked on Tia's door, too," he said. "I was there all night. They don't have shit. And plus, I don't leave no witnesses."

"You left one—your boy ain't dead," I said.

"Yes, he is," Black said. "He's brain-dead. He'll never be in his right mind again. Right now he's praying they pull the fuckin' plug. That niggah will never be in his right mind ever again. The same motherfuckin' way he wasn't in his right mind fuckin' with my peoples. Dee, every time I bust that niggah in the head with that Louisville Slugger, I thought about the way you said they just kept kicking you with Timberlands and busting you with the butt of the gun. That shit had me in a fuckin' rage. When I left, the niggah was barely holding on.

"Fuck him and everybody who fuck with him. My main concern is that people know where we are. With the sports bar, all our peoples, associates, and especially our enemies know where to find us. That scares me for you. I'm not ever there, but I don't need for them to catch up with you. The reason I buy houses on the down low and don't let people know where I'm at is not because of the Feds, but for niggahs—I'm hiding from niggahs. The Feds know where the hell you at if they need to find you. You can't hide from them. So be careful. Real careful."

Over the next couple of weeks, we had to make several changes in the business. Things were so slow that I started having parties in E's Cue on Friday nights. I got a DJ to come in on Friday nights. I had appetizers cooked up and would charged by the head, all free pool. Running it like a club turned out to be a good business move. Between the parties and the Cee-lo games, the business was still coming off.

I was still making moves back and forth Up Top, getting IDs. The phone had become a very lucrative business, but the Feds was on that shit. Black's move on Derrick and them Jersey kids put the street business right back where it should be. Niggahs in the street knew Black and Lo had done those niggahs' families. That made things run a lot smoother. Niggahs did not want to fuck with them.

Black had met this fiend who just enjoyed smoking. Black knew him from when he was on the corner. The man was a retired Norfolk cop. He had mad knowledge of the game and knew a lot of people. Black ended up helping him get a place out Campus East. A lot of business came through, and it gave him a spot to serve everybody. He no longer handled any business at the sports bar. He said the man was on it and felt it was best to chill.

I realized he was trying to keep me as far away from the bullshit as possible. Ever since they got me outside the sports bar that night, it seemed like he was just trying to protect me from everything. He knew I had to get this paper. It was the lifestyle he had established for me, and there was to be no turning back. But the way things were set up I had no problems. Money that came in from the Cee-lo games was more than enough for me to maintain my lifestyle. I also had the sports bar money, the fake IDs money, the cell phone money, and he never asked for a penny. He said that it was all good. Safe money. He said the shit he fucked with was low-down, treacherous money, and he didn't need me to play where there were no rules. He kept me away from it as much as he could but couldn't put all his trust in anyone, except for me. That made it hard.

The owner of Stampede's realized the country folks couldn't bring in the type of money black folks were bringing, so he changed it back to a black club and named it Picasso's. It took the hell off. He realized there was a demand for an R&B young adult club.

It was close to Labor Day when the club opened. We had gone to the big Labor Day weekend game. Norfolk State and Big State (Va. State) game always brought the big crowd.

As with every Labor Day, parties were off the hook. After the game me and G ended up in Picasso's. Black and the rest of the crew ended up in Magic's across the street. I was shocked as hell to see Black going to the club. He had never gone to the club, but Mr. Magic's hooked him.

The following day we were in E's Cue: Lo, Black, G, Carlos, and myself. We were sitting around talking about the time we had over the weekend. Suddenly the phone interrupted our conversation.

"It's a collect call from Norfolk City Jail," G said. It's Boot."

"Collect. Aw shit!" Black said. "Grab that, Lo."

"Say it ain't so," Lo said. "I hope this niggah ain't in no shit."

Boot got caught with half-kilo of cocaine. The police ran up on him and those Ocean View niggahs he was serving. They scooped him in DJ's parking lot on Tidewater Drive.

Lo hung up the phone. "Goddamn, I told him that spot was hot as hell. Back in the day that shit was fine, but not now. Not fuckin now."

"What the hell has he gotten into?" Black asked.

"Caught with a half brick in the Honda. Holding him on a hundred thousand dollar bond."

We stood there in disbelief, not knowing what to do. Lo was upset because he felt about Boot the way Black felt about me. He didn't want Boot fucking around with this shit, but Boot was chasing the cheddar the same way, except Boot wasn't rude like Lo. Boot was straight business, and that's how he figured niggahs was coming at him. Lo, on the other hand was also about business. But if you got caught slipping, even if it was over a couple grand, Lo would take your life.

"Page Junie. See what he say," I said.

It wasn't long before he called back. He said he had to make some calls and to not do anything until he called back. Half an hour passed before the phone rang, with him on the other end.

"Hello," I said.

"What's up?" he asked. "How you feeling?"

"I'm Okay. Just worried about Boot now."

"Look. Go downtown to the jail. I already talked to Madison down on Freemason. He's tied up right now, but his partner Bill Robinson is going to meet you down there. Take ten thousand, and after you talk to Robinson, you gonna meet with a bondsman name Frank Bowe. I already talked to Madison and Robinson. So go down there and bring Boot ass home. Don't let him sit no longer than he has to. Give me a call when y'all get back."

Before he could finish talking, I saw a black 5.0 Mustang pull in front, driving real slow. All of a sudden a kid popped up with a ski mask on. He extended his body out the window, holding an Uzi, and began spraying.

"Get down," I yelled as the bullets shattered the glass, hitting walls, pinball machines, and the big-screen television. Things got quiet as everyone stood looking at each other.

"This shit like motherfuckin' Cali," Carlos said.

"Niggahs doing drive-bys, trying to take my peoples out," Black said. "Everybody all right?"

"Y'all carry your ass," I said. "Don't need the police fuckin' with y'all. Go get Boot, and I'll take care of this shit."

Me and G sat until the police came, which was only minutes later. We got a report for insurance purposes only.

Then I called my landlord, GSH Realty, to see what had to be done as far as getting the glass and the holes in the walls repaired. I let them know that I was going to try and sell the business. I told them that before I opened my sports bar, I had no idea that the area was so bad and so drug-infested and that I had been beaten within an inch of my life. And then today I was almost caught in the crossfire of god-knows-what. I kept up my story by telling them I did not understand why people would act like this— I had no idea—and I could no longer subject myself to this type of environment.

They got everything repaired, and we decided to sell it.

I thought about Black saying that people always knew where to find us and too much shit was going down around the sports bar. He was on again and things were flowing fine.

The hair and nail shop out Greenbrier was coming off. The rent we were receiving from our building was a positive cash flow, and the other small investments I'd made were holding us down. It hurt to let something that we treasured so much go, but it was for the best. It took me almost $80,000 to open it, and I sold it for $60,000 to this young baller out Norview. We didn't lose anything, considering.

Chantel and I were going to dinner on the *Spirit of Norfolk*. She had never been on a dinner cruise, and she called me letting me know not to plan anything for the weekend. She had made reservations for us Saturday evening.

I didn't always play fair, but I knew a good girl when I saw one. She had respect not only for me, but for herself. She always carried herself like a real woman, and that gave me no choice but to treat her like the woman she portrayed. And so I decided to do something special for her. I called her and told her to come straight to the house, where I would be waiting. I went to Lynnhaven Mall to the Victoria's Secret to get her some elegant late eveningwear. I picked up a pearl white, long, silk gown that I could only picture her in and a robe of the same color and texture. I didn't want her to have to search for anything, so I picked her up two thongs and bras for the weekend occasion.

When she arrived I knew she would be hungry and tired from a long day's work and the additional stress of the drive to Virginia. She entered the house, and dozens of white roses awaited her arrival. One was on the dining room table with two tall candles. The petals from the others were covering the floor from the living room to the bedroom, with the rest floating on top of the hot water that filled the Jacuzzi. Candles were lit and sitting all around the bedroom and bathroom, there being no other lights in the house.

I thought this was some bullshit, but I had seen it done in a romantic scene on one of the soaps I had seen while laid up. When the guy did it, the woman was so touched that she began to cry. I realized bitches still like that corny shit and get touched over it.

When she knocked at the door, I opened it to let her enter into a candle-lit room with a fireside. I told her to drop her bags and strip. She obeyed then followed me down the hallway. I watched as she strutted her beautiful pecan-brown body with full breasts down the hallway, entered the bathroom, and stepped up into the Jacuzzi. It took everything I had in me not to dive in with her.

As she relaxed in the Jacuzzi, I laid her lounging wear out on the bed before checking the ribs in the oven.

I went back into the bathroom to bathe her as she sat there and absorbed all the attention I was giving her. I dried her off and escorted her to the bedroom, where I massaged her body with some massaging lotion that I had copped from Victoria's Secret. The soft, sweet-smelling shit made me want to eat her for hours. She began to put on the items I had placed on the bed. I watched in amazement and realized that I loved every inch of this woman, inside and out. She was a queen, and I promised myself to treat her as such.

We went into the dining area and sat for dinner. Afterwards we carried the unfinished bottle of Dom up to the loft and shared a toast. She began to show her appreciation, her love, or whatever you want to call it.

All I know was by the morning I knew she would be the one I would spend the rest of my life with.

The next several months I allowed Chantel to open my mind to different things. We checked out a Broadway play called *Cats*. Some shit, I thought, but I gave it a chance and actually enjoyed it. She left smiling, holding me closer and ready to show me love.

The Opera House was one of a kind—an experience. We began to catch every Black play that came to town. Most of them were in Portsmouth at Willett Hall.

We began to take trips in the States and abroad. She opened my mind to the different cultures that were out here. Some places and things I could appreciate; others I couldn't get with nor understand. Through everything, she kept smiling, and that made me happy. I knew something was really different with her, because whether or not she smiled or was all right could either make my day or fuck it up.

CHAPTER 15

"Family Ties"

Big G and I were at Black's house in Campus East looking at *Martin,* when Franklin, the retired cop, came through the door. He was looking for Black and was talking mad shit. We were waiting on Black so we could go to Mr. Magic's. Just then Black came in wearing Mark Buchanan, Pelle Pelle leather coat, jeans, T-shirt and Rockport boots. The back of the coat had Pelle Pelle across the back in studs that stood out like diamonds. This shit ran some paper, and I could tell. But he was on again.

He had made his connects in Suffolk and had kids from Franklin, Emporia, and Smithfield scoring from his peoples in Suffolk. So, as soon as Black put him on, he went from half a brick to several bricks.

Black liked the fact he only had to serve one kid, tax him, and make his money. He was making a lot of money with Muhammed now also. Houdini was gone on tax evasion charges, but his family still had to live, so Muhammed was the savior and Black was God. Carlos was Black's right hand man. He came in the crib, rocking black Guess jeans, black Timberlands, grey Guess T-shirt, and a black Nautica leather that was just as phat as the Pelle Pelle.

We began to spark, which was becoming an every-Thursday thing. We would get high as hell before going to the club. We arrived at the club with Black. He had gotten in good with the owner, Ray, and was getting his props as he arrived every week. He had his own parking space in front of the club, and lines were never a problem. When you blow several hundreds in a club every night you show up, why would lines be a problem? This club brought out every Big Willie in town, and Black wasn't the only niggah living like this.

On this night the line was wrapped around the building. Cars were across the street in the restaurant parking lot. When we parked the 740il BMW and got out to go inside, all we saw was a long line of mostly bitches. We eased to the front and were let in, everybody that rolled with Black. Almost all the security had been over to E's Cue or had worked for Lite and Smalls at The Bridge at one time or another, so we were in real good.

We went inside and ordered jugs. The club sold jugs of liquor. Black bought four jugs at $15 each, two filled with Hennessy and Coke for Big G and Carlos, and the other two filled with Tanqueray and juice. We knew the bartender, so she made our drinks damn near straight. She also knew Black. She knew if she looked out, her tips would be off the fuckin' meter. The jugs held almost a quart of liquor and, by closing, it showed. We got our drinks and leaned on the wall to check out all the hookers passing by. They were coming by, passing out hugs and begging for drinks. Most of them were phat as hell, but we knew the game.

It wasn't even two minutes before Muhammed and his peoples entered the club with the loudness, ordering four bottles of Moët. That started something; other niggahs weren't trying to be outshined. Big D and his clique from out Tidewater Park were sitting over in the corner by the picture man. They had a table full of drinks, and bitches gathered all around. When Muhammed ordered four bottles, they yelled for the waitress to bring them four bottles.

On the other side of the club sat the Jamaicans and New York kids; they ordered six bottles, as they lit the club up with the strong ism they torched. Black smelled the ism in the air and said something about sparking up. Carlos pulled a dub sack out of his pocket, and I was already splitting the blunt, dumping the useless tobacco on the club floor.

By 1:00 a.m. everybody was fucked up, and the bitches were parading around us like niggahs had something to give away. Muhammed had three bad-ass bitches up in his face. He was known for having and blowing cheddar, but only if he was feeling you.

Two bitches came strolling up. One hugged Black, and the other hugged Muhammed. Chris and Tangy were the young girls' names. Tangy was a cosmetologist who worked out of a shop off of Liberty Street. Her girl Chris worked downtown at Nations Bank as a customer service representative. Tangy had gotten mixed up with one of the niggahs from Up Top and ended up getting pregnant. She said she didn't fuck with him any more, but after looking at her, you would wonder why any niggah would let this go.

She stood in front of me talking, as I stared down at her jeans that were so tight it looked as if her ass was begging to be released. She wore black boots with a short, tight shirt, which exposed her pierced belly button. She could have hid her piercing with the leather jacket, but she went for that extra edge. And it wasn't that she needed it because the girl was tight.

Her friend Chris was dressed more to the conservative side, but recognizing that she had body wasn't hard. She had body, but her points came in because she was fine. The bitch was just fine—no make up, no fly hairdo, no tight-ass clothes—just goddamn fine, without an attitude.

I remembered Black mentioning her at one time or another. He was telling me that they went out, but she wasn't trying to come off no ass. Later, he found out she was fuckin' one of those Tidewater Park niggahs, who was taking real good care of her.

As their conversation went on, a voice blurted out, "What the fuck you doing in here, girl?"

"I can come out, Noriega," she said. "You're my baby's daddy, not my motherfuckin' daddy."

"Come here. Let me fuckin' talk to you," he said. "Now!"

"No. And don't start up in here, Noriega."

Before she could finish talking, he grabbed her by her hair and tried to slam her on the wall, but she fell into Muhammed.

Muhammed stole on the kid, then Muhammed's cousin.

Before you knew it, a lot of niggahs were all around. It was quickly brought under control by security, but the club was closed for the night.

When we got to the parking lot, Muhammed's cousin was still upset. He went to his Lexus, went under the seat, and pulled out the nine. After he let it go and the sounds of gunshots rang in the air, everyone began to scatter.

We all sat back and laughed. The night was good.

It wasn't even a year since Mr. Magic's went from

twenty-five and older to twenty-one and older, and the man was trying to shut it down. The shooting was on the news because it was a black club and because of previous incidents there.

One day I was sitting and talking with Boot when he said that he was there one night and heard a shot in the other parking lot at the Exxon. As everyone scattered he glimpsed over in front of the cashier's window and saw the young man lying there. He had been shot at point-blank range in the head and was lying in a puddle of blood under the well-lit gas station. He was dead by the time the ambulance arrived.

Boot said he looked down at the dude lying there, and all he could see was Black's face. This scared him and it was then he decided that this hustling shit wasn't for him. It was time for this shit to come to an end.

He talked to Lo and Black the next day. They said he was a paranoid-ass niggah and weren't giving up this life for nothing. They said they had worked too hard for the status and lifestyle that they had built, not to mention the empire of money. They vowed that no one was ever going to take this away and that only death could end this shit. This was their time to shine.

Boot had been talking to his lawyer Robinson and was told that because of mistakes in the arrest procedure and as it was his first offense he could probably get him off through loopholes; but it would cost him dearly. He also told him to sit tight because it would be a while before his case would be heard before a judge.

Black was with Boot as the lawyer ran everything down to him. Boot sat there in a daze, thinking about the time he could get.

Black brought him back to life when he told him

that only broke niggahs go to jail. "Let the lawyer do his job. Just relax and concentrate on school."

Boot didn't do a lot of balling, so he saved a lot of money. He put his money into his house, his girl, and savings. His only weakness was the mall. He loved to look good. He loved to shop, and his lifestyle had him in slacks, silk shirts, and dress shoes on a daily basis. He definitely had some adjusting to do.

Thursday was his birthday, and his girl had planned a surprise dinner for him at Grand Affairs on Pleasure House Road. We all tried to give her a hand in getting things together. She wanted something small, strictly for the family. We had the money to go all out, but she wanted it personal, something the family could get credit for, with everyone contributing something small.

Everybody did their little thing, but Moms and Auntie did the majority of it. Everybody had stuck to the plan until Black came in with 40lbs of crab legs and shrimp. I didn't bring any food. Me and Chantel stopped at the Italian Restaurant downtown and got four bottles of Crisi (Cristal champagne). I wanted to make this occasion special.

Emani, Boot's girl, really went out of her way to make this day special. She had moved in with Boot about a year ago. He met her one weekend we went to Washington DC to pick up Tony. Emani was working in the airport at the gift shop.

Boot was never impressed with no bitches. He just had that shit that bitches liked, and he never had to chase them. When he saw Emani, he just kept staring. I could tell, for once, a bitch had caught him. And, if he had the time, she was going to be got.

I was never a lover of red bitches, but when I looked over in the gift shop, I saw one of the finest red 'ho's I'd ever seen in my life. She was about 5' 6, with a body to kill. She had silk-like hair brushed back to a ball. Her skin was flawless—no bumps, no discoloration, no scars. Just straight smooth, with eyes to make any hard-ass niggah weak.

We walked inside, and Boot began to politic with this bitch, straight big-dick style.

When she spoke, her accent caught us both off-guard. She began by telling us she was from Ethiopia.

"We had gotten the wrong idea of Ethiopians," we told her. "We thought all of you were skinny, black, and starving—the shit we see on TV."

She began to smile and shake her head as if we were stupid. Then she took the time to explain things to us.

I looked into her beautiful face once again, turned to my cousin, and told him to handle his business. He talked for a few then came over to where I was standing. He tried to get a dinner date, but she wasn't having it. She was down for breakfast though, as long as she could meet him somewhere by the airport. The plan was to leave DC that evening, but he changed that, and I understood. I really did. He was hype as hell, as if he was getting with Janet Jackson or somebody.

"Niggah, you need to chill," I said. "She ain't all that, son."

"Shit. I'll be goddamn," he said with a wicked smirk.

"Yeah, son. You right," I agreed. "But my mother-fuckin' cousin ain't no slouch. You stepping to bitches, with linen on by Armani, silk shit by Versace, six-hundred-dollar gators, with mad ice on. Got bitches squinting just to talk to my fam. What the fuck she supposed to do? She trying to get with you tonight, but her peoples ain't having it."

He started smiling, because he knew I was telling

the truth. Me and Tony stayed in the Marriott the next morning, while he took her to breakfast.

He came back all smiles, on a natural high all the way back to Norfolk. She had him going to DC almost every weekend or just as much as Chantel was coming to the beach.

After seven months he moved her in with him and was paying for her to go to Tidewater Community College. The family fell in love with her, but our main concern was that she made him happy and had an abundance of respect for our peoples.

The party turned out to be a success. Everybody in the family showed: Tony; Dre; Junie; Auntie; Big G; Mom's; Black and Shereena; me and Chantel; and Lo and his girl. Boot came in acting really surprised, I guess for Emani's sake.

After toasting Boot's birthday, we all yelled, "Speech, speech, speech."

"Thank you. Thank you. Thank you. Please, no autographs. Just throw money," he said.

The family burst out laughing.

"No, serious. I thank God for letting me see twenty-three. I almost missed it several times, but I'm here. I also thank him for my family. I don't believe anyone could be blessed with a better family. I love you all."

He then turned to Emani. "Girl, you are a gift. The things you do, the way you make me feel, I could never love anyone more. I would like to know if you want to be a permanent part of our family?" he asked, reaching into his pocket. "Will you marry me?"

"Yes, Adrienne. Yes," she said, her eyes watering as she threw her arms around him.

"I heard that shit, Adrienne," Lo said.

"Watch your mouth," Boot said. "That's only for her."

He put a diamond on her finger that we saw clear

across the room. Lo said he picked it up from Zales for $5200.

My cousin was in love, and we had no complaints. She was a beautiful girl with a pleasant personality, ready to love and take care of Boot.

As we only had the spot until 11 p.m., the party was coming to an end. We gathered up all our belongings and left. Boot and Emani went home to celebrate their new engagement. Tony rode with Black and Lo—they had to go out Campus East to take care of some things. Me and G went to the condo to roll up. I gave Chantel the Land so she and Shereena could drop off Auntie and Moms.

By the time Black, Lo, and Tony arrived, me and G were blunted out and ready to ball. We got to the club, and just like every week, it was packed. It seemed like the more shit happened, the more people got shot, the more the club packed out.

We started inside, and security cleared the way. From the way we just strolled inside, people who didn't know us just stared, trying to figure out who we were. Our 600 Benz said it all: We had money and, in our world, that's all that mattered. The security guard yelled out the price had just gone up to $30. Every week it started at $5, by 11:00, it was $15, by 12 it was $25.

When it became so crowded that the Fire Marshall would close the club, the owner would up it to $30, $40 or even $50. It never made a difference; all heads were determined to be in the club, no matter what the price.

We went inside and got our jugs. Carlos and a few more kids Black had put on were inside. They would all come up showing him mad love. He knew that if he didn't have knowledge of how to get this money and make niggahs rich, niggahs' attitudes would be completely different.

Niggahs would come up to me showing me mad love, giving me pounds, talking and hanging like they were my peoples. But I wasn't stupid, I knew the bitches wanted my paper and niggahs wanted me to put them on with Black. Many niggahs knew that Black was my brother and I could easily put them in with him. I had the clout to carry a scrambling niggah to Black and, within weeks, the niggah would become somebody. Black taught niggahs how to blow up, not just how to make money.

I just never got involved in his business directly, so I didn't make a habit of carrying people to him. He knew if I brought somebody to him either they were somebody or they had mad potential. The only way I would even take a chance was if I knew you really well, because if you fucked up, that would leave my brother fucked up, and that would be on my head. And I vowed to always be there to protect him and hold him down, not throw wrenches in his shit. Most of the time if he didn't fuck with people himself, he would give them to either Lo or Carlos, until he saw they were capable of moving weight.

Since Black had blown to Big Willie status, I had taken two kids to him. One played fair; the other one fucked up. Black didn't blame me, but it bothered me that I had brought this kid to him. I had known the dude for a long time, since middle school. He came to me begging me to look out, and I did. I was thinking he was on the up-and-up, but people do change. I swore that if I ever ran into him again that I was going to put his ass to sleep.

Then I ran into him shooting pool at the Casablanca one night. I eased up behind him, scooped his ass up, and slammed him to the pool table, taking the five hundred he had. He owed Black thirty-one hundred. I pulled my nine and put it to his chest.

"I was going to come by your sports bar tomorrow," he yelled.

"Naw, niggah, tomorrow is here."

It took everything I had not to blow a hole in this niggah's chest. I knew Black had enough money to get me out of anything I got into. Besides, if shit went down in the Casablanca, who would give a fuck? But I knew Black would be pissed too, because he told me to leave it alone.

"Dee, I just got back from Atlanta. When I got that from you all, I went to Atlanta with some family. But they were on some bullshit, and we fucked around and got robbed. I tried to make it right before I came back, but it's right now. Dee, this is the number I'm at. I stay with my girl out Bridal Creek. I promise, kid, I will see you tomorrow."

"All right, kid, tomorrow. You know where I'm at," I said, walking outside to the pay phone to dial the number. If it was wrong, I was going to close the club for the night. This was the Casablanca—ENTER AT YOUR OWN RISK.

The number was right, but I never saw this kid again. When I ran into his peoples, they informed me that he had started smoking that shit. They said he caught beef with some more kids, robbed and shot one, and caught mad time behind it. Everything worked itself out, except for Black being out of $3100. Through that experience I learned not to turn anyone else on unless they were family.

I was over by the picture man in Magic's, and Black was by the bar chilling with some girls from P-town that I had met several times at the townhouse in Campus East. Black was fucking one of them, so their whole crew was getting special treatment—drinks, chicken, and fries.

Carlos walked over to me. Said he overheard these

kids talking about robbing Black. At once, I realized it was those broke-ass New York kids he caught wreck with in the sports bar that night playing Cee-lo.

I walked over by G at the bar and stood there. I was fucked up, and the Tanqueray had me going. When the kids walked by, I stepped out to ask them a question. "Yo, son, you know Black?" I asked.

"Who? Naw, niggah," he said, staring me down.

"Then what the fuck you talking about getting him for?"

"Niggah, don't step to me like that. You don't know who the fuck I am," he said, taking a step back.

His second step was involuntary because I caught him. Before I could catch him again, Black came out of nowhere and split the niggah shit wide open with a jug. Big G slammed him to the bar and was stomping him, when security came and tossed them niggahs out.

Then security ran back in to make sure we were all right. Matter of fact, many niggahs came to make sure we were straight. We knew niggahs were just showing their concern, trying to show love to this strong-ass money-making clique.

It wasn't long before we decided to leave. Sometimes you're just not pressed for anything but a drink and a peek at all the phat-ass bitches running around. Something to relax the mind.

We left the club fucked up. Black had drunk about three jugs, plus all those blunts, and he was driving us home. Somebody was looking out.

The following day Black and I took Shereena and Chantel to the movies at Lynnhaven. We were strolling through the mall, when we ran into Muhammed peoples.

"Where my niggah at?" I asked.

"Y'all ain't hear what happened?"

"Naw, kid. What's up?" I asked with a bewildered look.

"You know Muhammed was having problems with that bitch he was fucking with, right. They got into some shit, and he beat her ass. She heard him telling Cuz where he was going to serve this niggah, and she called the police."

"Oh, hell, naw! You gots to be bullshitting."

"Him and Cuz went to meet the niggah and as they were pulling off, police came from everywhere. Fam took the fuck off and started a high-speed chase through the streets, but Cuz hit a pole. Muhammed jumped out and ran. They scooped up Cuz and got him with a whole brick in the back of the truck."

"They catch Muhammed?" Black asked.

"Naw, he gone. Gone! Gone!"

"You know where I'm at," Black said. "Let me know something."

I got up and the sun was high and bright that next Saturday morning. It was going to be a great day. Chantel had quite a bit of work to catch up on, so she wasn't able to make it this weekend. I was in the house cleaning, the stereo blasting.

Big G knocked on the door and began letting me in on his plans for the day. He wanted to ride to Coliseum Mall to check on some shit. I was down, so I threw on my Nike sweatsuit and new Reebok classics, and niggahs were out.

By the time we got back, we were starving and trying to figure out what we were going to eat.

We decided to run by Mom's crib. Black's car was already parked out front, when we got there. We went inside and just as expected: fried chicken; greens; potato salad; cornbread; lemon cake; and a punch bowl full of that special brewed ice tea. Black said Boot, Lo, and Dre had just left.

After eating we stood outside talking when Boot and them came back. We stood around talking until we got on the subject of bowling and the outcome of the scores last time we went. Everybody had a different take on what happened. And so it wasn't long before we were in Pinboys, showing our skills. We all put up $50, so the high scorer of the evening got hit lovely.

Before long, pagers were going off and cell phones were active. We then began to disperse one by one, knowing everybody was going to hook up in a couple of hours at Magic's. Even Lo talked about going and he wasn't even twenty-one yet—but that was a small problem for Black.

It was already a quarter to midnight, and Big G and I were in Magic's with three jugs. I knew Black had to be on his way. I was standing in front of the bar on the wall, where I could see everything going on. Girls were gathering around, showing love, waiting for me or G to offer to buy them a drink, or waiting for the right opportunity to ask me to buy them a drink. But most of the time I wasn't pressed. Drink or no drink, I had fuckin' money, and that put me in control.

Black came strolling in looking fly as always. He was wearing new gear, with jewels swinging from the neck, wrist, and hands. His boy Carlos was looking just as fly. You could tell these niggahs were straight getting it.

I passed him a jug, gave the bartender a look, and she passed us another one, no charge. We were having a bomb-ass time.

My girl was in Charlotte, and I was trying to freak. I was talking to this girl, Rose. We had kicked it for a few. She had even given me a key to her crib, but she started tripping on the dick, instead of enjoying it, which created problems. I would come to the club, and she wanted to be right up under me while I was trying to trick. Even after I gave her back her key, she would still make sure she made her way over to speak. I was glad she got her feelings under control because I had enjoyed her company on many-a-nights, but tonight I wanted to see what was up.

I was just asking Black where Lo was. He didn't know, saying he thought he'd changed his mind. Out of nowhere this young kid came running through the door past security, causing a ruckus. He was out of breath trying to talk to Black. Security grabbed him, but Black realized he was one of the young boys from out Lake Edward. Black threw his hand up for security to chill.

The out of breath young boy broke loose, bent over, and pointing outside, shouted, "Black, don't your cousin got that phat-ass Acura with the three-tong rims on it?"

"Yeah," I said. "Why? What's up?"

"He's beefing with some niggahs in the parking lot."

He never had a chance to say any more. We burst out the front doors like bats out of hell. Soon as we came out the doors, we saw the crowd. Then we heard three shots, and niggahs began to scatter. As guys and girls took off in different directions, Black and me watched the Acura slowly roll up and hit the curb as the driver lay motionless. We ran over to the car. Black looked inside and threw two balled-up fists up, covering his eyes as he fell to the curb.

"Oh God, no. Oh God, please," he yelled, as he jumped back up and fell on the hood.

I walked up and opened the door. My heart dropped, and my stomach tightened until it hurt.

"Boot," I said. "Not my goddamn peoples. Come on, Boot. Please hold on," I yelled.

He lay there with his eyes open, not moving. I looked but didn't see any blood. I then pulled open his shirt and saw three little holes in his chest. I took the cellular and called 911 before paging Lo about three times 911. He didn't call back.

Black was still leaning on the car and breathing hard with rage. I felt Boot's neck for a pulse and got one, so I knew he was still alive. I just continued to talk to him, while people were all around the car looking, as if it was a show or something. I just kept on looking into his eyes and talking. He didn't respond, but I knew my cousin could hear me. I could feel it.

Finally the ambulance came and took him away. I rode in the ambulance with him. On the way I called Moms and told her to go get Auntie and meet us at Norfolk General because Boot had gotten shot and it didn't look good. Black had gone by Lo's crib to get him. We thought he had got with some hooker and wasn't answering his page. I called Boot's house to get Emani and didn't get an answer. I then called G and told him to go get her.

I was there all alone, when the doctor came out and told me that he had died on the way to hospital. I fell back in the chair and just began to cry. My brothers and cousins were all I had—how could this happen? I felt pain but never like this.

Moms, Auntie, and Dre came through the emergency doors. Moms had on pajamas and a robe.

Auntie was wearing nothing but a nightgown and robe, not even shoes. "Where is my baby?" she yelled. "Where's my baby?"

I just walked over to her with tears in my eyes, reached out, and hugged her.

She knew. She let out a scream that made my knees buckle, and then collapsed in my arms. Dre quickly scooped her up, set her back down, and they both let the tears just flow.

Moms came over and took her sister into her arms,

"What am I gonna do, sister?" Auntie yelled. "It ain't supposed to be like this. My baby gone, sister. My baby is gone."

Moms looked at me with disgust.

"Just like our brothers Bobby and Aaron—Will any of you Brooks boys live past thirty? Will you be able to see your grandchildren? Y'all make me sick, living the way y'all do," Moms said, tears running down her face as she squeezed her sister. She wasn't really mad at me but at the way all of us were determined to live. We wanted the best and were determined to get it at any cost.

I got a page from G. It was an unfamiliar number, but with his code. As I was dialing the number, Black paged me from the condo off Shore Drive with 911 behind it. I knew there was a problem because we never played with 911.

"What's up, G?" I asked.

"I just rode past Boot house. Unmarked cars and police are all in the crib. I kept going."

"Let me hit you back. Don't move," I said. Then I instantly called Black.

"What's up, man?" I asked. "G said unmarked cars and the police are all around Boot house."

"Dee, those are the Feds. They got Lo. I saw them putting him in the car, when I rode by. Carlos' sister called and said they kicked in his mom's house. He tried to keep going, but they knew his car and ran him off the road. They got him too. Listen to me, Dee—sell everything; you got papers to the houses, cars, everything. Sell it all and hit a lawyer off with some dough so he'll pick up Lo's case.

"Oh, what's up with Boot?" he asked with hesitation. "Is he going to make it?"

"He died."

There was silence for a moment.

"Yo, big brother, you've never been alone out here before, but you on your own now. You got to hold it down. I want you to get this shit done as soon as possible and get the fuck out of here. They're getting major players now. That's why they haven't fuck with you yet, but don't wait. Get things done, get money in your hands, and get out of here. I'm gone, man. Gone, gone. Yo, man, I love you."

Those were his last words, and the phone went dead. I stood there not knowing when or if I would ever see my brother again.

The next morning we were at Auntie's house, when Lo called collect. He lost his mind when we told him Boot had gotten shot up the night before and died. We just heard the phone drop and him bawling like a baby, but there was no way to comfort him.

The Feds had kicked in every house except for Franklin's out Campus East, mine, and the condo off Shore Drive. I guess we really kept that on the low. I called Freddie Mac and told him to get a handyman to fix all the doors them simple motherfuckers tore off the frame then sell all the properties without putting *for sale* signs in the yards. The condo off Shore Drive by Great Neck wasn't to be touched.

I moved the furniture out of all the houses and placed them into storage. Emani moved in with Auntie until she decided to go back to DC with her peoples.

I received a call from Jacqueline's brother that Thursday. He was threatening me about Black talking to the Feds. I told him that the Feds didn't have Black, but he thought I was lying. He told me that me and Black had ours coming. I paged Junie all day, and he never answered.

That Friday morning, Virginia Beach police knocked on Mom's door, saying that they found him somewhere in New Jersey, slumped over the Jag's steering wheel, two shots to the back of the head. My body was numb. I tried to be there for Moms, but I needed help myself. I was walking around like a zombie.

After burying Boot and Junie, I finished up Black's business and mine. I then bounced to Charlotte away from the beautiful houses, the foreign cars, the sports bar and clubs, and that lavish lifestyle that I had grown accustomed to, far away from the great Lake Edward, that housing area that sits off Route 13 and separating Norfolk from Virginia Beach. That housing produced many rude-ass niggahs whose names will ring in people's ears for years to come. Real niggahs who, just for a moment, got their time to shine.

It's been three years, as I sit here in the home I bought for me and Chantel. And even though she gives me all the love and attention a man can ask for, I still feel alone.

It was real hard trying to deal with my brothers' death, something I just couldn't seem to get over. Not to mention every night I saw Boot's face with his eyes open and lying back motionless in the Acura. Not a day passed that I didn't sit and recollect all the great times me and Black had. I missed my brother and every day I prayed that he was ok. All these years that I shared with my brothers, I never told them that I loved them. Now it was too late.

"God, I ask you, how did my family ever end up here?"